The Ghosts of Liberty

The Ghosts of Liberty

JUDAH HASTINGS

RESOURCE *Publications* · Eugene, Oregon

THE GHOSTS OF LIBERTY

All quotations of Scripture are done so from the King James Version, which is within the Public Domain. Such is the same for the Art of War by Sun Tzu.

Resource Publications
An Imprint of Wipf and Stock Publishers
199 W. 8th Ave., Suite 3
Eugene, OR 97401

www.wipfandstock.com

PAPERBACK ISBN: 978-1-7252-7840-0
HARDCOVER ISBN: 978-1-7252-7839-4
EBOOK ISBN: 978-1-7252-7841-7

Manufactured in the U.S.A.   08/24/20

I would like to dedicate this work to my family and friends who encouraged me to keep working and pressing to finish this book. I especially want to thank my wife for helping to edit and make grammatical suggestions as well as asking me to translate the "army lingo" as the work neared completion. I could not have finished without her.

List of Abbreviations

ASAP	As Soon As Possible
APC	Armored Personnel Carrier
BOLO	Be On the Lookout
Clicks	Kilometers
Charlie-Mike	Continue Mission
DMZ	Demilitarized Zone
ECP	Entry Control Point
ETA	Estimated Time of Arrival
FOB	Forward Operating Base
Freq	Shorthand for Radio Frequency
HUD	Heads-Up Display
HALO	High Altitude Low Opening
IED	Improvised Explosive Device
Intel	Shorthand for Intelligence
LACE	Liquid Ammo Casualty Equipment
MedEvac	Medical Evacuation
Mic/Comm	Microphone/Communication System
Mikes	Minutes
NET	Network; usually radio
OIC	Officer In Charge

RedCon	Ready Condition
R&R	Rest and Relaxation
RTO	Radio Transceiver Operator
SAM	Surface to Air Missile
SP	Start Point
VIX	Vehicles

Prologue

BILL COLLINS WAS, AS far as anyone was concerned, an average and ordinary sort of guy. He had been assigned a position at the Northern New York Food Distribution Center, and never missed a shift. He was married and had one daughter per the more recently revoked One Child Policy the People's Legislative Body had passed decades earlier. He had always strived to obey the law and live a quiet and peaceable life, never publicly speaking out against the State, or the Party. He kept mostly to himself, working in the freight dock preparing large totes of food and supplies for each family representative that came to receive their weekly allotment. The Equity Department had become responsible for "fair distribution of necessary items for sustaining the population," or at least that's what they claimed to do. Some days, the Equity Department would cut rations down, which was never a well-received event. Today was such a day, and Bill was concerned at the growing crowds outside. Normally people would begrudgingly accept the provision cuts, but this was day ten of increasing cuts, with no end in sight. Bill had witnessed firsthand food riots before, and they often got ugly very quickly. He just kept his head down and continued to work as the tumult grew outside the Center.

He could hear the onsite Peace Corps Officers through loudspeakers ordering the crowds to disperse or risk criminal charges. Bill listened a moment, pausing as the Officers threatened to charge the people with Sedition against the State, Unlawful Speech, Unlawful Assembly, Attempted Violence against the State, and other various things. Bill sighed sadly, shaking his head. He reached up and wiped the sweat from his brow. He just wished that everyone would go away, and let things be. These things tended to end violently, and usually were accompanied with a multiple year sentence at a hard labor camp. Bill had foolishly gotten himself arrested once as a young man. He was once full of ideas about how things should be, about how truly un-equitable things were. He had a five year stay at one such camp, working eighteen hour days with only one small meal a day to get him through. Following his incarceration, he accepted his current position after being assessed by the Labor Department and reaffirming his loyalty to the Party. He didn't mind the job, as he preferred physical labor to a desk job any day. His co-workers were very similar to him, quiet types that showed up, worked, and then left with barely a word spoken. Many of them had learned similar lessons about the way things worked as a citizen of the People's Socialist Republic of America.

Bill pushed his pallet jack, his back and shoulders aching. He felt old, and some would say being fifty two was in fact old. His body was pretty generally in pain, after years of pushing heavy freight following the labor sentence. He glanced at an informational poster on the wall about Labor Policy and workplace injuries. He stifled a contemptuous scoff, as the last time he'd been injured on the job he hadn't been able to see a doctor for months. The hospitals were just too backlogged. It seemed that giving the run around was the current Health Administration's version of healthcare. Bill paused for a moment; his old idealistic nature flickered with life as he considered the way things currently were. He had quite a lot to say about the matter, he decided, but his time at the labor camp quickly reminded him to stifle these notions. Speaking out would just cause no end of trouble and could land him back in a lengthy incarceration if he was particularly unlucky.

Bill sighed and returned to work, albeit nervously. The sounds from outside seemed to have intensified, the angry roar growing so loud that Bill thought they were about to smash the doors down. Bill and his colleagues exchanged nervous glances as the freight doors started rattling. Suddenly, pry bars were rammed beneath the doors and forced them open. Bill and the other workers froze, unsure as what to do as people flooded in and started to take as much food and supplies as their arms could carry. In the commotion, Bill was knocked to the ground. He was helpless before the angry mob as they picked clean the containers, leaving chaos in their wake. Bill pulled himself back up and shoved his way to the wall where he could be out of the way of the inevitable storm to follow. Sure enough, no sooner did he crash into the wall did he notice a phalanx of riot control officers descend upon the mob. Clubs and shields struck down looters in a most brutal fashion. Wave upon wave of riot control beat their way through the crowds, indiscriminately bludgeoning and trampling the people who fell in their way. Some looters dropped their stolen goods and tried to surrender, but even they were summarily beaten down. Bill couldn't believe his eyes. A most righteous anger filled him as he watched a riot officer continuously beat an already battered and bloody young man who was laying in the fetal position a few feet away.

Overcome by his parental instincts, Bill charged the officer, knocking him down. Bill threw a few heavy-handed blows into the officer's face, rendering him unconscious. He then turned back to the wounded young looter to assess his injuries. The young man's eyes shone with the smallest glimmer of gratitude as his lips weakly mouthed a "Thank you," and his breath slipped away gently. Bill cradled the young man's head, tears welling up in his eyes. His vision flashed hot white in an instant, and it was over.

Bill moaned, his ears ringing as he tried to move. His hands were restrained behind his back, his vision blurring in and out of focus. He was forced up onto his knees by a pair of violent hands. He tried to take in his surroundings. The warehouse looked like a warzone. Bloody bodies were strewn about, some currently being zipped up in body bags, others kneeling on line with Bill. The authorities had their made their obligatory arrests. Bill's gaze met with one of his colleagues, who stared him down with absolute panic in his eyes. A sharp strike on the back of his already injured skull racked him with pain.

"Eyes forward, terrorist scum!" A voice commanded him. Bill's vision blurred deeply as he tried to regain some measure of coherence.

"This one . . . perfect," a new voice said. "He's certainly old enough and has a prior conviction . . . The perfect ring leader for our terrorist cell." A gloved hand gently lifted Bill by the chin. Bill stared hard into the malicious eyes of a small, wiry man. He was wearing a fine black suit, far nicer than any average citizen could ever dream to acquire.

"You're with the Party," Bill barely whispered. The man sneered as he nodded ever so slightly.

"You are correct, Mr. Collins," he replied. "But more specifically, the Office of Progression." Bill's eyes widened ever so slightly.

"Ah, so you are aware of our reputation," the man chuckled. Bill sunk his head in acknowledgement.

"Unfortunately, the proclivity towards rebellion is a familial trait . . . and now it falls to me to sanitize the problem. I assure you, I will use every means to do just that." The man stood and crossed his arms.

"Don't you dare touch my family!" Bill roared, lunging against the strong hands holding him back.

The man sighed, shaking his head slightly. "It's a pity you won't be able to say goodbye to them," he said, turning away. His footsteps clattered loudly as he walked away. Bill heard him speak one last time. "We can manufacture the confessions later. Shoot them all."

Bill looked up and stared into the barrel of a carbine. Its flash was the last thing he saw.

Chapter 1

PEOPLE THRONGED THE BUSY streets that surrounded Alinsky square, all about their daily business. That is, whatever business the Party and Labor Department had deemed appropriate for them to conduct. Days were divided into twelve-hour work periods, but due to high population levels within the greater New York industrial area not everyone started and finished on the same time interval. The whole of New York itself had been converted into the regional backbone of industry, and with the existing cityscape, much of the area was a combination of lower-level occupied space given to factories while residential sections dominated the higher levels.

The city itself had a look of glum and filthy disrepair, and the atmosphere itself was choked with smog. Many citizens wore small disposable medical masks to try to counter the air pollution. If you were lucky to live in a relatively newer residential pod, or had connections within the Party, you could have an air filter that kept the pod air relatively fresh. Although, due to the age of many of the buildings themselves, it was next to impossible for the common citizen to enjoy cleaner air after the pod conversions took place. On the streets, pedestrians dominated much of the space.

Much like the situation with air filters, one needed connections within the Party to own a vehicle of some kind. For the most part the cars one would see were tiny, electric powered one or two seated vehicles. The Party had banned and disposed of internal combustion engine powered vehicles, due to the increased effects of air pollution the city had already been suffering from. The only other vehicles the average citizen would see would be their local Peace Corps patrol vehicles, larger SUV style vehicles which were sometimes accompanied by what the locals, in an unaffectionate manner, named "meat wagons." The meat wagons were large troop or prisoner transport trucks, featuring a large extended cab and rear "wagon" seating for approximately twenty. These trucks were heavily armored, and still ran on diesel fuel given their sheer size and weight made an electric motor impractical. Whenever PC vehicles were on the move people would clear out of the way, as these convoys were not likely to stop.

For the most part, average citizens commuted on the old subway lines and the newer high-level transit trams between the residential sections. The city almost looked like a large box, with the old towers all in one way or another leveled off to similar heights to aid in stabilizing them and connecting tram lines. People often frequented Alinsky square, whether to swap gossip or just to catch the news on the giant screens installed by the Department of Truth. Foot traffic came to an abrupt halt as a news bulletin broke the silence, the telltale music chiming in followed by the Truth Department graphics. A young woman, dressed in the Party-approved formal blue dress, began to speak.

"Greetings loyal citizens of the People's Socialist Republic of America! It is with heavy hearts that the Truth Department must inform you of a terrible event that took place just this morning: The Northern Food Distribution Center was maliciously targeted by terrorists who authorities have linked to the rebellious "American Army" in an attempt to cause mass starvation in New York City. The terrorists and their leader Bill Collins have been arrested and are awaiting trial. All are expected to plead guilty before our merciful system and will be rehabilitated and re-educated. As always, the People's Representatives are committed to your safety and security. In response to these blatant attacks, PSRA military assets targeted and destroyed several rebel cells throughout the Northwest and Central regions. General Reid also made a statement today confirming that 'These are the death throes of the rebel movement, and they will be finally defeated very shortly'. In other news, more sanctions have been imposed on the Texan regime for their blatant and repeated human rights violations. These sanctions will ultimately cripple the Texan economy, causing the people to cry out to rejoin our wonderful Union. Lastly, a word from your Leader of the Free People."

The screen cut to reveal an old woman, her countenance stately, yet tired in appearance. She had the face of one carrying a heavy burden, despite the make up artists' attempts to cover her worry lines.

"My beloved people, in these troubling times it is easy to lose heart. But, remember we are always stronger when we face adversity together! I call upon you, the people, to rise to the challenge! It is the duty of every citizen to contend against the will of these cowardly insurgents, wherever they hide! We will be victorious together!"

The people on the streets politely applauded, and some cheered, as the screen displayed the seal of the Leader's office, signifying the end of the news bulletin.

Chapter 2

LAURA SHOT OUT OF bed, frantic. Her alarm had been buzzing for the last half hour, and if she didn't hurry, she'd be late to work. Thankfully she'd set herself up for an easier morning with her coffee maker set to a timer, and most of her gear set out along with a small lunch. Laura immediately hit the deck, pumping out as many pushups as she could manage in a few brief moments. Immediately adjacent to her sleeping area within the living pod was the washroom, where she cleaned up quickly, skipping out on cosmetics due to lack of time. She grumbled to herself for moving too slowly for a twenty-five year old as she dressed into black cargo pants, dirty black boots, and a black shirt. Afterwards, she put up her short dark hair into a ponytail, not as well as she'd have liked, but it was functional. Laura was more of a tomboy to begin with, so the ponytail was about as much hair arrangement as she'd do. Next, she put on her duty belt, sidearm, and spare ammunition magazines. Hurrying over to the kitchenette, she grabbed the small protein bar she'd allotted herself as a breakfast. "These ration cuts are the worst," she mumbled as she took a bite of the chalky protein bar. Following that she quickly guzzled her coffee, which did not taste very good, despite the amount of effort and strings she had to pull to get extra coffee rations. She glanced at her watch. She needed to get out the door if she was to catch the tram to the precinct. Moving quickly, she grabbed her lunch bag and donned her NYPC ballcap and exited the small pod.

New York Peace Corps West Precinct was an old, run down building. Its brick exterior had been in disrepair for quite some time. There never seemed to be room in the budget for upkeep, let alone new equipment. Some of the only repairs to the building had been done by handy PC Officers who had a few free moments here and there to help. The main office floor area housed more officers than it had desks and computers, causing many officers to double up on each workstation. Laura shared a workstation with

Ben Fischer, her partner. The workstation itself, however, was conspicuously close to the Lieutenant's office. The LT, as they called him, had a short list of officers that he relied on, of which Laura ranked high on said list. She was an outstanding cop, to be sure, and nobody disputed that fact. However, much to Laura's chagrin, her colleagues razzed her about the LT being sweet on her. Whether or not it was true, Laura didn't mind getting a long leash to do her job the way she wanted to.

Laura entered the office floor, making a beeline for the relatively fresh pot of coffee that someone had brewed when they'd come in. She poured herself a generously large cup and headed for her desk.

"Mornin' partner," Ben greeted her, taking a sip from his own mug. Laura grunted a greeting as she was in the middle of a sip. "Geez Laura . . . what were you doing all night? You look like you haven't slept much."

Laura shook her head. "Yeah, didn't do so well last night. They finished the new tram line three levels down yesterday, so now instead of power tools keeping me up there's a fancy new train to make even more noise . . . until it breaks in a few months and we go back to power tools," she replied.

Ben chuckled, "That royally sucks. You could always take the pod next to mine; I think the Jimenez family is moving to the other side of the city."

Now it was Laura's turn to laugh. "Yeah, and be kept awake by your screaming kids? No thanks."

Ben shook his head, laughing. "Very true, Ben Jr. is a very noisy baby. Might have something to do with the Jimenez's moving . . ."

Laura smiled. Ben was a nice guy, and a good partner. On more than one occasion, he'd saved her skin, or covered for her when she had made a rookie mistake. He was the big brother she'd never had. He was about ten years older than her, around six feet tall and lean. His dark hair and similar complexion to her could lead someone to believe that they could be siblings. Ben was married, and had a four-year-old along with Ben Jr.

"So, when are you going to, uh, settle down?" Ben nodded toward LT's office. Laura shot him a look with spite-filled eyes. "Geez, relax! I mean, Hutchins is a good guy. Good looking. Single." Ben laughed as Laura punched him in the arm.

"Ben, c'mon . . . I . . ." Laura sighed, 'I just don't know. You know?"

Ben shook his head and threw his hands up in a mock gesture of surrender.

"Okay, that's fine . . . I will stop trying to play matchmaker, I get it."

Laura glanced at the LT's office. He was a good guy to be sure, but she wasn't looking for a relationship at the moment, and she just didn't like him in that way. He was a good boss and was in no way shape or form being creepy or overbearing; he seemed both kind and sincere. She just didn't feel the same way. Laura drifted off in deep thought for a while, until she heard Ben laughing at her.

"What's that?" she asked, snapping back into reality.

"I say again, Earth to Laura, come in Laura. Do you need the computer?" Ben said, waving in her face a little.

She gave him a sideways glance, and rolled her chair into his, knocking him away from the workstation. Ben, having raised his coffee mug to take another sip, ended up spilling some. He barely dodged the dark liquid as it splashed to the floor.

"Hey!" Ben cried out, offering a slight pout.

"Oh it's not like you actually like the coffee here," Laura chuckled.

Ben nodded, "Yes, I realize it's a struggle to get a whole mug down . . . kind of tastes like paint thinner to be honest, but I desperately need the caffeine."

"Okay, fair enough . . . here, let me top it off for you," Laura offered her mug, laughing.

Ben pulled away abruptly, "What are you trying to do, poison me?"

"You're impossible," Laura rolled her eyes, turning her attention to the computer screen, and logged on with a wave of her wrist.

"You know, my wife says the same thing . . . Can't imagine what she's talking about," Ben joked.

Laura choked on a laugh as she was taking a drink.

"Fischer! Can I have a moment?" The loud voice of the shift sergeant echoed from the other end of the hall.

"Be right back," Ben rose from his chair and stepped away.

Laura watched him for a second and gazed sleepily back to the computer screen. She skimmed through some of the previous shifts' activity reports, with nothing more interesting to note than a few juvenile charges filed against some teenagers refusing to participate in the daily recitation of the Guiding Principles of the Party during school. Laura took umbrage with things like that, and tended to steer clear from political police work in general. She focused on what she felt was real police work. She needed a clear picture of right and wrong, good guys and bad guys. She felt a strong sense of disquiet when the Party needed someone arrested, especially when a mountain of circumstantial evidence conveniently appeared to condemn them. Laura sighed and continued to skim through BOLOs and other reports, slowly finishing off the mug of poor tasting coffee.

"I hope that today is a slow day," Laura mumbled to no one in particular.

Chapter 3

AN EXPLOSION OF ACTIVITY, voices, and riot alarms disturbed Laura's would-be quiet day.

"Listen up people, we have a food riot at the Northern FDC, North Precinct has called us for support. They are being overrun as we speak. I need teams Alpha through Charlie to load up and move time now!" The shift sergeant's voice pierced the cacophony of activity.

Laura silently exhaled in relief. She was part of Delta team, and therefore, got to remain behind to cover any other calls. Her last food riot response hadn't gone so well. During that particular incident, her team's phalanx was broken by some rather large industrial workers, causing the whole lot of them to suffer no small amount of trampling. Laura was no pushover, standing approximately five foot eight, and built like an athlete, but on her own against men almost twice her weight she didn't have much of a chance. Despite wearing riot gear, she still received bruised ribs after the mob of people were finished charging through. The memories caused a sympathetic response in her body, her ribs ached for a flash, causing her hand to instinctively reach up and touch the place where it'd been injured worst.

She raised her mug once more but was disappointed to find it empty. She stood, waving her wrist once more over the computer terminal to log out of the system. There was a quiet chirping tone as the terminal read the implanted ID chip and signed her off. Laura moved fluidly through the outgoing crowd of officers, weaving expertly back towards the coffee pot. Upon seeing it was empty, she kicked a file cabinet in protest, and headed back toward her desk to finish writing up some almost overdue reports. She thought about the growing number of food riots, and how more frequently the government was making basic sustenance and supply cutbacks. Laura's stomach growled as she realized that she hadn't eaten a real full meal in a very long time.

"Jones! I need to speak to you," Laura just about jumped out of her chair, the LT's voice boomed loud behind her before he'd realized she was sitting right outside his door and subsequently decreased in volume. Laura was a bit puzzled, as the LT never yelled like that unless some heads were going to roll, or some other type of emergency necessitated it.

"Moving, sir," she replied. Laura sprang out of her chair and entered the LT's office quickly. Lieutenant Mike Hutchins motioned her to close the door as he stood and crossed the office quickly. He offered her a seat and took the one adjoining it.

"What's this all about, sir? Is there something wrong that's going to hit my performance review?" Laura asked as she sat, trying to read the face of her boss. Hutchins leaned forward in his seat; his expression worried bordering on panic. Laura took note of the trepidation in his eyes and then he began to speak.

"I just received a horrible report. The food riot . . . I . . . uh," Hutchins began, his eyes searching for the words. "Even though Fischer is Delta team, I sent him to coordinate ops and he sent me an encrypted message just a few moments ago . . ."

Laura's eyes narrowed, puzzling where this conversation was headed. Hutchins nervously rubbed his chin, and then turned his computer terminal to face them.

"Here, it'd be better if you just see this," he said quietly, starting the message. Ben Fischer's face appeared on the screen, a similar look of panic filled his countenance.

"LT, you need to get Laura out of there as soon as possible. The second they connect the dots, it'll be too late. It's a long story, sir, but she's been going by the name Jones to keep her clear of her father's record; it was so she could have a chance at the Academy. Her father is Bill Collins, a freight worker at the NFDC, and the Office of Progression just pinned him as the instigator of the riot, a terrorist, and executed him just a few seconds ago. They will come for her too, and her mother. Tell her I'll do my best to get to her mother first, but she needs to run now," Ben's eyes darted back and forth as the transmission ended.

Laura sat in shock as tears filled her eyes. "Mike . . . I . . ." she couldn't speak, emotions running rampant. Hutchins stood, deleted the message, and took her hands to help her up.

"Laura, you need to go right now. Any second a BOLO will be issued for you, and there'll be feds crawling all over this place."

Laura stifled her tears and nodded. Hutchins opened the door, took her elbow and led her towards the back of the building.

"You'll need to ditch the cop look and keep your head down away from the cameras outside," he said as they entered the back hallway. It led to the motor pool and the service entrance. "And lastly, don't trust anybody. Not even Ben. They'll find the message and coerce him into helping them find you. Head west; out of the city. I have a friend—"

Hutchins was cut off as they opened the service door and there stood before them two men in black tactical uniforms and armor. They were federal agents from the Office of Progression, as denoted by the emblem on their chest plates.

"Hold it! You're under arrest—" one of the agents was interrupted as Hutchins drew his weapon in a flash and fired, killing him.

The second agent fired, hitting Hutchins with a pair before turning his weapon towards Laura. It was too late, as Laura had drawn her weapon and fired, putting a round between the man's eyes. Laura kicked the weapons away from the two downed agents and confirmed they were dead before moving to Hutchins. He was bleeding heavily from his two chest wounds. Laura's eyes met his, and just as the life slipped out of them, he whispered, "Run . . ."

Chapter 4

LAURA SPRINTED WEST, FREQUENTLY changing streets to miss the ones she knew were more heavily patrolled. After covering a lot of ground without stopping, she dove behind an old rusty dumpster and tried to catch her breath. She coughed every few breaths, the intense amount of smog choking her as she tried to breathe. Sirens and shouting could be heard off in the distance as every officer at the precinct had heard the gunshots and was now searching for their fugitive; searching for her. Laura removed her pistol and stuffed it into the small of her back. Next, she took the two spare magazines and put them in her jacket pocket before turning it inside out to hide the obvious NYPC lettering. She then removed her duty belt and tossed it into the dumpster. A pang of remorse filled her as she saw her NYPC badge now sitting amongst the trash. She'd worked so very hard to earn that badge and now it was gone just like that. Lastly, she pulled her ballcap down to hide just a little bit more of her face. Now that she looked a little less conspicuous, she travelled the alleyways in a westerly heading, further and further away from the populated areas.

Laura was now in the Old Western District, where no respectable citizen would dare tread. It was a district stricken with poverty and disease and also suffered from no lack of gang related activities. The poor souls who called the Old Western District home were usually folk too injured or sick to continue to work the factories or had more than one outstanding warrant which kept them from more civilized areas. These people were outcasts in the eyes of the glorious Party, still technically citizens deserving of basic human rights, but the current regime saw them as a drain on the system not worth the precious resources. Hence, they chose to scratch a living through unscrupulous means, or by the charity of some good-hearted souls who'd deliver a portion of their weekly ration supply. Occasionally, Laura would donate some of her supplies when the donation runners came by and happened to catch her at home; but living the life of a cop meant that she was often too busy for charity. Laura shook the fog from her head, regaining focus for the task at hand. Looking at her surroundings, she tried scoping out a good place to duck away and hide should her former colleagues and the feds catch up to her. There weren't many people about the street as she continued on her way, keeping a brisk walking pace. She coughed again, the air quality even poorer in this area than she was used to. Up ahead, Laura saw a tall shady looking man in the distance, and made it clear to him that she noticed him as she closed on him. The man turned and went inside a dark building just next to him. Laura let out a small sigh of relief as she eyeballed the building he'd entered while she passed by. She could still hear sirens, but they grew faint. Perhaps they'd caught a sighting of someone who matched her description in another area. Laura moved a bit faster. Once they realized they'd gone the wrong way they'd most likely double back and pick up speed in their search. The sound of sirens disappeared entirely, giving her a small glimmer of hope. Laura reached another four-way intersection and looked to the north. Her hope was dashed to pieces.

Laura ducked and turned around. There was a convoy of dark SUVs approaching from the north. She doubted that any of the local gangs would have access to vehicles like them, which meant that they were more than likely OP feds. Laura spotted the building that the shady man had entered and hoped that it was either a good place to hide, or would allow her to at least give these feds the slip, should they follow her inside. Some of the older buildings had tunnel networks, or so she'd heard from the anti-gang section of her precinct. Perhaps she'd be lucky enough to have found one, enabling her to get out of the city. She decided the risk was worth it and charged up the steps into the building. Laura took in her surroundings quickly. She was in a large foyer that resembled an old office building, with large stone pillar supports lining the entry way. Confirming her suspicion was an area that clearly was a reception area, with old broken-down elevators lining the walls behind it. Near the elevators was a stair access door that looked like it was on the verge of falling off the hinges either from decay or intentional damaging. She figured it was the latter given the smattering of boot prints covering it. Laura moved to the westernmost pillar for cover and peeked around to catch a glance through the broken window at the growing activity she heard outside.

She felt exposed; there was a lot of space to cover if she needed to bug out. Confirming her worst fears, the convoy stopped nearby, the lead two vehicles pulling out to the east side of the entrance, the trail two completing the blockade midway through and west, respectively. The doors opened, and OP agents poured out, weapons trained on the building. Laura stole another quick glance to size up the force and noticed a man in a dark suit taking cover behind the trail SUV. The agents moved up to storm the building, scanning the broken windows and nonexistent front door. Laura drew her weapon and prepared for the fight of her life. She'd counted about twelve agents in all, but had no idea how skilled they were in a firefight. Laura pressed her back against the pillar nervously when she heard a metallic clatter nearby. She managed to shut her eyes and cover her ears as the inevitable flash bang shook the foyer. Just after the burst finished, Laura rolled and took aim at the entrance. She opened fire as a mass of black clad agents began to pour through the entrance way. She wasn't sure how many went down as she ducked back around her pillar. The pillar expelled a mass of rock debris as automatic gunfire peppered and chipped away at its mass. With many rounds striking too close for comfort, Laura returned fire, hitting a few more targets before they could reach good cover. She heard some of them crying out in pain, others cursing and crawling either to cover or back towards the entrance. Laura reloaded and burst out of cover, forcing down as many heads as possible with fire as she leaped over the old receptionist desk. It was immediately turned to scrap as return fire slapped against it. Laura waited a few beats, and her enemy capitalized on her delay, laying down more suppressing fire. They took up positions around the foyer, utilizing the large stone pillars to their advantage. Laura decided it was time to move and sprang towards the stairwell door. She fired wildly at her assailants and ran as fast as she could. Bullets whizzed by her, nearly missing as she lowered her shoulder and charged through the door. Once through she slammed the door behind her and was greeted by more rounds pinging against the door. Laura looked up and decided to take the relatively intact looking stairwell up. She went up two levels and paused before moving through the door. She could hear the agents moving through the door below and fired a few rounds at them, striking the second man and dropping him. Laura ducked through the door nearest her, more bullets zipping up the stairwell. She stumbled in the dark room, bumping against desks and file cabinets. Finding a steady desk, she took refuge behind it, training her weapon towards the door. She waited, knowing that once they opened the door their silhouettes would be illuminated, giving her targets if but for a moment. She held her breath, listening intently at the sounds echoing up the stairwell. There was a brief silence, and then the door swung open. Black silhouettes appeared, firing at random around the room as they began to breach. Laura steadied her aim and fired four well placed shots. Two more agents went down, and more dove for cover in the darkness. Laura heard them curse as they sprayed more bullets in her general direction. Laura watched closely from her position at the location of the muzzle flashes, aimed, and returned fire. She heard more cries of pain and anger, reloaded her weapon, and continued to surgically strike.

The OP agents, emboldened and angered by their losses, closed in brazenly while pouring fire at her. Laura popped up, firing at the encroaching agents. Time seemed to slow as she took down a few more, but a hot radiating sensation filled her. In the few microseconds that passed, she realized that her left bicep had been shot. The hot sensation sparked into the most intense pain she'd ever felt, causing her to cry out in pain. She fell back, tumbling over another desk and crashing down hard.

"Target is hit, repeat she's hit!" She heard an agent announce in the darkness.

Laura crawled away from the voice, leaving a trail of blood behind her. She found a good spot to prop herself up and checked her magazine. Three rounds left. She became disoriented, the pain beginning to override the rush of adrenaline she'd been riding. Her gaze drifted in and out of focus, but her mind snapped it back as she fired at a black mass, dropping one more agent. Two bullets left.

"Over there!" She heard another voice whisper.

Her vision blurred again, and her body felt cold, weak. Laura sat up, breathing heavily. She could make out a few more dark masses, and, picking one, fired her last two shots at it. She missed. The enemy fired a few pot shots at her, continuing their advance. Laura dropped her pistol and steeled herself for the inevitable. She wanted to at the least look her killers in the eye when they finished her off. She heard boots shuffling closer and closer. *This is it*, she thought, *it's over*. She saw a dark silhouette standing before her, weapon raised. There was a flash and hot white light filled Laura's vision. Her ears rung and she was confused. She should be dead by now. She blinked, her ears slowly tuned back in, and she realized she was hearing muffled gunshots. Blinking a few more times, she noticed that there was now light. Laura saw a small wiry man standing before her, a lost and confused look on his face. He was wearing a nice black suit which was now being quickly wetted with blood. His arm dropped, lowering his weapon. Her gaze locked onto the malicious eyes of the man, and she saw fear flooding into him as blood poured from multiple orifices. He made a weak gurgling sound and dropped. Laura gasped in shock, her vision starting to blank out again. The light died out, and she caught a glimpse of another dark figure approaching. She blinked, and the figure was kneeling over her. It sounded like he said something. She blinked again. *Be okay? Is that what he said?* She thought. She felt the prick of a needle and quickly blacked out.

Chapter 5

LAURA FLUTTERED IN AND out of consciousness many times. She heard voices, softly spoken, and saw a dim light above her when she was awake long enough to notice. Her eyes finally held open, her mind totally unaware of how long she'd been unconscious. The light above her buzzed softly and flickered every so often. She noted that she was lying in a bed, or perhaps a cot and it creaked a little when she shifted slightly. There was a soft humming close by, a nice melody that was simple enough, yet the voice from which it emanated gave it a soothing quality. Her gaze went to her left arm and she saw that it had been hooked up to an IV, and that her wound had been treated. She turned her head to the right slightly, looking in the direction of the humming. A large man sat beside her bed in a folding chair. He was reading a small black book that had a little red ribbon hanging out from the spine. The man turned the page and continued humming his song. He was bald, with a black goatee that was speckled with white. His dark skin hid some of the lines etched around his eyes, but Laura determined that they were more like laugh lines than anything. He had a large, impressive build, broad shoulders and huge hands that made the little book seem even smaller, and was wearing a dark blue polo style shirt, dark cargo trousers, and black combat boots that looked quite worn.

Laura managed a raspy question. "That song . . . what is it called?" she tried clearing her throat a little. The man looked up and gave her a huge grin, his eyes bright, giving Laura a sense of warmth.

"It's called Amazing Grace, little sister, and if you'd like to you can hear it properly sung later. But first, it sounds like you need a glass of water," the man said to her.

Laura nodded gratefully, as her throat was very dry and hoarse. The man stood up and walked out the only door the room had. Laura looked around the room. It was small, poorly lit, as the dim light above her was the only source of illumination. Over in the corner stood a few folded-up cots and a few more folding chairs. Laura sat up a little, and the big man returned with a cup of water and was accompanied by another man.

"Here you go, hopefully it tastes okay. The water filter's been a bit testy." He said, handing over the cup. Laura whispered her thanks and sipped down some water.

"Oh, I'm Jack, by the way. Jack Bridger, but folks around here call me Rev," the large man, Rev, said, offering his hand. Laura shook it, giving him a quizzical look. *There must be a story attached to that*, she thought.

"I'm Laura, good to meet you," she said, offering a warm smile. She glanced over as the other man began to check her vitals, bandages, and withdraw the now empty IV. Laura watched him work and did a double take when she noticed that there was an extra bandage on her wrist.

"I'm Rich Armstrong, but you can call me Doc," Doc noticed Laura examining her wrist. "Oh that. So, I had to do a minor operation on you. Don't worry; nothing bad, it was just to remove your microchip."

Laura was a bit confused. "The feds were tracking you with it. It has a built-in transponder with quite an impressive range," Doc added.

He finished up his medical exam and stood. He was much shorter than Rev, standing at about Laura's height, and was built lean but looked tough. His skin had an olive complexion, his hair was dark, which he kept short in a high fade, and he had a dark stubble beard which gave the impression that he hadn't shaved in a few days. He wore dark blue coveralls and black boots. His gaze fell on Laura, seeming to give her one last scan before meeting her eyes.

"Well, you seem to be looking good," to which Rev gave him an elbow accompanied by a booming "Hah!" Doc shot Rev a chiding look, and then chuckled. "I'm sorry, Ms. Jones, or do you prefer Collins?"

Laura was taken aback. They knew more about her than she'd already revealed. "Uh . . . Collins," Laura said slowly, guarded. She was grateful for the obvious help they'd given her, but she was ill at ease with them holding all the cards. "You can call me Laura though," she added, offering her hand to Doc. He smiled and shook her hand.

"Very well, Laura," he said, "As I was saying, you seem to be recovering quickly. You took a round to the left bicep, but it went through cleanly, so the only real danger was blood loss. Other than that, you just had some bumps and bruises, so at this point you should be good to go."

"How long was I out?" Laura asked. The water she'd just consumed awakened her hunger, and her stomach growled with the awareness.

"Well, this is the morning of day three," Doc answered. Laura's eyes went wide, and her stomach let out another angry gurgle.

Rev laughed, "Hollywood was starting to call you Snow White, you know, 'cause you got all pale from the blood loss and all." Doc reached under the cot and produced an arm sling, which he gently helped Laura to don.

"Tell you what, Rev, why don't you grab her some food? Not too much too soon though," he said.

"Sure thing! I'll whip up the finest field ration I can find," Rev joked, heading out the door.

"Hey, um, Doc? Could I have a few minutes alone?" Laura asked.

Doc, nodding, said "Absolutely. If you need anything, feel free to come out and ask. We'll be having lunch in a little while." He smiled and moved towards the door.

"Hey Doc . . . thanks for patching me up," Laura said, a small smile crossing her lips.

"No problem, see you soon," Doc replied and stepped away.

Laura let out a large sigh. She just needed a bit of time to process everything that'd happened. A few moments later, Rev came with food and left, and Laura just sat and stared at it. As hungry as she was, she didn't seem to have much of an appetite. Her father was dead. Just like that. Her mother was missing, as far as she knew, and had no idea of how to find her. Her mind reeled, as she also had to come to terms with taking lives. She'd never shot a person before, and now she was pretty sure she'd killed at least six in the span of a few hours. She watched Hutchins die before her very eyes, trading his life to try to save hers. Tears streaked down her cheeks and she hung her head low. Her life as she knew it was done, and now, she had no idea what to do with the pieces that remained. She grappled with the anxiety that accompanies uncertainty, feeling both trapped and lost in equal measure. As time passed, and the waves of fresh emotion subsided, she looked at the door to her room and decided to grab a little hope. Hope that these people she'd met were associated with the "friend" that Hutchins had mentioned. Laura took a deep breath, appreciating the relative cleanliness of the air, and slowly started eating her food.

Chapter 6

LAURA FINISHED THE MEAL in the quietness of her little room. She was feeling groggy again and decided that she should probably get more rest soon. Her thoughts, and the silence, were disturbed by a soft knocking on the door.

"Come in," Laura said, clearing her throat. Rev peeked in and smiled.

"I figured you'd be done with the food and came to clean up the tray and stuff." He gestured for the tray, and Laura offered it to him.

"Oh sure, thank you Rev," she replied with a smile. Rev took the tray and turned to leave. "Rev, would you mind staying a while?" Laura asked impulsively.

He turned and asked, "Sure, what's on your mind?"

Laura felt a little embarrassed but decided to push aside her introverted apprehensions. "Earlier you were reading a book, what was it?" Rev's eyes lit up again as he reached into his cargo pocket and produced the book.

"You mean this one?" He said, holding up the little book. Laura nodded, curiosity taking hold. Rev sat on the folding chair again and handed it to her. "This is the Bible," he said. Laura examined the little Bible, flipping through the pages.

"Is it any good? Who's the author?" she asked inquisitively.

Rev chuckled, running his hand over his bald head. "Well, I'd say it's a real page-turner!" He crossed his arms, thinking. "As far as the author, well, a lot of people were inspired to contribute to it, but ultimately the author is God."

Laura looked him in his eyes, unsure if he was making a joke or if he was serious. "God? Wait; are you people part of the terrorist cells? The Party says that generally people who participate in deity worship are associated with them."

Rev had a hearty laugh at her statement and reached out for the Bible again. Laura handed it over, not sure why he was laughing. He opened the book and flipped a few pages until he found what he was looking for.

"Let's see here . . . '*But I tell you, love your enemies and pray for those who persecute you.*' Does that sound like the manifesto of terrorists to you, Laura?"

Laura's gaze fell as she shook her head. "Not really . . . I'm sorry, I didn't mean to offend you," she said.

Rev smiled. "It's okay Laura. I understand you've been raised and trained in a system of strict atheism. There's no way the Party would ever let you have access to any sort of materials they've banned."

Laura looked up, nodding in understanding. "I am curious about that, actually . . . I mean, what kind of things do I accept to be normal, true even, that you'd associate with . . . with brain-washing, I guess?" Rev nodded and smiled warmly.

"Absolutely, I can imagine you have a lot of questions, and the answers to them will only produce more questions. Tell you what, why don't we start with this book, and then in time we can discuss political views. Sound good to you?" Laura nodded a bit more eagerly.

"Yes, I'd like that. What's your favorite part of the book?" she asked. Rev shook his head, smiling a toothy grin.

"Oh boy, well, I have a lot of favorite parts. Hmm, let's try here . . ." He began to read out loud.

Laura listened, transfixed by the usage of language but she was even more curious as to the meaning of what he read. The time passed quickly, and Laura eventually made herself comfortable as Rev continued to read to her. Her eyes grew heavy, and she drifted off to sleep.

It was the next morning. Laura blinked the sleep from her eyes and sat up. She felt grungy and was self-conscious upon discovering that she had morning breath. Looking around, she realized that she must have passed out at some point during the time Rev had been reading to her. She was about to feel embarrassed about it, but then based on the way he quickly forgave her for potentially insulting him earlier, she realized that he more than likely didn't take any offense. The blanket on her cot had been pulled up for her, and she assumed that Rev had done so once she fell asleep. He seemed to have a very caring and paternal nature to him, and Laura guessed that he had kids somewhere. Laura got out of bed, her feet while thankfully still covered by socks, could feel the floor was rather cold. She tried her best to stretch, despite the sling on her arm, needing to get the sleep stiffness out. Moving to the door, she reached for the knob and hesitated a moment. There was a flash of anxiety, but then she pushed past it. There was no real reason for her to feel nervous. She pushed the door open slowly and it creaked loudly. Wincing at the sound, she pushed it faster the rest of the way. Her cheeks flushed a little as she could feel every eye in the next room on her.

"Um, I hope I'm not interrupting anything," she said. There was a group of people seated at a large table, having breakfast.

"Laura! Good morning! Come join us," Doc called out from the table.

Laura moved towards the table, taking in the room itself and scanning the faces. There was an ordinary kitchenette oriented across from her room, with the table taking the room's center. There were three other doors, probably leading to other rooms like hers, or outside, she wasn't sure. She figured that this was in an old apartment building somewhere in the Old Western District. Thankfully, the group she was about to meet had brought some life back into it. The floor was worn out and damaged, yet it looked as if it was regularly cleaned, as was the kitchenette. She didn't see Rev anywhere. As she approached, Doc rose and pulled out his seat for her. Laura thanked him and sat down, offering a polite smile. Doc went to get a plate for her.

"What a proper gentleman!" exclaimed the woman who Laura was now seated beside. She had a southern accent and she smiled warmly at Laura, extending her hand in greeting. "Hi! My name is Jamie Bell, or Cowgirl, as young Mr. Park so affectionately but rather unoriginally calls me. You just let me know if you need anything."

Laura shook her hand. Jamie appeared to be in her mid-thirties, had blonde hair, and despite her generally petite build, her grip was surprisingly like a vice. Doc returned with Laura's breakfast, setting the plate of scrambled dehydrated eggs gingerly before her. Laura thanked him as he pulled up another chair.

"Jamie is our liaison from the Republic of Texas, she's here to, uh . . . what is it you officially do again, Jamie?" Doc teased, an obvious smirk marking his face. Jamie shot him an "I'm not amused" look, before turning to Laura.

"I liaise . . . But more accurately, I am here representing the Texan peoples' commitment to supporting the Underground Railroad out of the PSRA. Once in a while I'll get my hands dirty with these boys during an operation, but mainly I'll be assisting Hollywood with communications during missions." Picking up on his cue, a young man, Korean by the look of him waved from across the table.

"Hello, Snow White, nice to see you're looking better," he said, prompting another contemptuous look from Jamie. "I'm John Park, resident genius, hacker, magic working electronics wizard. These guys call me Hollywood, obviously because of my amazing good looks and rapier wit!" There was a collective sighing accompanied by eye rolls as he continued his introduction.

"Okay, okay, I make a lot of obscure film references and come up with all the call-signs," he finished, looking like the wind had been taken out of his sails.

Laura wasn't quite sure what to make of him, but ultimately decided that he seemed nice. Next to Park sat a lean, rough looking man. His eyes were intense, overshadowed by a dark ball cap pulled down low. He had a dark beard covering a grim and serious face. Although he didn't smile, he seemed to be attempting to be at the very least amicable.

"Hank Wells," he nodded at Laura, arms crossed.

"I call him Valkyrie," Park cut in abruptly. Hank flashed an icy gaze in Park's direction, giving Laura a strong indication that this was a man who did not like to be interrupted.

"I'm the team's sniper, amongst other things," he finished, clearing his throat. He did not appear comfortable talking about himself, let alone to someone who wasn't a part of their team.

"Pleased to meet you," Laura said softly, meeting his gaze.

His eyes seemed to be fixed into a thousand yard stare, but for a brief second he looked a little more at ease with her demeanor. Laura guessed a thousand yards was mere target practice for a man like Valkyrie. Next to him sat a tan, dark haired man who also sported a beard. He looked to be shorter than some of the others she'd met, although his build conveyed athleticism as well. After shuffling some papers he'd been reading, he looked up to introduce himself.

"Hello Ms. Collins, my name is Beniah David Spectre," his voice was colored by an accent she'd never heard before. "Similar to Ms. Bell, I am an operative, but I come from Israel. My role here, however, is more hands on, if you take my meaning. My nation has suffered greatly since the fall of the USA, and the Israeli government has a vested interest in helping the American Army restore what was lost."

Park chimed in again: "Yeah and his call-sign is still Spectre, because, well, it already sounds cool," he laughed. Laura reached across the table and shook Spectre's hand, offering a greeting.

"It is good to meet you, please, call me Laura," she said. Spectre nodded, smiling.

"Then you may call me Ben," he replied. A few moments passed, and conversations were struck up until Doc's voice broke through the buzz.

"Hey, boss! We saved you some chow!"

Laura turned to look at who Doc was calling out to, and, along with Rev, walked in another man. There was a burst of loud greetings and more chatter. Laura's heart beat increased a little bit as the man walked toward her, along with Rev. He was an imposing figure, though not as built as Rev, he was taller. Laura estimated his height at around six foot five and he looked like he easily could take on multiple opponents without much effort. His eyes were an intense blue, and his brown hair was cut short in a very militaristic style. He smiled as he approached, yet his gaze still held a sense of seriousness.

"Good to finally make your acquaintance, Ms. Collins," he said, offering his hand. Laura shook it, feeling like his huge hand could easily crush hers. "I am Captain Titus Hansen, and these are my Ghosts." Laura raised an eyebrow, unsure of what he was saying.

"Likewise, Captain Hansen . . . I am afraid I don't really understand what is going on here." Titus pulled a chair over and sat facing her. He looked younger up close, probably not much older than Laura.

"Well, what do your police instincts tell you?" He asked, leaning back a little. Laura studied his face a moment, and then glanced at each person in the room.

"Well, you're either a military, or some kind of pseudo-humanitarian operation. You have foreign agents, military personnel, and one of you teaches Christian religion . . . from what has been said in this room, it seems to me that you're trying to either undermine or overtly overthrow the PSRA regime while simultaneously utilizing an Underground Railroad system built to move people from Party controlled turf to . . . Texas? Rebel territory? Not sure yet on that, but I'm still trying to figure out where I fit in."

Laura took a drink of water. There was a glint of amusement in Titus' eyes.

"I am a cop targeted by my own government, and yet, you people, or "Ghosts," swooped in to save my life. You need me, or at least, something that I know, to aid your cause in some way." Laura glanced over at Jamie, who quietly made applause. She looked back at Titus, and was surprised to see guilt written on his face.

"Ms. Collins, you're correct. And I sincerely apologize." Laura was confused yet held eye contact with him, searching.

"What do you mean? I was about to end up in a body bag, you saved my life," she said slowly. Titus cleared his throat, shifting in his seat.

"You misunderstand. I used you, and for that I am sorry. Over the past few months, I've been waiting for an opportunity to follow someone who'd been targeted by the Office of Progression. We hit their agents and learned locations of labor camps, prisons, as well as radio frequencies and SOPs. We're trying to disrupt their operations as much as we can, while still aiding the efforts of those associated with the Underground Railroad. So, I sincerely apologize because we followed you while using you as bait for our own gain." Titus looked deep into her eyes, nothing but sincerity filled them. He paused, taking a moment to measure his words before continuing.

"I am sorry that you got hurt . . . and lost your father . . . and that we couldn't save Mike Hutchins . . . he was our friend."

The room was silent, heavy, as everyone observed a moment of silence for their fallen friend. Laura reeled, her emotions running wild in waves. Anger and resentment washed over her countenance, followed by remorse and sadness. She hadn't had a very good relationship with her father. He had sacrificed so much to make her life better, and yet, she had pulled away. Now he was gone. That was it. Laura's eyes welled ever so slightly with tears. She felt a large hand on her shoulder and reached up and took it. She looked up to see Rev's big smiling face, and felt reassured, calm even. His eyes were filled with compassion, and Laura smiled a little in return. She looked Titus in the eyes once more, resolute.

"I forgive you and . . . I understand; I really do. I don't feel like you used me, you saved my life. You didn't have to, and you did. I appreciate what you all have done for me, and I hope that I can repay you somehow. Thank you all for being so very welcoming," she said, wiping away a little tear.

Park cleared his throat, "Well, everyone except Hank," he said. Laughter started to break the seriousness. All eyes were now fixed on Valkyrie's face as it went beet red.

"Park! You're such a . . ." he started, shaking his head and cursing under his breath. The laughter grew, and conversations were struck up once more. Jamie nudged Laura getting her attention.

"You're one of us now, sweetie, and we're glad to have you with us."

Rev's big voice boomed out in agreement. "Welcome to the family, little sister!" The suddenness and volume made Laura jump, startled a little, then she laughed.

"Geez, Rev! You almost gave me a heart attack!" He laughed, obviously aware that he had that effect on people sometimes.

"Oh, Laura would you like to come to our church meeting after breakfast?" he asked. Laura shot him a quizzical look.

"Is that . . . oh! Is that your designated religious gathering? Is that what it's called?" she asked. Rev let out another booming laugh.

"Yes, ma'am, although the folks that attend just say it's a get together, to avoid any Party intervention."

Laura thought for a moment then nodded. "Sure, I'm curious to see what about this religion has got the Party so concerned."

"Great! We'll sing Amazing Grace, so you can hear it properly done." Rev wolfed down his eggs, obviously excited about the upcoming event. Laura was intrigued, albeit unsure of what to expect from a religious gathering. After a few more moments, Rev led her away to participate in "church."

Chapter 7

LAURA STAYED SEATED, EVEN after most of her new family had cleared out from the religious meeting. She had chosen a corner seat near the door to the gathering area, which was a few floors down from where they were staying. It appeared as if some walls had been knocked down in several apartments to create this space. Hard metal folding chairs were scattered in clumsy rows facing the front area where Rev had given a speech. She had been surprised to see how many denizens of the Old Western District trickled in prior to the meetings' start. The room was soon filled, and the meeting began. Rev stood before the assembly, greeted everyone, and then started singing "Amazing Grace," with the crowd quietly joining in. The people were wary of making too much noise, as the threat of secret police or even agents from the Office of Progression loomed like a cloud over the proceedings. As they sang, however, Laura could feel a sense of peace fill the room. It was strange to her, but it was a welcome feeling given the circumstances. Once the song ended, Rev said some words to his God, and began to speak to the crowd. He talked about a man named Paul who had endured much suffering a long time ago for telling people about his God, Jesus. Rev then encouraged everyone to stand strong and keep their faith, no matter the circumstances.

Laura enjoyed listening to him speak; he was filled with passion and sincerity. He shut his eyes and once more spoke to his God. As he did so, Laura could hear some people begin to weep softly, and she had no idea why. The feeling of peace she'd had now pulsated within her, calling out to her. She didn't know what to do with it, and decided that the people in the crowd who were weeping were feeling what she felt, too. Some of the people approached Rev, who'd lay a hand on their shoulder, or give a hug, while he spoke to God on their behalf. These people would walk away with joy on their faces, despite the harsh lives they were going back to afterward. Laura just wanted to linger and enjoy the feeling that was so tangible in the room.

She shut her eyes, and when she opened them, she noticed that much time had passed. People were on the way out the door, being handed rations and supplies donated by anonymous citizens from the more well off areas of the city. Laura sat and waited, and as the last people exited she noticed that Titus was sitting in the front with Rev. The intimidating man she'd met earlier now seemed small and humble, she saw what appeared to be tear streaks on his face. Laura closed her eyes, simmering in the now waning atmosphere; not wanting to disturb the two friends as they talked. She just listened, as she was unsure of what she was supposed to do now that the gathering was technically over. She peeked again, and saw Titus hang his head slightly.

"Rev . . . this part of our lives . . . it's just never easy," he said finally.

"Saying goodbye to an old friend is never easy, brother," Rev answered.

"I just feel responsible," Titus said, "I should have had Jamie's contacts get him out months ago. I should have gotten him out myself!" Rev spoke softly, but firmly,

"If you'd tried, it would have blown a lot of people's cover, Titus. That's all part of this cloak and dagger business we've gotten mixed up in. The boss gave you this team to make a real difference, and we are doing just that. C'mon, mighty man of valor; rise up! I know you're feeling like Gideon did, hiding in the winepress, but that is *not* who you really are!" Rev's eyes welled up with tears.

"You are strong. You're a warrior. I know better than most the pain of losing loved ones in this fight, and we've all lost someone. It's not your fault, you have to believe it. Mikey-boy is with our Lord now. Free from all this pain, sorrow, all of it. Someday, we'll get to join him," Rev paused, tears now flowing freely as he looked to the sky. "Lord, tell Mikey hi for us . . . and tell Annie and the kids I love them."

Titus pulled his friend into an embrace as the two shared tears for their loved ones. It was all Laura could do to not start bawling in sympathy for her new friends. She buried her face in her hands, choking back the tears. The two men stood and made their way towards the back, in her direction. Laura looked up, and when they came near, she jumped up and threw her arms around them both, tears streaking her cheeks. They both chuckled, and returned the hug.

"Now we have another loved one to watch over, brother," Rev said, smiling. "We'll make a warrior of you yet, little sister."

Laura accompanied Titus and Rev back to the little apartment the Ghosts had holed up in. Park had pulled out a cot and was busying himself on his tough case computer. Laura saw the screen flashing a myriad of holographic images and work windows that he furiously swiped, tapped, encoded, decoded and read. Spectre was reading a book while stretched out on a cot next to Park's. The cover had some Chinese lettering, and the book itself was very thin. He looked frustrated as he shifted again and again, trying to find some way to be comfortable on the loud creaky cot. Jamie and Doc were over in the corner cleaning weapons, seated on more metal folding chairs and chatting together. Laura could read some of their body language, and, apart from sitting together at breakfast to help her theory, it seemed to her that the two were interested in each other. Titus caught Hank's eye and excused himself. The two men went through another door, beyond which Laura hadn't had an opportunity yet to see. Rev walked over to the kitchenette and, grabbing a glass, filled it with water after struggling with the filter that Park had set up.

"Yo, Hollywood! Why are there little black flakes in the water?" his loud voice carried across the room. Park didn't even look up from his work.

"It's charcoal; it's technically good for you! Look, just tighten the filtration actuator on the bottom and then the two nuts on the side!" Rev stared at the very obviously jerry-rigged contraption in frustration.

"The wha-? Pssh . . . wish he'd stop actuatin' his mouth and fix the thing himself."

Laura, witnessing the drama unfold, shook her head and smiled. She moved over to where Park and Spectre were racked out, curious about what they were doing. Spectre smiled as she approached, and sat up, gesturing for her to join her.

"Hello, Laura, please have a seat." Laura grabbed a chair and sat, motioning at the book.

"What are you reading?" she asked.

"Ah, this is Sun Tzu's *The Art of War*. It is very short, yet the principles it teaches are very broad when you take time to think deeply about it." Laura crossed her arms, curious.

"So . . . philosophy?" she asked.

Spectre nodded. "Yes, military philosophy. In my opinion, however, it'd be a good read for anyone in a leadership role. Consider this: '*Treat your men as you would your own beloved sons. And they will follow you into the deepest valley.*'" Laura bit her lip unconsciously; thinking.

"So, a good leader should treat their followers like family, which will garner the best response from them . . . not just because they have to obey, but because they'll want to."

Spectre nodded. "Yes, one could say that love is the greater motivator, even above fear or selfish ambition." Laura studied his face a moment.

"Why are you telling me this? What do you have to gain?" she asked, holding his gaze.

"It is my belief that you will be presented with a choice, Laura, very soon. One path will lead you to a life of freedom, whether it is in Texas, "Rebel Territory," as you call it or elsewhere. The other path, well, you will take freedom and share it with your brothers and sisters currently held under the iron grip of the Party. This second path will not be easy, but it is one that means so much more." A smile crept onto his face. "As to what I, we, have to gain . . . well, I think someone with your skillset and knowledge of this city would be a beneficial asset to this team. So, to come full circle, I bring up the philosophical discussion to shed light on whom it is you would be following, should you so choose."

Laura's eyebrows rose. "I thought so . . . you guys are planning another mission, and you need my help with it."

Spectre nodded. "Although, it is not my place to officially extend an invitation, I would be very glad if you'd agree to participate."

Laura considered the thought. "Alright, Ben, I'm intrigued . . . I guess we'll just have to wait and see what happens, though, right?"

Spectre nodded, smiling. "I'll be sure to convey my opinion, and recommendations upward," he said.

Chapter 8

LAURA HAD CONTINUED CHATTING with Spectre for a while longer, Park eventually joining in the conversation. She learned more about both men, but more specifically, why they were engaged in their current struggle. Spectre elaborated more on the economic and diplomatic isolation his nation was suffering without the support of the once great USA as its staunch ally. Israel continued to struggle to survive amidst decades of prolonged conflicts waged by its neighbors. Thankfully, they hadn't needed to put to use the nuclear option, as the threat of mutually assured destruction kept at bay the Iranian Caliphate's nuclear arsenal, and the conflict at large conventional. Spectre was hopeful that a resurrected American alliance would tip the scales back into Israel's favor. Laura could see the pain filling the eyes of both Spectre and Park as they shared their experiences.

Park had grown up under the puppet regime the People's Republic of China had installed forty years ago in the "Unified Korea" initiative. The North Koreans, backed by their Chinese allies, invaded the South in a short and brutal conflict that saw Seoul razed and millions of people enslaved. Park's parents escaped when he was ten years old, making their way across Southeast Asia and then eventually were granted asylum in Texas. He then was able to dedicate himself to the good education afforded him by his new home. While in college, he was recruited by the Texan Army's Intelligence Division, putting to use his technical skills and learning new ones. He eventually met Jamie Bell and volunteered to aid the Underground Railroad. Laura was a little surprised at how much information they were willing to volunteer to her, given that she still hadn't committed to helping their cause as of yet. Maybe it was an act of faith, she wondered. Everyone's attention shifted suddenly as Titus came back into the room. He moved over to the table and glanced around the room and spoke.

"Alright people, we have a new directive from Haunted House. In three days, we are moving to Site Kilo and linking up with the Underground Railroad cell there. We will have plenty of time to prepare in the meantime, as the Kilo cell is handling most of the logistical support. Our mission: infiltrate Newark Rehab Center, liberate any prisoners being held inside, and grab any intel we can find. We will then transport them back to Site Kilo and exfil back to friendly turf. I will have the final plan ready for you soon. Any questions?"

Rev raised his hand. "Yeah, where's Valkyrie?"

"Valkyrie is en-route to Site Kilo at this time to help them secure transportation, most likely a meat wagon," Titus responded.

"Are we headed for Texas afterward? I could use a vacation," Jamie joked. Titus chuckled a little, before replying.

"Yes, arrangements are being made with the Underground Railroad to move us to Texas. I don't know if we'll be there long enough for R&R though." He looked around and, seeing no one had any more questions, started to move. Laura caught his eye, and he stopped as she approached.

"Captain Hansen, I don't want to be a bother, but I do have a few questions if you have a moment," she asked.

"Please, Ms. Collins, call me Titus. You don't need to sir or captain me; I try to keep things informal around here. What's on your mind?" Titus replied, giving Laura his undivided attention.

"Well then you call me Laura . . . miss sounds like I'm an old lady or something," Laura smirked and continued. "What's actually happening at the Rehab Center? All I'd ever heard of it was that they took the occasional junkie or loon in and zapped them straight."

"Well, Laura," Titus began. "In truth it is a regional Office of Progression facility. They house political prisoners that are waiting to be either executed or transferred off to a hard labor camp indefinitely. It serves our purposes to hit it, as we can save some lives and disrupt the activity of our enemies' more ruthless arm, albeit temporarily." Laura paused, considering the information.

"It's beginning to sound like the Party really has no end to its cruelty. . ." she trailed off, feeling disgusted that such things were going on in plain sight, and that she may have inadvertently had a hand in it. Titus narrowed his eyes, studying her.

"You okay?" he asked. Laura shook her head, meeting his gaze.

"I don't know, I'm . . . angry, to say the least. Sick, even. I feel like my time as a cop, and my colleagues as well, was just being used to help prop up a disgusting and tyrannical system." She sighed, crossing her arms. "I was loyal, you know? I wanted to do a good job and try to do what was right.

In reality, I did what *they* said was right, and now I'm left here wishing that nobody got hurt because of me. I won't have any way of knowing . . ."

"You didn't know any better, Laura. How could you have? You were told to accept what they said as truth," Titus broke in, his tone reassuring. Laura managed a small smile.

"I want to help, if I can. With this mission, at least," she said, standing straight and firm.

Titus nodded. "Absolutely. Tell you what, link up with Park. He has our primary routes through the city. I need you to determine if we'll run into any checkpoints or patrols that we may have missed in our recon."

"Sure thing; I'll get right on it," Laura said.

"Oh, and talk to Jamie about getting some gear. She has a cache here with all sorts of things . . . just be sure to get all black, we have a specific look we're going for on this mission," Titus added, smirking just a little.

The days passed quickly for Laura, a combination of her continued convalescence and contributing where she could towards the mission they were about to embark on. They packed into an SUV they'd "acquired" from their last engagement with the feds. The plates were swapped, and the electronic ID tags were hacked, changing the status of the vehicle from listed as "missing" to "active." Laura felt a little off put, as they had elected to wear the black armor and gear they'd acquired from the OP federal agents. Doc sat behind the wheel, with Titus seated in the front passenger seat. Titus was dressed like a senior agent, wearing the ensemble of dark suit with bullet proof vest, shoulder holstered sidearm, and even dark glasses. Laura sat behind Doc, with Park and Jamie next to her; Rev and Spectre sat in the rear. They rode in relative silence, although occasionally somebody had commentary to make on the Old Western District. Laura learned that technically they were in New Jersey, according to Rev, and at some point, New York essentially absorbed much of its' territory. Not that it mattered, as the PSRA consisted of five District-States and many of the former states no longer existed in people's memory, let alone history books. Laura absorbed all the information, caught up in the new filter from which she was now observing her previous life. It seemed so alien to her now, despite the short span of time. Nothing was the same anymore, she decided, and she had quite a learning curve. The distance they had to travel was not a great one, but the route that Laura plotted for Park took them away from all the checkpoints she'd been aware of. The trip was significantly longer, but the benefit of missing the chance of being discovered prematurely was worth it. They were silent for a while, until Park chimed in.

"Guys . . . we really look like the space troopers from . . . oh what was it called?" he said. Laura gave him a perplexed look.

"What are you talking about?" she asked, wondering if it held any significance to the mission. She'd come to discover that it was hit or miss with Park.

He chuckled. "Ah, well there's this film from the 1980s . . . the bad guys had black armor kind of like this, wore big bulbous helmets. I'm spacing out on what it was called though. It's really funny, maybe I'll find it and show it to you once we get to Texas."

"You spacing out? That sounds like a Freudian slip!" Rev piped up, laughing. "We might not get the time; we could be sent home fairly quickly."

Laura was curious. "Home? Is that a base in Texas, or something?" she asked.

"Home is classified," Doc answered. "We don't call it anything else, in case unfriendly ears or electronics are listening."

"Whoa now, Doc, don't you trust my ability to make this a clean ride?" Park asked, sounding defensive. He dramatically placed his hand over his chest and sighed, feigning a wound.

"Can it, Hollywood!" Doc ordered. Park tapped Laura on the shoulder.

"He's just a grump. We'll find out what it's called and watch it without him," he whispered. Doc glared at him through the rear-view mirror. An awkward silence followed.

Titus turned to look behind him in the vehicle, his gaze studying everyone. He started to smirk, prompting confused looks from Laura, Park and Jamie. Doc glanced over at Titus, perplexed. Titus turned back around.

"I know what movie he's talking about. He's right, though, I see it now!" he finally said, breaking into laughter.

"Oh c'mon boss, help a guy out!" Park complained. Titus just shook his head, still smirking.

Park looked flustered, as the others laughed at his expense. Doc just shook his head, a small smile creeping across his lips. Laura looked at Jamie and shrugged. Park leaned forward and poked Titus on the shoulder. After a moment, the laughter subsided, and Titus reeled them back in.

"Okay, okay, focus up. We'll be at Site Kilo soon . . . " his voice trailed off. "I just hope the old man got the meat wagon or this is going to be a real short trip," he added. Park let out a quick bark of laughter,

"Oh, good one, sir . . . I see what you did there! I applaud anyone who can integrate or modify a quote from the galaxy's greatest smuggler into a conversation."

Titus smiled, pleased with the quip. "Alright, for real now, heads up."

Laura didn't bother to ask about the quotation, as she was sure it wasn't worth it. She turned her attention back to observing the goings-on outside the vehicle, hoping that they didn't get stopped and run the risk of anyone recognizing her. People on the streets moved out of their way as they rolled towards their objective, their gazes filled with either terror or spite. Laura felt for them and didn't take any offense at the nasty glares she caught. She commended them for even being brave enough to conjure up that form of silent protest. A few more moments passed, and they drove into an old railyard. Laura noticed some men obscured in positions that looked as if they were prepared for a fight. They had arrived at Site Kilo.

Chapter 9

THE TEAM DISMOUNTED THEIR SUV and gathered around an old rail car. With them stood the members from the Site Kilo Cell, along with their leader Bruce Conway. Bruce was a short, stocky man in his sixties, his hair very short and grey. Laura looked around, taking note of her surroundings. This railyard appeared to still be in use, as nearby the sounds of shipping containers being loaded onto trains permeated the area. Laura wasn't sure just how many people were associated with this cell but suspected that at the least a significant portion of the individuals working at the rail yard were involved in one way or another. In this case, it was literally an Underground Railroad. There was still an old system of railway infrastructure, but alongside it was an underground hyperloop system that had been emplaced before the PSRA's rise to power. Laura glanced around the rail car and noted that Valkyrie's grand theft auto had been successful. He'd acquired a meat wagon for them to use. Titus and Bruce stepped forward a few paces, moving to a place from which they could address the crowd. Bruce let out a loud whistle, and everyone turned their attention to him and Titus. Titus spoke first, loudly.

"Today, we have an opportunity to do some real good, to save some lives. Our goal is to get in and out as quickly and cleanly as possible. However, as we all know, no plan ever survives the flames of action, so I ask for your continued vigilance and professionalism to ensure that the mission is ultimately a success. I'd prefer not to take any lives tonight, but if you are in danger do not hesitate to protect yourself, your buddy, and the people we're saving." Titus scanned the crowd, then reiterated. "I say again, if we are compromised, weapons are free. Now, for the strategy: Hollywood has rigged up micro chip spikes embedded in the wrist plates of your armor. These will defeat any ID scans, allowing us access to the facility. Once in, the meat wagon will stage at the prisoner loading dock. A small contingent and

34

I will enter the administration section and order a prisoner transfer. Bruce?"
Bruce stepped forward.

"That's where our Kilo Strikers come in. The prisoners will be escorted by agents, and because of that, I want one Striker shadowing each agent in the event that weapons go hot so we can neutralize the threat and secure the dock ASAP. Kilo Movers," he paused as a section of men and women let out a bark. Bruce grinned and continued. "Movers, you will stand by here to aid this last load of refugees. I want the container on the train in no less than two minutes from the meat wagon rolling back in. I need two to dispose of the truck once it is offloaded." Bruce nodded back at Titus.

"Ghosts, I'll need Rev and Doc to take the gate after we roll in, Valkyrie is providing overwatch. Hollywood and Cowgirl will remain in the meat wagon to run comms. Spectre, Laura, you're with me," Titus added.

The Ghosts vocalized their acknowledgement. Laura did as well, offering a loud "Roger." Bruce then shouted for everyone to load up, and movement began. As Laura and the Ghosts began to load into the cab of the meat wagon, Bruce caught Titus by the arm.

"Titus, if things go south, as they tend to these days, those feds will be gunning for you with everything they've got," he said, his gruff voice carrying loud enough for Laura to hear.

Titus nodded. "What did you have in mind, old friend?" Bruce pointed over at a shipping container that a Kilo Mover had opened. The Movers rushed in, reappearing with a number of shoulder-mounted anti-air missile launchers.

"We've been seeing more choppers recently, so we made a request from some friends and they hooked us up with these bad boys." Titus studied his friend for a moment.

"You're going to follow us, aren't you?" he pried. Bruce held his gaze for a moment.

"You just worry about getting those poor souls out of that hole and let me worry about covering your escape. I've got you." Bruce extended his hand, which Titus shook. "Until we meet again; in this life or eternity."

"Godspeed, Bruce . . . and thank you," Titus said, his jaw clenching slightly with emotion.

"Just promise me one thing," Bruce said. "Make sure you win, sonny boy . . . make sure you win."

The Ghosts rode in silence toward their objective. Laura considered what may happen should their mission take a deadly turn. Although she'd never ridden in a meat wagon, she was aware of its capabilities. The armor would protect them from small arms, but Laura wasn't sure about heavier weapons. The vehicle was equipped with re-inflating tires as well, should someone decide to attempt to immobilize them. They slowly approached the main gate, where two guards scrutinized the vehicle through the dark visors of their helmets. Laura dropped her visor down slowly and turned to glance at Park as he stole a quick last second check of their chip spike status.

"Let's hope these codes were worth the price we paid . . ." he muttered quietly.

Titus shook his head, a small smile on his face. One gate guard directed them to stop. The vehicle came to a slow chugging halt and the guard approached the driver's window. The driver, one of Bruce's Kilo Strikers by the name of Ace, rolled down the window. He extended out his arm, palm down, and the guard waved a scanner pad under his wrist. The guard looked back at his partner, who gave a thumbs up.

"What's the purpose of your trip tonight?" the guard asked.

"We've been sent to pick up a load for Camp Unity," Ace replied. The guard nodded and gestured toward the facility.

"Roger, they seem to be going through a lot of 'em lately. You guys are good to go, just be careful on your way out; there's been some terrorist activity along that route lately."

Ace nodded and lumbered the truck forward. Once the window rolled back up, there was a collective sigh of relief. Laura looked over at Park and gave him a thumbs up. He mouthed thanks and pounded fists with Jamie. Ace pulled the vehicle wide around to the loading area and backed into the bay. The squads dismounted and headed for their designated areas, ready for anything. Laura watched the Kilo Strikers enter the bay door as she, Titus and Spectre went through a set of double doors labeled "Administration." Laura listened as Park and Jamie began to coordinate with the Strikers and Ghosts via their in-ear comms. Laura and Spectre followed Titus, keeping an escort detail formation close behind as they followed Jamie's directions through the winding hallways. As they walked, Laura felt a chill go down her spine. The building felt very eerie to her, as if there was some sort of seeping darkness that dimmed the already poorly lit hallways even deeper. The atmosphere was cold and had a strange unpleasant odor. The building itself must be old, Laura decided, and not somewhere she wanted to be any longer than she had to. Jamie directed them toward a main door at the end of the hallway, where Laura read a sign that said, "Administration and Processing." She was given a strong indication that the people who manned this facility looked at their prisoners as little more than meat. The doors opened as they approached granting them access to the office. There were three men in the room, given that it was late into the night they hadn't expected more than that. *So far, so good*, Laura thought. One of the men was clearly busy with clerical work, another monitoring security feeds from his work station, and the last one sat behind a desk in the middle of the room. He seemed to be the man in charge, given the placement of his desk which included a large plaque proudly bearing his name, reading: Agent Gordon P. Brewer. Titus stepped forward, and Agent Brewer casually glanced up.

"Be with you in just a moment . . . too many reports to review," he muttered, turning his attention back to his computer.

His fingers typed away furiously as he tried to finish whatever business he'd been attending to. Laura's gaze tracked over to the agent monitoring the security feeds. He had his feet kicked up and looked like he was only trying to entertain himself with whatever caught his attention on the screen. The other man looked visibly frustrated with his clerical work, probably facing down an ever-increasing workload. Laura looked back at Brewer, amazed at how someone could just flippantly ignore his fellow agents. He seemed as if he had forgotten they were even there.

"What's the holdup?" Jamie's voice crackled through the in-ear comm channel. Titus stood still, hands folded behind his back, posture rigid and imposing. He cleared his throat, catching Brewer's attention.

"Agent Brewer, are you deliberately wasting my time?" Titus asked as he took a step toward the desk.

"My apologies, agent . . . ?" Brewer said, worried.

"*Special* Agent Grant Mitchel," Titus replied, playing the part of a very irritated senior agent. Brewer and his men snapped to; caught off guard by the title.

"Beg your pardon, sir!" Brewer apologized again. "We don't usually receive guests of your prestige." Laura detected the attempt to brown nose. Titus continued the pompous air, looking down at the sniveling man.

"Yes, that much is apparent to me," he said. Laura glanced at Spectre, and despite their helmet visors being down, they shared a collective eye roll. Brewer fixed his tie, visibly nervous.

"Now, what can I do for you, sir?"

Titus slowly moved about the room, glancing towards anything that could potentially be intel to grab should Park say so as he watched the HUD feed from Titus' glasses.

"I have a prisoner transport outside; I need more prisoners for Camp Unity. Have you any available at your . . . *disposal*?" Titus emphasized the last word. Laura cringed at the thought of it, despite knowing they were there for a different purpose.

"Yes, yes of course sir, but, as you know, I need to clear it." Brewer said, springing to action, resuming his work station to begin the transfer orders.

"Yes, be quick about it. I do not have all night," Titus replied, feigning more irritation. A few minutes passed, Park sent through a few short commands to Brewer's terminal, and then Brewer looked up at Titus.

"Excellent, it appears that I have twelve prisoners currently, my men will begin loading them onto your transport. It'll be a few minutes, sir; I will draw up some paper work as well."

Titus nodded at Brewer and continued to scan the room. Laura moved over to the security monitor, stood behind the guard, attempting to get a better look at what he was watching. The man moved his feet off the desk and scooted away a little for her.

"You ever work this side of the shop?" he asked, casually.

"No, I've only been out in the field," Laura lied. The man crossed his arms and let out a sigh.

"I used to be a field agent like you, until I took a bullet to the knee. Been riding the desk ever since."

"Tough break," Laura replied.

"Yeah, but the bright side is I get to watch some artists put on quite a show," the guard gestured to the monitor, grinning widely. Laura leaned closer to the screen, scanning over the feeds. She noticed a small, lone figure, seated in a chair, but she couldn't discern the face due to the darkness.

"Can you zoom in on that one?" Laura asked, pointing at the feed.

The guard complied, enlarging the screen. Laura's heart started pounding so hard and fast it felt as if it were about to explode. Her palms were beginning to sweat, her jaw clenched in unquenchable rage and horror in equal measure. Jamie chimed in suddenly.

"Laura, what's wrong? Are you okay? Does anyone have eyes on Laura? Her heart rate is spiking!"

Titus and Spectre both spun to look as subtle, yet quick, as possible. Titus walked over, stopped next to her, and looked at what she was staring at. The guard piped up again, with a loud chuckle that startled Laura back into reality.

"Oh yeah, this one's been one of my favorites. They just finished the old fingernail factory treatment on her, here look," he zoomed the camera on the prisoner's hands, showcasing the damage.

Laura quietly reached over and squeezed Titus' arm, her grip tighter than a vice. There were several tiny, shimmering needles protruding from beneath the prisoner's nails. The guard pulled the camera back and maneuvered the feed to view the prisoner's face.

"Yup, this one was brought in about a week ago; associated with that terrorist ordeal at the food distribution center. Hang on," he allowed the camera to focus on the face and then the computer displayed the prisoner information. "Here we go . . . Collins, Jackie . . . Scheduled for sanitation tomorrow morning," the guard finished.

Laura looked up at Titus, she let go of his arm and said nothing. She was mortified, angry, and unsure of what she was going to do. She had to save her mother, no matter what. She was an innocent woman, having done nothing to deserve the horrific torture she had to endure. Her only crime, like Laura, was that she was part of Bill Collins' family. Sanitation. That's what they called murder now. Laura clenched her fists, her right hand then dropping to squeeze the grip of her pistol in its' holster.

"Dear God," Jamie said.

"Laura, it's okay, we will get her out," Park assured her.

"This one . . . I want this one as well as any other scheduled for sanitization," Titus said to Brewer, pointing at the screen. "They will make excellent examples for the others at Camp Unity."

"The terrorists? Ah well, I don't see why not. There's this plus two more . . . I will amend the transfer order," Brewer replied, typing away.

Laura was nervous, as this operation seemed to be taking an eternity. Now her mother was part of it, only adding to the tension. A moment passed, and Laura turned her attention back to the monitor. She watched as her mother and the last of the prisoners were being loaded onto the meat wagon. Brewer stood up from his desk, walked around to where Titus stood, and presented a biometric scan pad.

"Just one last box to check sir; to close out the transfer and custody orders."

Titus waved his wrist over the pad and it flashed green. Next, he placed his palm on the pad and it flashed white a few times sporadically before flashing red. Brewer looked confused, pressed a few buttons to reset the system, and presented the pad once again for Titus.

"It must be a glitch, sir, let's give it another try."

Laura saw Titus clench his jaw as he placed his hand back on the pad. It flashed red. Brewer let out an exasperated gasp, shook his head, and started to backpedal. His hand started to reach, slowly, within his jacket. In a flash, Titus punched his throat hard, crushing Brewer's trachea. As the choking man collapsed to the ground, Laura and Spectre quickly drew their weapons and fired, killing the other guards. Blood splattered all over the stations where they'd been working.

"Weapons free! I say again, weapons free!" Titus commanded through the radio.

He kicked Brewer in the hand, knocking away the weapon he'd drawn as he continued struggling for air. An alarm began to bellow through the facility as Spectre then took aim and put the man out of his misery.

"Move out," Titus ordered.

Laura heard bursts of gunfire erupt nearby. They charged down the maze of hallways, heading for the main entrance. Laura looked out the window as she noticed enemy agents dropping in rapid succession. She heard Valkyrie's voice finally, as he chimed in.

"Courtyard clear, Rev, Doc proceed to gate."

Laura stole another glance as she ran, noting the two figures charging the gate in the dark. A couple muzzle flashes lit the night, beginning and ending the maneuver in rapid succession.

"Gate secure, dropping combat lockout," Rev reported. Spectre kicked open the main entrance door leading to the courtyard.

"Meat wagon inbound, ten seconds," Park said. The loud truck rumbled around the building, sliding to a halt in front of them. Laura, Titus, and Spectre jumped into the cab.

"Punch it, Ace," Titus said.

Ace complied, revving the motor loudly and barreling toward the gate. Bullets struck the armor plating, as more OP agents swarmed the courtyard in pursuit. Rev and Doc returned fire from the gate and Valkyrie continued to snipe from his overwatch position. The truck slowed to clear the gate and stopped for Rev and Doc. Laura leaned out as the door opened and laid down covering fire for the two men. She witnessed Valkyrie's handiwork as heads began to explode in fountains of gore. The OP agents fell back, momentarily suppressed by the sniper fire. Doc deployed the gate combat lockout; the heavy barriers shot up loudly. He jumped aboard the truck, grabbing a handrail as Rev tossed a grenade inside the gate shack, destroying the controls. Doc clambered into the cab as the truck shot forward again, bumping down the road. Laura scanned everyone in the cab of the truck, visually conducting a quick blood sweep on herself and those near her.

"Kilo Actual, Ghost One," Titus called via the radio.

"Send it, Ghost One," came the reply.

"Ghost Team inbound with one-five guests, say again one-five guests, break," He paused a beat. "ETA three-one mikes, how copy, over?" The radio crackled a second.

"Good copy Ghost One, we'll roll out the welcome mat, out." Laura looked out the window, weapon ready as she scanned her sector of fire.

"Ghost One, Valkyrie. Enemy VIX closing on your location. ETA two minutes, how copy?" Valkyrie reported.

"Good copy, Valkyrie. Proceed to exfil, out," Titus replied.

"Here we go people," Rev shouted, reloading his carbine. Laura checked her magazine, replaced it, and slapped her spare mag pouches to verify they were still there.

"You good?" Doc asked her, glancing at her arm.

"Yeah I'm good," she replied.

Titus looked at her, nodding. She gave him a half smile. Despite being physically good, she wasn't good mentally. She was worried for her mother, who was stuffed in the back with the other prisoners and Kilo Strikers. Her thoughts were interrupted by more bullets pinging off the truck. She took a deep breath and readied herself for another round.

The meat wagon swerved all over the narrow two lane road as Ace attempted to run the OP SUVs off the pavement and into surrounding trees. It was all Laura could do to hang on as a hail of bullets struck the windows and the truck shifted left and right violently. The truck shuddered and shook as one of the tires was blown and struggled to re inflate. A pair of SUVs surrounded the truck and agents fired from their windows. It was getting to the point where it was difficult to see due to the spiderweb cracking from bullet strikes against the windshield.

"We need to shake things up," Titus said.

As if on cue, Spectre wrapped a seat belt around his torso, braced, and opened his door. He leaned out the door a little and sprayed the neighboring SUV with automatic weapons fire. He hit the side passengers and then the tire, causing the vehicle to swerve wildly. It careened off the road and smashed into the forest. Doc and Laura repeated the maneuver on the other side, disabling one vehicle and causing another to fall back. Laura's attention turned ahead as she saw another SUV careen onto the road from the right.

"Ghost One, Valkyrie. I've got this one," came the voice of their sniper.

They saw Valkyrie wave from the window of the new SUV before he swerved around the meat wagon and disappeared behind. Laura craned her neck, trying to catch a glimpse of the action. Unable to see, her curiosity was sated by the sound of gunshots and crashing of metal as Valkyrie disabled the enemy vehicle.

"Tango down," came the report. A cheer arose in the cabin of the meat wagon.

"Yes! We got 'em!" Ace shouted in celebration. Laura rolled her window down.

"I hear something," she murmured to herself. A sense of fear skyrocketed from within her. "Chopper inbound!" She roared, ducking her head as she rolled the window back up.

"Heads down!" Titus shouted.

The road ahead of them began to explode with chunks of pavement sent airborne by strafing weapon fire. Ace tried to swerve out of the path of the bullets. He was too late. Armor piercing rounds tore through the engine block, the windshield, and finally Ace. There was a cry of horror;

Laura wasn't quite sure from whom, as she saw what was left of their driver. Spectre clambered forward, taking the wheel of the out of control vehicle. He shoved the remains of Ace out the driver door, muttering an apology. Laura was too shocked to feel sick.

"Get down!" Doc yelled, seeing the fast attack helicopter making another run, this time from their left side. Laura ducked as glass showered the cab, hot bullets and broken metal screaming above her head.

"He's trying to take our heads off!" she called out.

Doc was breathing threats, amongst other unintelligible curses, as he leaned out his door again to return fire. His shots missed, but he didn't care. The chopper turned to make another pass. This time, however, it didn't attack the meat wagon.

"Taking fire!" shouted Valkyrie. Laura heard the harsh thumping of rotor blades pass overhead and automatic fire strike pavement.

"Valkyrie! Status!" Titus called.

"Nearly lost my melon, but I'm okay," Valkyrie replied. Laura sighed in relief, making eye contact with Titus. He shared the relief and replied.

"Good copy."

"Uh, boss," Spectre pointed forward.

They had just crested a hill and Laura's heart stopped at the sight before them. There was a roadblock up ahead, just shy of the outskirts of the city. OP SUVs occupied the road space, agents training their weapons toward the meat wagon. The chopper hovered above the road block, daring them to proceed. Titus looked at Spectre, then back at his crew. Laura offered him a grim stare. He took a deep breath, looked forward again, and said:

"Run it."

Spectre stomped on the accelerator pedal causing the vehicle to lurch as it struggled to comply. The agents began to open fire, pelting the already compromised armor with more damage. Laura winced as the distance rapidly closed. She could see the rotary machine gun on the chopper begin to spin, poised to end them. Laura took a deep breath. Then the chopper erupted into massive ball of flame before dropping onto the vehicles below. The meat wagon swerved right, missing the flaming hulk, but smashed into an SUV. They emerged through the road block, smoking but intact.

"Ghost One, Kilo Actual. Looks like we showed up just in time," Bruce's voice cracked through the radio. A cheer erupted from the cab.

"Many thanks, Kilo Actual . . . be careful out there," Titus replied.

"Yeah Bruce!" Park cheered.

The meat wagon lumbered toward Bruce's position further up road. Laura could see him and two other Kilo Movers firing automatic weapons and rockets at their pursuers. The crew waved and saluted the bold Movers as they passed by.

"I'll see you on the other side, Ghosts. Kilo Actual signing off," he replied. Laura watched him and his two brave Movers for as long as she could.

The meat wagon choked and sputtered its way into Site Kilo. Time had passed by quickly as they grew closer to their destination, adrenaline still running hot. Spectre brought the truck to a skidding halt just short of the shipping container that they were going to be loading into, followed by Valkyrie. The Kilo Movers wasted no time rushing people out of the meat wagon and into the container, clasping their chip-wrists with a signal blocking cuff. Laura and the Ghosts aided the process, before loading themselves into the container.

"Welcome to the Conex express!" Park joked, jumping in.

"Hurry, people, let's move!" Titus ordered the remaining few as they clambered in.

Laura could hear the thunder of more explosions off in the distance as Bruce and his men encountered a raging onslaught. The Conex doors were slammed shut as Laura strapped herself into a crash seat built into the wall. She felt the container lurch upward as the Kilo Movers loaded them onto a hyperloop freight train that was scheduled to depart in less than sixty seconds. The Conex thundered as it was hefted aboard and dropped down.

"All aboard!" Rev boomed. Laura felt the train lurch and then nothing after that. She looked over at Park, who was interfacing with a control module near his crash seat.

"Hey Park, are we moving?" she asked. He nodded, typed a few more commands and then replied.

"This train is electromagnetically suspended, giving the reduced sense of inertia." Laura then noticed that she did indeed feel it, however slightly.

"We've hacked the train to go faster, thereby causing it to get ahead of schedule so that when we stop it later to offload, it arrives at its' eventual destination on time," he added. Laura looked around frantically for her mother.

"Is it safe to stand?" she asked.

"Give it another minute, we're dipping underground now," he said.

Laura felt her stomach rise and dip back down as gravity played with them. Once it was steady, Park nodded to her, and Laura unstrapped from the crash seat. She searched, scanning faces amongst the people they'd rescued. There. Jackie Collins was seated toward the other end of the container, with Doc tending to her wounds. Laura rushed through the now mingling crowd of teary eyed and grateful people.

"Mom!" Laura called, causing more than a few to be startled by the sound. Jackie shot out of her seat, much to Doc's protest, with a wild look in her eyes as she recognized the voice of her child.

"Laura? Laura!" Jackie replied as her daughter nearly tackled her in a tight embrace. Both sobbed freely, not wanting to let go. "Is it really you?" Jackie finally managed through her tears. She took Laura's face in her hands, studying her daughter as if she was caught in a dream.

"Yeah, mom, I'm really here . . . I'm here," Laura responded holding her mother's gaze through teary eyes.

"I was so afraid, they took me, and I was so worried that they'd taken you as well," Jackie said, hugging Laura again. Doc gestured to Laura that they should take a seat, and Laura eased her mother back down so he could tend to her wounds.

"They tried to, mom. They tried hard," Laura gestured to Doc and the other Ghosts. "But, these people saved me and kind of adopted me into their family, so to speak." Laura then recounted to her mother everything that'd happened to her, not skimping on details as Doc assured her that they had plenty of time.

"You were shot!?" Jackie exclaimed as Laura mentioned it probably too casually. "She was shot?" Jackie looked at Doc, who chuckled and nodded. It really didn't feel so drastic to Laura anymore, in light of recent events, more like a distant memory.

"Oh, don't fuss over me, mom, I'm okay. Doc got me all patched up," she smiled at Doc, before continuing, "I'm more worried for you, what with all the horrible things they did to you."

Jackie looked at her bandaged hands, emotion flooding her face. Laura felt horrible the moment she realized what she'd said. *Tact . . . I need more tact*, she thought. Jackie looked her daughter in her eyes, as if reading her mind.

"Laura, don't go beating yourself up, I'm fine," she insisted, "Seeing you alive and well fills me with hope and erases anything they've done." Laura smiled sheepishly.

"Sorry, mom. It seems that I inherited dad's uncanny ability to say the wrong thing at the wrong time . . ." Laura put her head on Jackie's shoulder.

"I miss him too . . ." Jackie whispered as they shared a long moment of silence together.

Chapter 10

LAURA STIRRED, FEELING A gentle hand on her shoulder. It belonged to Jamie, who smiled at her and whispered that she should follow her. Laura had taken Doc's advice to catch some sleep, as did Jackie and the other refugees. Laura hesitated, not wanting to leave her mother's side, but acquiesced to Jamie's request, deciding it must be something important. She yawned, stretched, and followed as Jamie led her to the other side of the Conex back toward Park's command module. Park continued to work at the module, displaying graphics and other things for Titus to scrutinize. The other Ghosts gathered in a close semi-circle, talking quietly. Some of them looked very tired as they'd elected to stay awake rather than take a quick rest.

"Hey there little sister," Rev beamed a large smile at Laura as she approached with Jamie. "How's your momma doin?" Laura returned the smile and answered,

"She's holding up okay, sleeping pretty hard right now though."

"Glad to hear it," Rev said.

Laura looked over at Doc, who looked exhausted. He'd been tending to the refugees non-stop until now, consuming most of the medical supplies provided within the Conex. The dim lights flickered a little, causing him to blink sleepily. His gaze fell upon the sleeping refugees, his tired eyes full of compassion.

"Poor souls," he said. "This is the first time many of them have gotten to sleep in days, let alone eat." Jamie reached out and gave him a gentle squeeze on the shoulder.

"Well, Doc, you fixed them up best you could. They're all grateful." Doc allowed a tired smile.

Laura looked over at Titus. He looked as if he hadn't slept yet either. His normally clean shaven face was covered with stubble, and he had tired circles under his eyes. She wondered how he was holding up. As she studied his face, her gaze traced down his neck. He'd unbuttoned the top few buttons on the shirt he'd been wearing as part of his disguise. She noticed a scar that began at the base of his neck, on the front, that continued downward and grew wider as it went down before disappearing underneath his shirt. Her gaze lingered too long on the scar, for his gaze caught hers for a microsecond. She averted her eyes, looking down and away, cheeks flushed as she felt incredibly awkward for staring for so long. She took a breath, pushed away the embarrassment, and then caught herself looking back at him. She noticed his cheeks had flushed a little, too, despite his attention having returned to Parks' work. Laura looked back to where her mother was still sound asleep, the feeling of embarrassment returning slightly. She found Titus to be handsome and was unable to help but be drawn in by his mysterious nature. She wasn't ready to feel attraction, however. There was too much change, too fast. Her emotions, her life over the last few days had been completely turned upside down and tossed about on the winds of fate. She scoffed at herself for drawing such a conclusion, attributing it to Rev's growing influence on her. He'd probably say his God had something to do with it. She still wasn't sure what to do with that, however. She couldn't deny what she'd experienced at their underground church meeting, but wasn't ready to accept Rev's conclusions just yet. Still too much, too fast, she decided. She still needed time to process.

Her gaze unconsciously wandered back to Titus. She still had a lot of questions for him, not the least of which was whether or not he'd ask her to join their team. She then noticed he'd buttoned the shirt back up, concealing the scar. She looked away again, gritting her teeth, and scolding herself in her mind. The embarrassment washed up again. There was a part of her that wished that he'd enlist her for the team, but was that just the part that kept making her look his way? She'd prided herself in the past in her ability to control her feelings, to mask her reactions so as not to betray her intentions. She needed the sense of control and security. Perhaps she never really was truly able to be in control, but instead was just too busy? She'd always been busy with athletics and schoolwork as a child, before busying herself with study of the law. She'd been busy as she shadowed the Peace Corps Officers on non-school days, then busy through the Academy and finally her job as an Officer. She'd felt in control the entire time, but, as she reflected, she saw that it was an illusion. She was not in control, as current events obviously pointed out, and her feelings were completely haywire. Laura looked back over at her mother, feeling a twinge of guilt. She was an only child, one who'd been too busy for her parents. They'd sacrificed so much for her, especially her father, who'd worked so hard to generate extra income to bribe the right people so she could get into the Academy. At some point, she'd distanced herself from him, according to the plan, but unwittingly in her heart as well. Guilt beat her hard as she recalled what a straight-laced little future Party member she'd started to become, only checked by her father's strong will. She'd pronounce whatever dogma she'd been force fed by the Party and he'd push back. She now knew it was she that drove the wedge between them. She busied herself at the Academy, stopped talking to her father, and rarely to her mother. She wanted control, and she'd gotten it. Tears misted her eyes as she gazed upon her mother. How crushed she and her father must have felt, all because Laura wanted to ignore her real feelings and feel like she was in control because of it. Laura stood and allowed the guilt to pass its way through and then resolved to be a better daughter. She'd lost her chance with her father, but now she could make it up to her mother and do things right. She'd stop trying to be a robot, stop wanting to control, and simply feel.

She took a deep breath, still inwardly conflicted as her gaze returned once more to Titus. If he did ask her to join them, she didn't know what she'd say. She still felt the pull within her to follow him wherever he would lead, but now she needed to weigh it against her responsibility to her mother. Laura's thoughts were interrupted as she noticed Jamie watching her. Jamie's eyebrows were raised suspiciously, her eyes full of mirth and curiosity. It shook Laura out of her mist of heavy thought finally. A large grin formed on Jamie's face. She glanced over her shoulder at Titus, then back at Laura. Laura blushed hard, her eyes entreating Jamie not to say anything. She had no idea for how long Jamie had noticed her watching Titus. Jamie's hands raised and waved a little and she whispered a little "Eeee!" Laura gave her a glare, putting a finger to her lips to hush Jamie. Jamie scooted her way next to Laura, pulling her elbow, leading her out of the group.

"Ooh, you like him!" Jamie whispered. Laura shushed again, scolding her friend with her eyes. "I can tell, just by the way you keep stealing glances at him!"

"Please, knock it off, Jamie," Laura whispered back. Jamie crossed her arms and gave Laura a look.

"Okay, geez, I don't know. I haven't really, you know, liked someone before . . ." Laura confessed sheepishly.

Jamie grinned at her. "You should go for it, hon! He's cute. Single," she chuckled. "I didn't take you for one who'd like the tall, mysterious type." Laura shrugged, unsure of what to say; especially now that someone had caught her with a little crush.

"I like the rugged, to be sure, but I prefer my men to look good in scrubs," Jamie said finally, throwing a glance toward Doc. Laura smirked, lightening up, and thankful for her new friend's transparency.

"What's so exciting and hushity-hush over there?" Doc asked, having just caught Jamie's look out of the corner of his eye.

"Nothin' but a little girl talk," Jamie laughed and replied, finally adding "Mind your own darn business, boy!"

Doc shook his head and chuckled knowingly. Laura saw his lips mutter "Girls," as he returned to the conversation with the others. Laura stole another quick look in Titus' direction, and then looked back at Jamie. The two laughed and continued their own conversation.

A long while passed before the next stage of their journey was made known. Thanks to Park's work, the train was brought to a halt briefly in a demilitarized zone just north of the Texan border, in a below ground "station" that the Underground Railroad had tunneled out. This way, no eyes in the sky could visibly spot the stoppage, as the train's control computer was falsely sending data that it was still moving. Once they unloaded, the train would continue to its' destination on West Coast, ending up on time, and none would be the wiser. The shipping container, as well as several others that'd been loaded before, were quickly removed from the train so that it could continue. Laura was ready to be free of the cramped container and see the sun again. Titus had told her that this train line was one of several that ran a similar route that were essentially the lifeline between the East and West sectors of the PSRA. Currently, the PSRA kept an uneasy truce with Texas mainly because this railway could easily be taken away. Not only that, but Laura learned that something called the "Panama Canal" was cut off from PSRA use by a United Nations peace-keeping fleet, a sizeable multinational force that the PSRA did not want to openly challenge. To the north, Canada, having been largely absorbed by the PSRA after its rise, was a difficult and roundabout way to move supplies. This was largely due to joint-forces of Alaskan and Canadian rebels who had destroyed much of the infrastructure running east to west. Anyone who traveled the existing routes was almost certain to be set upon by large groups of bandits, robbers, rebels, and the like. Laura absorbed as much as she could, though much of it directly coming into conflict with what she'd been told by the Truth Department.

The doors to the container swung open, allowing fresh air to rush in. Laura took a deep breath, savoring the lungful, despite the heat. The refugees and other Underground Railroad operatives were ushered and aided out through the makeshift terminal by the Site Liberty Movers. Laura took Jackie's arm and followed the Ghosts. They were led up a long tunnel, which opened up into a large vehicle pool, still mostly underground save the opening. There were many long bedded, tan camouflage colored trucks standing by that they were all loaded into. They exited the vehicle pool and began a trip through the desert. Laura looked behind her as they departed. The vehicle pool entrance was built into a large hillside, aiding its concealment. They bumped along a dirt road for about thirty minutes, when Laura saw a huge concrete wall.

"That's the border fence," Rev laughed.

"More like the Maginot Line if you ask me," Spectre put in.

A section of wall opened for them as they approached, Laura saw large automated gun systems built in near the top. Shortly after they'd crossed the DMZ, they rolled into a forward base operated by the Texan Army. Laura watched, mystified as some soldiers cheered at their arrival. Others, dressed in duty uniforms, continued their daily business, seeming to be in a high state of readiness. The convoy came to a halt in a big open area, near a large tent, where medics stood by with water and medical supplies. Laura watched them quickly tend to some of the non-ambulatory refugees, conveying nothing but heartfelt care. Her attention was caught by a large formation of soldiers conducting physical training nearby, reminding her of her time at the Academy. She was greeted warmly by a medic who handed her a bottle of water. She thanked him, but then declined a quick medical exam. She heard some new words, which seemed to draw the ire of some higher ranking personnel, apparently words that "shouldn't be spoken in the presence of a lady." Some kind of chivalry code, she figured, and continued to gather as much information on the Texan culture as she could in these brief moments. The medics were also de-chipping the refugees, and again, Laura declined as she'd already had hers taken out. The medic eyed her suspiciously for a moment, but then Doc vouched for her. That seemed to satisfy them.

As the refugees were checked, de-chipped, and greeted they were ushered into the large tent. Laura and Jackie entered, filing in along with the others. Due to the space and seating availability, Laura decided that this was a mess tent. She and Jackie found seats about halfway down the main aisle and sat, sipping on their water. Laura scanned the crowd that shuffled its way in, a diverse group of refugees from all over the PSRA. She didn't see the Ghosts come in, but then Jackie pointed out Titus and Jamie standing at the front of the tent, accompanied by a large, old man. Laura studied the man, quite curious about his clothing and manner. He wore a white button-up shirt, blue jeans, big brown cowboy boots, and lastly a white wide-brimmed cowboy hat. He also had a big bushy dark mustache and when he spoke, Laura had to struggle to understand his accent. It was very similar to Jamie's, but his deep voice and slow speech pattern threw Laura's ears off. She'd come to learn that this was called a "Southern Drawl" after asking Jamie about it earlier. The man raised a hand to gain everyone's attention.

"Ladies and gentlemen," he cleared his throat, "May I have your attention please." The crowd's murmur died off as people leaned forward to listen to the large cowboy.

"My name is Arthur Jackson, I represent the Texan Government's commitment to humanitarian efforts," he began. "For whatever reasons you are all here today, let it be known that you are now safe. You are now protected as refugees seeking political asylum," he paused to let the information settle in. The more she listened, the easier it became for Laura to understand the old cowboy.

"Over the course of your lives, you have been told what to do, what to eat, what to wear, even what to think . . . No more, dear friends, no more," he smiled, opening his arms in a grand gesture. "Texas is a free nation. Our government does not do the things that you've been forced to be accustomed to . . ." he continued to provide more general information about Texas, painting things in sharp contrast to the way the PSRA operated.

Laura listened intently, baffled at the prospect of such things as free speech, the right to own weapons, to choose your own occupation, and the like. She looked back at her mother, mouth agape. Jackie shared the sentiment.

"This sounds like a dream!" Jackie whispered to her.

Laura nodded enthusiastically, returning her attention to the cowboy. At this point, the cowboy had activated a large projector screen that accompanied his speech with photos of life in Texas. Everything seemed so . . . individual. A concept that was as foreign to Laura as the life that Mr. Jackson was unveiling to them all. She'd been brought up with the doctrine that it was the individual's responsibility to sacrifice for the collective good of the Party. In doing so, one became part of many, building together the strength of the nation and the Law of the People, as set forth by the Party. Here, she was staring in the face of a different kind of freedom. Not at all like the Party's definition.

"Now, it is my distinguished honor, and privilege, to formally invite y'all to join us here in the wonderful Republic of Texas. Should you accept, we will help you to transition to your new lives. You will be provided a transition coach who will set you up with living arrangements, education, and career counseling once y'all are settled in nicely. From then on, you can choose your path. That's the main point, my friends; you now get to have a choice!" Jackson grinned widely, his voice raised in excitement.

"Speaking of choices," he continued. "Should you decide that you'd like to live elsewhere, we have available to you representatives from the United Kingdom, Australia, as well as other warm-hearted nations who'd be glad to assist you with settling in to a new and better life, should you so choose," he chuckled, amused by his own overemphasis on the word *choose*. Jackson then clasped Titus on the shoulder, gesturing with his large hand that he was turning the floor over to him.

"Without further ado, I would now like to invite Captain Hansen to offer you one more option that is available to you." Titus smiled and stepped forward.

"I'll be brief, but you may find my offer is quite different," he began. Laura cocked her head sideways a little, curious as to what he would say.

"To the north lies what is left of the United States of America, still formally recognized by much of the world as a sovereign nation despite much of her territory now absorbed by the PSRA. I am looking for volunteers to join our fight to restore freedom and liberty to all who are oppressed by the PSRA. Many of you have suffered greatly at the hands of the Party, and I offer you this chance to fight back. Should you join us, you will enjoy many of the same liberties and rights offered by our gracious ally, Texas, although you will be required to fight for them. Not everyone is a soldier, I understand, but everyone has something that they can contribute," Titus spoke with passion, yet his tone carried a degree of gentleness as well.

"Our cause is just, and God willing, we will overcome. Mr. Jackson," Titus offered back the floor, stepping back. The old cowboy nodded and cleared his throat dramatically.

"Thank you very much, Captain. And may I say that Texas is ever committed in supporting your cause," Jackson said, to which Titus offered a smile and thanks.

"Now we don't expect y'all to give us an answer just yet, but rather we will give you time think it over," he glanced at his watch. "We will reconvene at 10 o'clock in the morning, tomorrow. I understand that it isn't a great deal of time, but it's the best we can offer with all the logistics. But, we do have some transition coaches as well as representatives from our partner nations available to you, should you have questions."

At that, the meeting was informally adjourned, the crowd rose to its feet and dispersed around the tent to meet the aforementioned aid workers. Laura remained in her seat, lost in thought. She felt someone's gaze upon her and turned to see Jackie watching her.

"Daydreaming?" she asked.

Laura shrugged, smiling. "I guess so . . . that was a lot to take in." Jackie nodded in agreement, then reached over and squeezed Laura's hand.

"Sleep on it and decide in the morning. Wow, just imagine that . . . " Jackie trailed off.

"Imagine what, mom?" Laura asked.

"Decide. Choose. Nobody is telling us what to do; it's unbelievable," Jackie's eyes were distant, yet her face held wonder.

This was all a dream come true for her. Laura remembered as a child eavesdropping on her parents when they thought she was asleep. They'd whisper the stories and memories of their own parents who could remember life before the Party. It seemed as if they reminded each other so that they could try to have an accurate account of things. Even despite his time in the labor camp, Bill Collins would not give up what his parents had told him. Laura could see them daydreaming, lost in what used to be, what might be once again. They yearned for freedom. They never openly told Laura about it, in an effort to keep her safe, especially as things continued to worsen and the dream seemed impossible. Laura could understand that and was unoffended. She'd never truly understood as a child anyway, not until now. Laura looked over a pamphlet that had been passed around. It contained more information on Texas; photos, lists of career fields, living conditions, activities and more. Laura thought that it sounded too good to pass up on.

"Mom, I really think we should stay here and live in Texas. Look," she pointed at the careers. "I could learn their laws and be a cop again. Or, I could learn to do something else. You could do whatever you want to, mom." Laura searched her mother's eyes, trying to read her.

"We can stay together, and, eventually, when we've got a handle on things, we could travel the world. We could go see things that we'd never have been able to before."

Laura felt a little anxious, worry crossing her countenance. Jackie touched her daughter's cheek, knowing her well enough to read the emotion.

"Laura, dear . . . what about your new friends?" Jackie prodded gently, trying to get her daughter to pass the sensation and get to the facts. Laura felt ashamed, slightly, and averted her eyes.

"What about all they have done for us? Have you thought this through so quickly?"

"Mom, that's not fair . . . "

"Isn't it? They risked their lives, some gave their lives, to bring us here," Jackie tried not to come across too hard, but the gravity of the situation deemed it impossible.

"Wasn't that their own choice, mom? Aren't we supposed to have a choice in all of this?" Laura shot back, raising her voice. Jackie was silent for a moment.

"Laura, what do you really want? Skip the head, I want to hear your heart," she said, locking a firm gaze into Laura's eyes.

Laura was silent as she gathered her thoughts. She was truly torn on the inside. She felt an obligation to follow her new friends. Both she and

Jackie owed them their lives, not that they'd ever make such a demand. Laura was almost angry about that as well, they were too kindhearted and giving. How could she ever think to leave them? On the other hand, she had resolved to be there for her mother, and refused to leave her. She'd let family come second her whole life and did not want to make that mistake again. Yet were not the Ghosts now her family? Laura took a deep breath. She thought about Jamie, Doc, Rev, Hank, Park, Spectre, and Titus. She felt awful about the prospect of never seeing them again; after all they'd been through together. Laura looked up.

"Mom, more than anything . . . from my heart . . . I want to keep you safe," she spoke with finality. There was a glimmer in Jackie's eye as she nodded.

"Okay, sweetie; I will let you do just that." The two shared a long hug, Laura offering thanks. Jackie pulled away and smiled warmly.

"Now, you go spend some time with your friends," Laura started to protest, but Jackie wouldn't have it. "I insist. I am tired, dear. Doc's orders were to catch up on sleep, and that's exactly what I intend to do."

"Okay, mom . . . I'll come check on you later," Laura conceded.

Jackie rose and left the mess tent, the speed of her stride belying both her age and physical condition. She was strong, Laura knew. She had to be with how stubborn a daughter Laura had been. Laura stood, deciding that she should go find her friends. She still carried a guilt that weighed upon her soul, but she pushed it away. It didn't take her long to find the Ghosts, as their living area was only a few tents down as well as having the telltale laughter of Rev echoing throughout the camp to guide her. She smiled upon hearing it, bringing back good memories of the time she'd spent getting to know him. She followed the sound into a large tent, where upon entry she saw her friends talking and laughing together. She hesitated just beyond the entrance as the guilt punched her heart again. "Laura!" it sounded as if everyone cheered her arrival. She smiled, blushing a little at the raucous greeting. Her guilt washed away as she joined the revelry.

"Here! Try this!" Rev called, handing her a large mug. She inspected the dark liquid with a foamy substance on the top. "We're celebrating!" he added. Laura noticed Hank sitting in the corner, also holding a mug. A small grin twisted his lips as he took a sip.

"Oh c'mon, Laura! Stop inspecting it and drink!" called Doc, as he proceeded to drain his mug. Laura took a sip; her tongue was greeted by a dark, bitter, yet smooth taste. Fascinated, she took a larger drink, finding the odd taste somehow appealing.

"What is this? It's interesting, but good!" she inquired. This was followed by a hearty laugh, before Jamie answered.

"It's an Irish stout; my favorite beer procured straight from the brewery. I have a friend amongst the visiting nations who brings me supplies like this occasionally."

Doc refilled his mug and then raised it. "I propose a toast! Many thanks to our dear Irish friends for providing us with life's basic necessities!"

"Here, here!" everyone echoed, mugs raised high and then struck together with a loud *clink*.

Laura laughed at the display, continuing to drink her beer. She heard the flap of the tent open behind her, causing the Ghosts to once more raise a cheer as Titus entered. Park quickly furnished him a drink as he dropped a large bag on the ground. He reached in and began producing bags of chips, popcorn, pretzels, and other snack foods.

"Tonight, my friends, we feast!" he proclaimed in a dramatic voice. Another cheer arose as the sound of plastic snack bags being tore open filled the room.

"Hollywood, my good man, what is to be tonight's entertainment?" Titus continued in the ridiculous manner. Park stood regally, pressed a few buttons on his computer, and a projector screen flashed to life.

"Ah, this one is a classic film, dating back to the late twentieth century depicting a struggle between an evil governmental system and a small band of rebels, much like ourselves," Park carried on the dramatic tone. "And much to my liking, it's a sci-fi!" everyone clapped politely.

"Get on with it!" Doc threw a handful of pretzels at Park, which spurred on a few more to do likewise. More laughter erupted as Park dodged the barrage and started the film.

Laura didn't know what he was talking about, but one thing was sure, she liked popcorn. She was genuinely interested in seeing a film from "before," as the only films she'd seen had been produced by the PSRA propaganda machine. She shoveled another handful of popcorn into her mouth, transfixed by the film no sooner than it started. What she was seeing, through the filter of her life's experience, would be tantamount to illegal speech, yet this used to be common, and very normal. She was amazed and enjoyed the experience of it. About halfway through the film, she felt a poke on her shoulder, giving her a startle. She spun her head around, noticing for the first time that Titus had taken a seat next to her. She had been oblivious, so engrossed was she in the film.

"Laura, blink," he laughed. "You've been staring without even a flinch the entire time!"

Laura smiled, letting out a laugh as the self-awareness finally kicked in. She felt at once silly, embarrassed, but also curious. He'd noticed, but had anyone else? She quickly glanced around. Doc and Jamie seemed visibly more interested in each other than the movie, while the rest were equally engrossed in the movie.

"Wow, was I? I guess I got lost in the story." She replied, watching Titus' face as he glanced back at the screen. He smiled and finally said,

"I like this part . . . See the tall furry guy there? I wish I could understand him; he seems like he's got some amusing commentary on their situation." Laura nodded, and then turned a little to be able to face him. He noticed and gave her his attention fully.

"How are you doing?" Laura asked, trying to read him.

"I'm good, nothing to report, ma'am," he replied jokingly. His mouth smiled, but his eyes didn't. She held his gaze and crossed her arms.

"How are you really doing?" She pressed, genuinely concerned for her friend. He continued to smile yet averted his eyes for a second. Laura saw a twinge of pain in them.

"I guess it's the burden of command," he finally said. "I plan and execute missions, and sometimes, not everybody gets to come home. Sometimes, I have to ask someone that I care about to do something that will cost them their life in order to succeed and save everyone else's lives."

"Like Bruce and Hutchins," Laura said softly. Titus nodded; his smile faded slowly. He looked around the room at everyone before continuing.

"Everyone on this team trusts me to make those tough calls, and they'll gladly charge into harm's way in order to win. Honestly, it's a lot to bear." He returned his gaze to her. She reached over and took his hand without thinking. Normally, she'd be nervous, but this was a serious matter.

"Titus, from what I see, you're a great leader. They all love you, and they know that you'll never ask them to do something that you wouldn't do yourself." Her tone was reassuring "That, and I guess you're kind of competent," she joked.

He smiled, allowing himself a little laugh. He looked deeply into her eyes and she was lost in it for a long moment. Then she realized that she'd been holding his hand, and let go, her cheeks flushing, feeling embarrassed. He looked awkward as well, and stood,

"I'm going to get more popcorn . . . uh . . . do you want any?" he stammered.

"Oh, um no thanks, I've had a bit too much," Laura responded quickly.

He left, and Laura's frustration mounted. She muttered under her breath before catching a glance from Jamie that said "Well?" Laura returned the look with one that was flustered and then turned her attention back to the film.

After the movie had ended, the festive mood lifted, giving way to drowsiness. The male members of the Ghost team crashed in the tent where

they'd had their party, while the females departed to separate accommoda-
tions. Laura was tired, which made the irritation she felt that much more
potent. She had a strong suspicion that Titus genuinely liked her, but now
she felt like she'd blown it. She chided herself for allowing herself to become
so emotionally invested, as she'd intended on leaving them in the morning
anyway. What did it matter, then, in the long run? She'd probably never see
them again after the morning. She'd settle into a new life, new home, and
new people. Maybe meet someone. She felt guilty, unable to suppress it this
time. She groaned angrily and allowed herself to wallow in it as she made
her way to the female tent where she, Jackie, and Jamie had been assigned
to stay. As she entered the tent, she could see her mother sleeping peacefully
on the cot. Laura tried to climb onto hers as quietly as she could, despite the
loud creaks it made. She felt more than a little envious of her mother in this
moment, sleeping so peacefully, her conscience clear after their talk earlier.
Laura was quite the opposite, as she tossed and turned, trying to sleep. After
what seemed like an eternity, sleep finally came.

Chapter 11

THE NEXT MORNING CAME too quickly for Laura, and she unenthusiastically rolled off the cot, and put on her boots. It had been several days since she'd last taken a shower, and she felt dingy. Jackie had already gotten up and was gone, early bird that she was, probably off to breakfast. Laura exited the tent, making her way toward the mess tent as well. It was bustling with activity when she arrived; the length of the line for breakfast caused her to decide to skip out. She glanced down at her watch, noting that she had plenty of time before the meeting, and she set out in search of hygiene items and maybe even a shower. After returning to her tent, she raided the "community" items that Jamie set out from her cache of things and found toiletries and a towel, and then set off with an extra pair of clothes. She encountered a group of soldiers and asked them where she could shower and was led to the shower point. The water was cold, but she didn't mind given how hot it already was outside. After cleaning up, brushing her teeth, and feeling at least a little bit clean, she decided to catch the tail end of breakfast chow and wait for Jackie. Thankfully, the crowds of soldiers had mostly come and gone, although there wasn't much food left. One of the cooks offered her a cup of coffee as an apology, which she graciously accepted. She hadn't had time to miss coffee during the whirlwind that was the last few days, and her body rejoiced as she drank it down, perhaps too quickly. The cook let out a loud chuckle and pointed to a large drink dispenser, telling her to help herself to all the coffee she could want.

"You're my hero," she joked, pouring herself more of the hot liquid.

This cup she savored, taking in the aroma with each sip. It was much better than what she was used to and her spirits lifted a little. She finished the cup, refilled once more, and then found a seat near where she'd sat the day before, so that it'd be easy for Jackie to spot her. A few minutes passed, and people started to file in slowly, a noticeably smaller group than previously. Jackie settled in next to Laura eventually, offering her an apple and a protein bar.

"Here you go, I know how you sometimes end up skipping breakfast," Jackie said.

Laura smiled. "Thanks mom. Here, have this before I overdose." She handed the coffee cup to Jackie, who seemed visibly pleased at the taste.

"Oh, that is so much better," she chuckled, taking in the aroma.

"Where have you been all morning?" Laura asked.

"Oh here and there," Jackie took another sip. "I went and spent some time getting to know your friends as well." Laura didn't quite know what to do with that.

"Oh, okay. I figured you'd turn up eventually." Laura felt her mother's eyes on her and turned.

"Did you make up your mind?" Jackie asked. Laura was a bit annoyed, as rehashing the topic would go nowhere.

"Yes, mom, I did," her tone betraying her frustration. "I'm going to keep you safe and this is the best way I know how," she finished.

"Okay, just wanted to check in, is all," Jackie said. In walked Arthur Jackson, the old cowboy, finally. Laura glanced at her watch; he was a few minutes late. He stood, hands in his pockets before the crowd and cleared his throat.

"Mornin' everyone," he began. "I'll keep it short and sweet, since y'all remember what was said yesterday; ain't no use beating a dead horse," he chuckled.

"More than half of the folks gathered yesterday have already decided where they wanted to go, those going international have already left, and you all are the rest of those undecided . . . so, let's get to it: On your left there yonder is the doorway out to live in Texas. On the right, the first flight out to the good 'ol USA. God bless you, whatever choice you make."

Jackson stepped out, leading the way for those heading into Texas for good. Everyone rose from their seats and moved to follow him, save Laura and Jackie, who waited. Laura paused and then followed another refugee headed out the left. She stopped, not sensing her mother behind her. She spun around and saw Jackie standing by the door to the right. Her eyes were misted with tears as she smiled at her daughter.

"Mom! What are you doing?" Laura asked, perplexed. "I thought we decided-"

Jackie cut her off, "Sweetheart, you decided you wanted to keep me safe."

"Yeah, mom, but-"

"No buts about it! I want to help the wonderful people who helped us. I believe in what they're doing. Maybe I'll even be able to help more people like us, to save them . . . to give them the same chance we've got. Who knows? Maybe we'll even see the dream realized, see what was lost restored." Jackie studied her daughter's face intently, hoping she was getting through. Laura watched her mother turn toward the door, resolute.

"If you want to keep me safe, you'd better hurry up and follow me out," Jackie spoke firmly and with finality as she exited the mess tent.

Laura stood mouth agape in disbelief, unsure of what to do. She'd meant one thing, to keep her mother safe by staying in Texas, but now her mother had just charged off on some idealistic crusade. Many emotions surged through her, but the dominating feeling was that of confusion. Laura took a deep breath, clinched her fists in frustration, and followed through the door. The sunlight was hot and intense, causing her to shield her eyes as she stomped through the dust. She squinted, searching for her mother and caught a glimpse of her briskly moving toward a bus that was waiting nearby.

"Mom! Wait up!" Laura called, jogging to catch up. Jackie looked over her shoulder and smiled triumphantly as Laura caught up to her. "Just for the record, you're crazy." Laura said. Jackie chuckled and put her arm around her daughter as they walked.

"Yeah, stubborn and strong willed too. You take after me, sweetie," Jackie sarcastically whispered in reply.

Laura shook her head, grinning. They boarded the bus and were warmly greeted by their Ghost family. Laura had to shake her head once again as she noticed her bag of supplies was packed and waiting, placed on a seat; her mother and Jamie had obviously conspired together. The Ghosts all high-fived her and Jackie as they moved down the aisle; with Jamie and Rev offering hugs. Laura forgot the guilt that had been plaguing her, now re-placed by a sense of acceptance. Wherever these misfits were, she was home. The bus pulled away and headed for the airport.

Laura was nervous, but also very excited. She'd never been on a plane before, and here she was, strapped in and ready to fly. *Come to think of it,* she thought, *I've never even seen one before!* There was an airport in New York, she recalled, but it was restricted to the highest levels of the Party, and only used for official business. It was rare to even hear activity out of it. She looked out the window and saw a myriad of airplanes. Some small, some huge, some looked quite old, some fresh off the line, and though they shared a common general shape, there were some of obviously high technological design. They had boarded on a smaller, sleeker plane that resembled the other high-tech ones she saw out her window.

"Hey you, you're fogging up the window!" Jamie joked as she settled in next to Laura and Jackie.

Laura shot her a look, and they laughed. In the next row across the aisle sat Doc, Hank, and Spectre. Spectre too had his nose pressed to the window, stating that he'd always been enthusiastic about planes. In the row in front of them sat Titus, Park, and Rev. Laura looked around the cabin, counting only five rows of seats, which were sparsely populated by fellow agents and operatives making the return trip to US territory. She next checked her safety harness, which was a five-point system with a quick release buckle in the middle. Soon, the sleek plane started to taxi out onto the runway. A moment later, the pilot chimed through the intercom informing them that'd they'd been cleared for takeoff. Park looked back over his shoulder, a smirk on his face, and spoke in some kind of impressionistic voice: "Hold on to your butts."

The engines roared to life incredibly loudly, accelerating the aircraft faster and faster until it blasted off the ground. Laura clenched her arm rests tightly, eyes fixed out the window despite her head, and whole body even, being pinned by the inertia. The plane climbed quickly, banking left toward its new heading. At some point, Laura heard Jamie call out.

"Umm, boss? Why are we heading south? I know I haven't made this trip before, but I thought that you guys lived up north." Titus and the other Ghosts who'd made the trip laughed.

"Oh, don't worry Ms. Bell, we're going to get north all right, just a little differently!" Titus replied. Laura looked over at Doc, Hank, and Spectre. Their faces were lit up with excitement as they gave her a thumbs-up.

"We're going into space!" Park shouted exuberantly.

Almost as if on cue, the nose of the plane pitched up a few more degrees, and the pilot hit something that made the aircraft lurch with extra power as it tore through the sky. The inertia had everyone pressed immovably against their seats as they continued to climb. Laura could see the clouds drift below them, shrinking away into little tufts. A loud chime sounded as the pilot made another announcement.

"Cabin prepare for low Earth orbit."

Within a few more seconds, the sky faded from blue to black, and suddenly Laura felt weightless. She twitched her arm and watched it float in front of her. A big red countdown clock situated at the front of the cabin began ticking away, starting at fifteen minutes.

"Well, you wanted to see the world . . . just look at that," Jackie said, eyes filled with wonder. Laura looked out her window again, sharing the sense of awe.

"Low Earth orbit achieved, be back in your harness before times up," the pilot chimed in again. "But have some fun."

Rev whooped as he and the others tugged on their quick release handles and began floating.

"This is amazing!" Park cheered.

Spectre did some flips, grinning widely. Jamie started bouncing off the walls of the cabin, laughing.

"I could never get tired of this!" Rev said.

Jackie reached over and grabbed Laura's hands, spinning in circles with her in an impromptu space dance. Laura had never felt so exhilarated; the new experience was almost overwhelming. Hank "swam" over to Titus, giving him a fist bump as he approached. Laura stopped her spin, trying to find some sense of balance as she floated to join them. Titus floated in place, legs crossed like he was some kind of levitating guru.

"Do you guys always travel like this?" Laura asked.

"Not always, just when we're in a hurry," Hank replied, eyeing Titus inquisitively.

"Haunted House called yesterday," Titus said, giving Hank the answer he'd be satisfied with. Laura was confused.

"Higher HQ?" she asked.

Titus nodded, "They informed me they needed us back ASAP, this being the fastest way which keeps Texas honest in not violating the DMZ airspace and grants us an undetectable flight home."

"Uh oh, Jamie," Doc teased. "Looks like somebody out liaised you!" laughter erupted.

"I do wish I had access to that level of string pulling!" Jamie admitted, sharing the laugh.

"See, this aircraft is equipped with the latest kind of radar-defeating technology, and given its profile and design, it is quite difficult to spot to begin with," Park had begun to nerd out.

"Well it certainly helps that we're missing much of their radar scanning zone on this flight path," Hank cut in, deflating Park slightly.

"As I was saying, this aircraft is able to hide from their satellites in orbit as well," Park added defiantly. Laura looked back down the cabin, noticing one of the other passengers. He did not look well. Hank looked where she was and noticed him as well.

"Hey, man, use the puke tube! It'll float all over this place if you blow chunks right now!" he hollered. The man nodded, giving a nervous thumbs-up. Hank scoffed quietly, shaking his head. "Weak stomach," he muttered. The countdown clock hit two minutes and once again, the pilot chimed in.

"Ladies and gentlemen, at this time please return to your seats and strap in, we are two minutes to re-entry."

"Two-minute warning guys; just like football!" Rev joked.

Everyone floated back to their seats and strapped in, bracing. Laura looked up as the clock clicked to zero and felt the plane start to shake. She looked out the window again, watching the brilliant flames of re-entry into the atmosphere. The wings seemed to glow red hot as they descended back towards Earth. A few minutes passed, and the burn ceased as they lowered further in.

"Hey! I think I see Santa's house from here!" Park called, his nose pressed against the window. Nobody laughed.

"Man, you try too hard sometimes," Rev poked. The announcement chime sounded once again.

"Ladies and gentlemen, we will be landing shortly. On behalf of the crew, allow me to be the first to welcome you home."

A few cheers and whoops sounded in the cabin. Laura too pressed her nose to the window, trying to watch their approach. They passed quickly over what seemed to be an endless number of mountain peaks, flying so close that she began to worry that they'd clip one. Then, they were suddenly swallowed by darkness, save the guiding lights on the runway.

"We landed in a tunnel?" she wondered aloud. Titus looked back at her and nodded.

"It was cut into one of the mountain sides," he explained.

The plane continued to slow, now at a taxi speed before coming to a halt somewhere deep within the artificial cavern. Another chime sounded, and the harness light shut off, indicating it was time to debark. Everyone pulled their harnesses, and stood by to deplane. Laura looked back at the sick man and couldn't help but smirk a little. He looked visibly relieved to be on the ground as he wiped away sweat that had beaded on his forehead. The boarding hatch opened, and a ramp lowered to allow them out. As she stepped out, Laura's head was on a swivel searching the cavern. It was massive, filled with various military aircraft; planes, helicopters, and several more of the space capable passenger craft like the one they'd arrived in. The ceiling seemed to stretch as high as a mountain itself, the ramp they'd come through trailed off so far that the light down at the end seemed small. Opposite them was the launching area, a continuation of the same tunnel, allowing for fluid air traffic movement, stretching down not nearly as far but still a long way off. There were air crew men and women scurrying about, performing various maintenance services and flight checks. This place was a hub of activity, it seemed. Movement nearby caught her attention and she looked to see a tall old man approaching them. He had a full head of snow-white hair, and, despite the thinness and apparent age, he carried himself with a strong sense of authority and dignity. Laura was taken with his eyes, however. They were imbued with a certain kind of softness, as if he were someone that kept his authority in check with humility and kindness. He took long strides toward their group, specifically at Titus, who immediately snapped to attention and rendered a hand salute. The old man returned the salute, and then smiled and shook Titus' hand, clapping him on the shoulder. Titus visibly relaxed at the gesture, accepting the more informal interaction.

"Titus how are you doing, son?" he asked. His voice carried strength.

"Very well, sir," Titus replied. "Our mission in New York was an overall success, as you've most likely been briefed."

"Yes, of course, but I prefer to hear it from those who were actually there. I heard you aided an Underground Railroad operation as well."

"Yes, sir. We hit an OP site and exfiltrated some political prisoners. We . . . lost Bruce Conway and some of his Kilo Movers, as well as Mike Hutchins," Titus' tone dropped slightly. The old man nodded solemnly.

"Good men and women, all of them. They will be missed greatly," he brightened a little. "We will have a memorial for them soon, I will see to it personally. For now, however, we will celebrate your safe return. I understand you've brought some new recruits?"

"Ah, yes sir, we have," Titus motioned for Laura and Jackie to join him. "Allow me to introduce Jackie and Laura Collins." The old man shook Laura's hand, his face filled with a kind smile accompanied by many laugh lines.

"A pleasure to meet you, Laura," he said. Jackie's hand he shook and held a moment longer. "My dear, surely you two are sisters!" he chuckled. "For you are certainly far too young to be mother and daughter!" Jackie blushed, laughing with the old man.

"Unfortunately, yes, I am that old," she said. Titus now introduced the old man.

"Laura, Jackie, this is James Alexander, President of the United States of America." Laura's eyes widened. The President? Meeting them? She was at once dumbfounded and humbled. Alexander winked toward Jackie.

"Now, now, you my dear can call me Jim," he then turned back to Titus. "Oh, Titus?"

"Yes, sir?"

"Be sure to check in with Colonel Nelson soon, he's bound to try to give you another task right away . . . and Titus?"

"Sir?"

Alexander's eyes lit up as he smirked. "Tell the old fool I said he can go pound sand if he tries to task you out. You and your Ghosts have earned some R and R."

Titus smiled, "Roger that, sir."

President Alexander shook both ladies' hands again, smiling warmly as he bade them farewell. Laura and Jackie exchanged a look that said "Did that just happen?" as the President walked away. Laura would never have expected any kind of politician, let alone a head of state, to give anyone the time of day if it weren't first to advance their own agenda. He seemed like a sincere, kind man who cared about every person he led. Laura watched him as he continued down into a corridor where a protective detail formed around him, escorting him away. Titus turned and gave a hand signal to his team that meant "Rally on me," prompting the Ghosts to horseshoe around him.

"Well, Commander-in-Chief says we get some R and R, team," he began, pausing for the brief cheer from the Ghosts. "I'm going to check in with Haunted House, see how much time we'll be off. Other than that, go download your gear and do something fun. Dismissed!"

Park took off in a hurry, like a kid that'd been let out of school for summer. The rest slowly meandered their way into the main corridor. Titus looked at Laura and Jackie.

"Come with me, I'll see about getting you set up some living quarters, and get you linked up with the transition processing folks." Laura nodded as she and Jackie followed Titus away from the main group.

Chapter 12

AFTER A FEW HOURS, Laura and Jackie settled into their new home. It was, as one of many, a two-bed dormitory with a single restroom, some closet space and a pair of dressers. It wasn't very large, around the same size as Laura's old pod, but definitely in better shape overall. It was home, at least. They'd each been supplied with two large duffel bags packed with uniforms, boots, cold and wet weather gear, hygiene supplies, and other various clothing items in their sizes. Titus told them, and they were reminded later by the transition coach, that soon they'd start accruing pay and they could head into the civilian sector to purchase clothes and other things they may want. Laura still was unsure of where they were in relation to where they'd been but was assured by the coach that she'd be brought up to speed and all of her questions would be answered soon. She glanced down at the book in her hands, entitled *The Blue Book*. Titus told her that it was essentially the how-to for being a soldier; covering customs, courtesies, and other centuries-old traditions. She flipped through the book, skimming over the pages, taking a moment here and there to read whatever caught her interest. She'd read it cover to cover soon, but for now she was just curious. Soon, it would be dinner, and she'd agreed to meet up with Rev for a post-dinner tour of the civilian sector, although she'd overheard many people refer to it as simply "going to town."

Jackie was nose deep in another book they'd been given. It was a historical treatise, covering the history of the USA in depth all the way to its decline and the rise of the PSRA. It was required reading as part of their transition course and was supplemented by other history volumes provided by friendly nations as a way of verification. They were going to be having classes covering world history, social integration, personal finance management, and the Constitution of the United States. Following that, they'd take a battery of tests to identify and eventually choose some type of military occupational specialty. Once they completed all the learning and training to come, they'd be sworn in as citizens. Jackie expressed enthusiasm over the process, happy to dive into study. Laura shared the sentiment, thankfully being a quick study, but mainly was excited to see how she'd do in military training. She glanced at her watch, seeing that it was currently 1745 hours. She was going to meet Rev down near the entrance to the female dormitory bay in a few minutes. She got up, told Jackie what she was doing, and walked out of their dorm into the hallway. Just like everything else, it seemed, in this subterranean complex, the hallway was very long, filled with similar dormitories for female service members. As such, Laura noticed no small number of women coming and going from the area. Laura traversed the hallway that led to a large stairwell, making her way down. She spotted Rev quickly at the bottom of the stairwell, waiting for her.

"Hey, little sister! You ready for some hot chow?" he smiled.

"Absolutely!" Laura replied. "I'm hungry for anything other than packaged meals."

"Well, then you're in luck, because I know of a spot in town that makes the best jambalaya this side of the Mississippi!" Rev boasted as he led the way into town.

Home was comprised of a labyrinth of endless corridors, hallways, tunnels, elevators and stairs scattered all over the place. Laura felt lost at first, but then Rev explained the system of colored lines on the floor as they went. At main junctions were placards with helpful diagrams and directions as well. Laura noted that the line system was not too dissimilar to that of a hospital, which helped her grasp the concept quickly. They reached an elevator hub and rode one a few floors down. As the doors opened, Laura gazed in wonder at what lay before her. The civilian sector, or "the town," was situated in a huge open room that expanded further than she could see from where she was standing. They walked through the security checkpoint, Rev nodding at one of the guards in recognition, and made their way into town. The huge room was filled with shops, diners, and many things that Laura had never seen before. A sea of people milled about the large market space, bustling about their business. It was very loud and for a moment Laura felt as if she'd was having sensory overload. Rev steered her through town and they eventually found what they were looking for. A young woman stood behind a large counter, the face of the diner lined with menu options, and Rev approached her to place his order.

"Two house specials, biggest bowls you've got!" he said as he reached into his pocket.

He pulled out his wallet and removed a few pieces of green paper, which he handed to the young woman. She took it and exchanged it with other papers. Laura watched, intrigued by the concept of paper currency. She still didn't know what jambalaya was, but like this paper exchanging, she'd soon learn. A cook poked his head out from the kitchen.

"Hey! Rev! Is that you, old man?"

"Tommy!" Rev laughed, "How you doing?"

"Good, man, good! It's good to see you! You back for a while now?" Tommy asked.

Rev nodded emphatically. "You bet, boy! At least long enough to embarrass you on the court again!"

The two men shared a hearty laugh, and then said goodbye as the food was then served. Laura and Rev took seats at a table situated out in front of the diner. Rev bowed his head for a few seconds, silently saying a prayer.

"Are you talking to your God, Jesus?" Laura asked loudly, giving him a bit of a start. Rev laughed before he answered, having forgotten she was still observing and learning things about his way of life.

"Yep, I'm just telling him thanks for the delicious food." He said as he scooped his spoon into the bowl.

Laura paused. "Shouldn't you rather say thanks to the cook? Not that you didn't, but . . ." Rev laughed some more at that.

"I get you, yeah. Well, I say thanks to Jesus because ultimately, he is the one who provided the opportunity for me to be here, now, enjoying this food. He provided the means for the cook to have access to the ingredients, the drive to develop the skills of which are necessary to prepare the food correctly. He also provided the safety in which we, and everybody here, get to sit and enjoy all the good people and things around us." Rev paused, smiling as the concept began to sink in.

"Right, okay. So ultimately, to spare us the time of delving into each individual way events and people's lives have been orchestrated, we can then attribute it all back to Jesus?" Laura asked, reasoning it out. Rev nodded, enjoying a large helping.

"Which is why I like to take a moment to be grateful for what he's provided," he said through a mouthful of food. Laura dipped her spoon in her bowl, thoughtful.

"Do you think you could tell him thanks for me as well, you know, for getting me here safely and for this food, too, I guess?" Rev smiled warmly at her, looking her in her eyes with his loving paternal gaze.

"Of course, I have many times, and I did just then as well. You know, you can talk to him yourself, if you want?" Laura's eyes widened. She didn't know how to speak to a religious deity.

"How? Is there some kind of special ritual, or . . ."

"No, no, not at all!" Rev almost spewed his food laughing. "Just talk to him! Ain't no different than you and me talkin' right now." Laura nodded in acknowledgement, still uneasy at the prospect.

"Here, let me help you," Rev said, offering his hands. Laura took them and followed his example as he bowed his head again.

"Lord Jesus, thanks for bringing us here, safe and sound. Thank you for my wonderful little sister, Laura. She wants to say something to you, so help her not be afraid," he squeezed her hand, indicating she could begin.

"Um, hi, Jesus . . . Laura here, um, thank you for keeping mom and I safe . . . and thanks for my new friends. Oh! And food." She finished, peeking her eyes open.

"Amen!" Rev said. "Oh, which means, let it be done. Now, eat up little sister!" he continued to shovel the hot jambalaya into his mouth, savoring every bite. Laura took a quick taste, and then subsequently devoured the rest. It was delicious.

"See, what did I tell you? The best!" Rev chuckled.

"Is there more food like this, like, this good all over the place?" Laura asked after clearing her bowl completely.

"Yes ma'am!" Rev said.

"Oh, I can't wait to try everything, I've never had anything like this," Laura said, absent mindedly patting her stomach.

"How about we take that tour and then finish it off with ice cream?" Rev suggested, standing and taking their bowls.

"Yeah, sounds good to me! More things to try!" Laura beamed. They then left the diner, seeking out all manner of new things for Laura to see.

Chapter 13

SEVERAL DAYS FLEW BY in rapid succession, deluging Laura with a whirlwind of information, crammed into presentation after presentation. Laura's instructor had joked about the consistency within the US government over the decades with subjecting people to what he referred to as "death by PowerPoint." Laura had to agree that the endless hours of sitting staring at one slide deck after another was killer. She often found herself becoming groggy, so instead of being rude and falling asleep in class, she'd go stand in the back of the classroom and sometimes do some form of exercise. During her time in the transition course, she learned that "Home," as everyone referred to it, was an elaborate "doomsday shelter" the US had built within the Rocky Mountain range, which formed the natural divide between the two halves of the nation. At the start of the Second American Civil War, forward-thinking top military staff had captured the strategic fortress, along with its arsenal. These leaders had been the founders of the fight against the rise of the PSRA, attracting many like-minded individuals, many of whom were veterans of World War Three. At the height of the conflict, the PSRA had attempted to level the mountains completely, using every kind of ordinance at their disposal, save nuclear. The original complex within the mountains sustained severe damage, yet many of the personnel survived thanks to the ongoing expansions and fortifications to the fortress. Unfortunately, despite their resiliency, the sheer manpower the PSRA could muster overwhelmed and drove back US forces to the present existing boundaries. The PSRA believed that they'd effectively dealt a final blow to the remnant of the USA; the latter allowing said belief to grow unchallenged. The world watched as the greatest super power it had ever known shrank into obscurity. Behind the scenes, however, the US was slowly rebuilding, working not only to undermine the regime from the inside out, but also preparing for a renewed offensive.

The PSRA lay claim to large swathes of former US territory, even having some member nations of the UN recognizing its' legitimacy, alienating US citizens not aligned with the Party in the process. In equal measure, however, many nations were outraged at the situation as a whole, choosing to instead break off economic and diplomatic ties. The PSRA struggled to maintain control under the heavy economic strain. Some nations even went as far as to supply the new Republic of Texas with arms as they declared their independence from the PSRA. Years passed, with Texas fighting desperately, pushing her borders into Oklahoma to the north, New Mexico in the west, and Louisiana to the east. A desperate and violent offensive from the PSRA left the two warring nations in an uneasy truce, developing the DMZ that exists to this day. The PSRA now existed as an ever increasingly isolationist state, hostile towards foreign governments that overtly try undermine its legitimacy, with only China to call on as a friend.

Laura glanced over at the clock on the wall, beginning to daydream. She appreciated the history lessons, but felt that she'd rather read about it in a book while sitting outside, in the sunshine. She yearned for some fresh air, as she'd been cooped up for the entirety of her time without making a trip outdoors. She had difficulty judging the time of day, which threw off her internal clock. She wanted to run, not on a treadmill, or track, but simply outside. Suddenly, class was over. She snapped out of her trance, springing out of her seat and beelining for the door. She wasn't paying any attention to where she was going and plowed into someone.

"Oh! I'm so sorry! Titus?" Laura was doubly caught off-guard. Titus chuckled at her.

"Whoa there, speedy!"

"Sorry, I . . . what are you doing here? I'd heard they were keeping you really busy with your working, or scheming, or something?" Laura poked some fun at him.

"Oh nice, thanks," Titus laughed. "No, I decided to take a walk, you know, clear my head or something." His gaze drifted downward, a little nervously. Laura knew full well that his area, called the "Haunted House," was well off on the other side of the complex.

"Actually, I was hoping you'd accompany me to get some coffee," he offered, finding his courage again.

"Um, yes please! I'm dying in there! I could really use about a gallon or so," she joked.

"Sounds like we'll need two gallons then," Titus replied. They shared a laugh as they walked the corridor.

Titus led Laura back into the massive hangar bay they'd arrived in. He walked over to an area where the maintenance technicians kept their toolboxes and extra gear, looking for something. He motioned for her to follow, finally finding what he was looking for. Laura moved around a large toolbox and saw a large container labelled "Go Juice," as well as paper cups.

"The mechanics brew the strongest coffee you'll ever taste," Titus said as he poured a cup and handed it to her. He then poured one for himself and raised it.

"Phew, here we go . . . bottoms up!" he said as he and Laura drank simultaneously, both making faces as it went down.

"Ouch, that's a punch in the mouth!" Laura said, working up the courage to take another drink.

"Yeah, rumor has it that they put some grease or gear oil in it or something," Titus said, busting up laughing as Laura just about spewed the sip she'd taken. She grinned, wiping the liquid that'd dripped down her chin. She gave him a mischievous glare and then slugged him in the shoulder.

"Ow! Man, you can hit hard!" he laughed, rubbing his shoulder. Laura refilled her cup, raised it dramatically in the air before downing it quickly. He followed suit, although unable to stop his face from contorting as the strength of the brew took hold.

"Hey Titus, can we go outside?" Laura asked, her tone suddenly less jovial and a little more desperate. He looked at her, puzzled for a moment.

"Oh! Of course, I'm sorry. A lot of us tend to forget that not everyone is used to living like a troglodyte," he said.

"A troglo-what?"

"Cave dweller; usually depicted as monsters . . . but yeah, follow me." Titus led her back into the complex, making their way to the central elevator hub.

They took a ride upward, before exiting into another long corridor. He led her down the corridor until they came to a heavy steel door. Titus walked up to it and waved his access badge over a panel. The door's electronic locks popped, allowing the door to slowly swing open. Intense sunlight shone through, causing both to squint.

"C'mon, you're going to love this," he said, stepping through.

Laura followed and was immediately treated to a magnificent view of the snow capped Rocky Mountain peaks. The area was sparsely populated with trees and other vegetation, and as Laura looked, she saw Titus walking down a path leading toward a small lake. The water looked still, yet not frozen as it sat underneath the warmth of the sun. The air was still very chilly, however, and a light wind caused Laura to cross her arms and shake a little. Ultimately, she didn't care about the cold. She was just happy to be outside again. She ran down the path, passing Titus by as she made her way to the shore of the little lake. The water was crystal clear, all the way to the bottom, despite it not being very deep. Laura bent down and dipped her hands into the cold water, leaving them submerged for a few seconds. Titus came to a halt next to her, silently admiring the picturesque scene around them. Laura suddenly felt an urge of playfulness, and acted on it. She splashed Titus with the freezing water, and as he ducked in an attempt to avoid it, she put her hands on the back of his neck.

"Gah!" he yelped. "That's so cold!"

He turned and splashed back at her, laughing. She ran away, ducking around a large bush for cover. He ran after her, hands still dripping with water and returned the icy touch. She let out her own cry, and batted at his hands, laughing.

"Okay, okay! No more! You got me!" They stood laughing together for another moment, eyes locked. Suddenly, a gust of wind blasted through, chilling them as they stood partially wet. "Oh! That's even colder!" Laura shivered.

"Yeah," Titus' mouth quivered. "We should get back inside before we freeze!"

They started back up the path together, until another sustained gust of wind drove them into a sprint. They raced back up the path, Titus pulling ahead. They burst through the door, slamming it shut behind them.

"Not fair . . . long . . . legs," Laura laughed as she sucked in air.

"This elevation really kicks your butt!" Titus said, also panting. Laura nodded in agreement, feeling just a little dizzy from the thin mountain air. She took a step and stumbled into Titus, who caught her.

"Oh! Your hands are still freezing!" she laughed tiredly, looking up at him.

He remained holding her, gazing into her eyes, smiling. Laura smiled back, suddenly feeling both nervous and excited. His head started to dip downward, very slowly, and Laura became aware that she was closing the distance as well. Her heart was pounding a million beats per minute. Was this really about to happen? She was afraid, but she also really wanted to kiss him. His communication device chimed abruptly, causing them to jump. The moment was totally disrupted, both feeling at once embarrassed. Their heads snapped back and he let go of her.

"I . . . um . . . I should answer that . . . probably my boss," he said awkwardly.

"No, that's fine, um . . . go ahead," she replied, face downcast. Titus answered the call, learning that it was indeed Colonel Nelson. He was being summoned back to whatever duty he'd been playing hooky from.

"Laura, I'm sorry, I've got to go back now. If you'd like, we . . . we could come back here soon, maybe bring lunch out and actually dress for the cold?"

Laura nodded at him. "Yeah, that'd be great. Sure." After he bade her goodbye, she watched him walk back toward the elevator, disappearing inside. She let out a huge sigh of frustration. "Good luck at the bad timing awards, Colonel Nelson," she muttered.

She wished that the call hadn't come through when it did. However, she still had strong feelings of confliction. These feelings were still alien to her, having never been in anything close to a relationship. She wasn't sure if it was all just a big crush that'd pass, or the real thing, whatever that was. She walked back toward the elevator, unable to help herself but replay the events in her mind over and over again. She made her way back home almost in a daze, so deep in thought was she. She decided that she'd wait for Jackie to come back, where then they could go get dinner, and perhaps she could pick her mom's brain.

Weeks passed, and Laura felt as if her life as of now was on fast forward. She'd been pretty exhausted with the busy schedule surrounding her transition course, devoting many hours to study, as well as exercise. She'd been preparing for her final written exams, which was a long and tedious process. As the in-class portions finally drew to a close, she began her basic combat training. She was grateful for the opportunity to spend a lot of time outdoors and enjoy nature, but the operational tempo her training company kept was quite high. She once caught herself falling asleep on her feet while standing at attention. Thanks to the time she spent exercising on her own, she was well on her way to adjusting to the thin air, not suffering nearly as badly as some of the other trainees. She excelled at whatever task she'd been given, gaining stellar performance reviews from her trainers. She felt very motivated to do the best that she possibly could, and it showed. Now she found herself at the end of ten weeks of military training, where upon graduation she'd receive not just her new duty assignment and Military Occupational Specialty, but also her citizenship. Laura stood proudly next to Jackie as they took part in the ceremony. All of their friends, new and old, had come to support them, and when it was over gave a raucous ovation. Laura felt good about it all; she would honor everything she'd sworn, giving it her all, of course. But, she couldn't help but feel a twinge of disappointment when she noticed Titus duck out early, taking another call. She felt like he was avoiding her, since the lake, and she didn't know why. They'd had a blast together until they . . . was that it? Was he embarrassed? Or did he change his mind about her? Laura was full of questions, being frustrated about not able to speak with him. When she'd ask the Ghosts about him, she'd only get answers such as "Oh, he's been stuck at Haunted House," or "He's off on a Ghost Walk." It seemed as if his duties were keeping him from their mutual friends as well. When she'd seen him at the ceremony, he looked exhausted. Her instincts told her that something big was coming down the pipe and he was mixed up in it. She just wanted to have five minutes, to see if he was okay, at least. The feelings that had been stirred up within her back at the lake suddenly surged back, having been ignored during her training. She bit her lip and then looked at her mom. Jackie looked so happy, genuinely filled with joy as her friends congratulated her. They'd already learned that Jackie was going to be assigned to Cyber Ops, as she'd displayed a high level of proficiency with computer systems. She would spend some time training at a more advanced level with Park, who was not the least bit excited to have an "intellectual equal" that he could "communicate with on a higher plane." Everyone, true to form, razzed him in equal measure in an attempt to deflate his ego. Laura still hadn't learned where she'd be assigned, the information was still forthcoming. For now, she celebrated.

As the weekend arrived; and after constant invitations from Rev, Laura found herself back in a church gathering. He'd quickly become a good friend to her, always ready to lend an ear or answer her plethora of questions about God. This time, Jackie came with her, as her own curiosity was piqued on the subject. It had been a while since Laura's last experience, but the memories of her last time at church flooded back into her mind. Once again, she found herself at a loss to explain what her eyes witnessed. The gathering proceeded in an orderly way, music, praying, speaking, yet the presence she felt in the room was so undeniable. It was so good. She felt the peace once again, welcoming it readily this time. During the course of the gathering, a woman came forward to ask for prayer. Laura watched as the minister put his hands on the woman's ears and began to pray, giving Laura the impression that this woman was deaf. Suddenly, the woman cried out in joy, as did many of the people gathered, as the woman's hearing was restored. Laura and Jackie just looked at each other in shock. All that had happened was a simple request to Jesus, as Rev had been talking to her about, and this woman could now hear. Rev had given her and Jackie Bibles of their own and had encouraged them to read about Jesus and the things he did. This certainly fit the bill, Laura decided. She'd read about healings and now was actually seeing it happen. As the gathering came to a close, she still didn't feel totally ready to decide, but would keep an open mind as she continued to investigate it. With the weekend now drawing to an end, she began to prepare herself mentally for what lie ahead.

Chapter 14

It was Monday morning and Laura regretted existing. She'd been given a conspicuous message from an unknown sender the previous evening instructing her to sleep up in the hangar bay along with a packing list of items to include in her rucksack. She'd found a cot out in the bay, which was one among a handful of others currently occupied by sleeping trainees. As she joined the group of sleepers, one gave her a "pro-tip" that she should sleep in her uniform and boots. They probably meant *try* to sleep, as the sound of flight crews conducting maintenance at all hours made it difficult to catch even a few winks. Laura looked at her watch in frustration, the soft glow telling her that it was 0230. She groaned a little and rolled over. She suddenly let out a gasp; startled at what she saw when she rolled over. Hank Wells was standing over her, out of nowhere, brandishing a huge knife which he held to her throat.

"You're dead," he growled in the dark. "You're all dead!" his voice boomed with intensity. He removed the blade, allowing her to spring off of the cot. The other trainees scrambled up as well, realizing that they were surrounded by knife-wielding Ghosts.

"Form up, maggots!" a different voice roared. The trainees complied, shuffling quickly into a single line. Laura quickly caught that there was ten of them in total. They stood rigidly, at attention. Hank paced back and forth before them, drilling holes into them with his eyes.

"Listen up, you little pukes! You've been selected for Ghost training! Congratulations!" he spoke with a condescending fierceness. "When we're done with you, you will either *be* an elite soldier, worthy of joining the Ghost teams, or you will quit and remain an insignificant pile of dirt!" he continued. "Now, we have a lot of work to do. Let's get to it!"

"Yes, sir!" the squad of recruits bellowed.

"What? I can't hear you over the sound of how pathetic you are! What did you say?!" Hank increased in volume.

"Yes, sir!" came the reply, even louder.

"Good! Now get your gear and follow me!"

Laura's throat already felt scratchy from yelling so hard. She tossed her rucksack on her back and followed the group out.

Valkyrie led the recruits out into the forest after they'd taken a bumpy ride out on an old forest service road. They walked in silence for about an hour before he stopped them and instructed them to ground their gear. Laura felt the strain, having only recently completing her initial combat training with its increased physical demands. Her ruck was heavy, adding around forty extra pounds with the gear she'd been instructed to bring.

"This is your new home until either you quit, or you successfully complete training," he said. Laura looked around as she drank water, scoping out a good place to crash later in the partial clearing.

"This morning, you'll be going for a little walk through the forest," Hank continued as one of the other instructors dropped a box containing maps, compasses, protractors, and a list of grid coordinates. "You have six hours to make those points starting now!" Hank finished.

Laura scrambled, grabbing what she needed from the box and began plotting her course. She went to the ground, under her field jacket with a red lens light, practicing good light discipline.

"Clocks ticking!" one of the other instructors boomed.

Laura finished plotting and stood up to shoot her azimuth with her compass. Once her direction of travel to the first grid point was set, she felt ready to go. Grabbing her gear, she stepped off, counting her paces. She heard another announcement of time remaining as she disappeared into the darkness.

Laura counted off around thirty days of grueling training and felt like a zombie. There was no indication of how much longer she'd spend in the field, although she hoped that the end was near. She'd hiked countless miles each day through the forest, up the mountains, and through rivers until her feet felt as if they were going to simply detach from her ankles. She was in pain physically as well as mentally. The Ghost instructors were trying hard to break her and her fellow trainees, to get them to quit. At this point, she was the only one left. Whenever someone made a mistake, they were later made to sprint up a steep hill that Hank seemed to be particularly fond of or low crawl for a few hundred meters. Hank said that if they were going to act stupid, then he'd make sure that they were at least strong. More than once it seemed as if they were given an impossible task, subsequently causing one or more trainee to call it quits. The latest event to claim a recruit involved dragging a one hundred-fifty pound "casualty" to a notional medevac site located two miles away, while wearing their full kit. They had been given thirty minutes to do so. Laura hadn't made it in time, nobody had in fact, but she still finished. As punishment for not meeting the time requirement, she had to low crawl until told to stop while yelling "I let my buddy down" consecutively.

As time progressed, and once the other trainees dropped off, however, Laura seemed to note a shift in the general tone. The instructors had her ruck less, instead increasing the amount of time conducting specialized survival training and hand to hand combat. They no longer berated her, still occasionally punishing her mistakes, but more so treated her as a colleague. Hank taught her hand to hand skills, helping her to be aggressive, yet controlled; swift, yet stealthy. She quickly became proficient with a knife as well as how to successfully stalk a target. He had her building traps, snares, pitfalls, and other various lethal tools. He'd taken a city cop and transformed her into a ghost of the forest, a predator. She'd greatly enjoyed some of the latter training events. Hank had arranged for some basic training squads to walk patrols, as well as some other established infantry teams. Her mission was always seek and destroy, silently. She'd set her traps and stalk her prey, often taking to the night to eliminate her opposition, stealthily taking down surprised and subsequently frustrated soldiers. It was a challenge for them as well, a competition between the different disciplines. Laura did have a real incentive not to be spotted, however. Hank briefed her on the stun rounds that they'd be carrying, demonstrating their effectiveness by shooting her arm with one. The round didn't break skin, but it released an electric impulse that rendered a limb useless for about an hour, and it hurt very badly. Laura was very motivated not to be shot again, as she took down four patrols successfully, each with more seasoned soldiers than the last.

As she performed her tasks, she could sense growing approval from Hank and the other instructors. They granted to her a couple extra hours of sleep over the course of the next several days, informing her that she'd need to be rested up for the last two culminating events. The first event was a simulated "Ghost Walk," which she'd have to complete alone. The mission, in a nutshell, was to locate and neutralize enemy patrols in the vicinity of a friendly town nearby. Hank told her that in reality, PSRA troops often raided local farms and towns, searching for food and supplies in the guise of searching for "contraband." The enemy troops would strip the local "rebel country" farms of any valuables to sell on the black market. The Ghost Teams, when on a Home deployment cycle, would conduct their "Walks" out into friendly territory to silently eliminate such enemy incursions. The locals were more than happy to support the US troops in return for protection, while the PSRA believed that wandering squads of their soldiers were simply ambushed by highwaymen of sorts. For her Ghost Walk, Laura would be pitted against two squads of skilled infantrymen who were "raiding" a nearby mock-up town. Using everything she'd been taught, in the course of the night, she prevailed. Laura was now on her way to the second event.

Laura didn't get to sleep after the Ghost Walk; instead she was transported via truck back to the little clearing where Hank helped her toss her gear into the back. They bounced down the old dirty road until they reached pavement. Hank pulled the truck out onto the old highway and pressed the accelerator, getting up to speed. They rode in silence for the better part of an hour as they shot down the highway, until Hank pulled off onto another dirt road. The road curved and climbed up, finally ending at a trailhead. Hank exited the truck, made his way to the back once again, producing a large container of water.

"Here," he finally spoke. "Make sure you're topped off." Laura filled the two canteens that were attached to her load-bearing vest, as well as the Camel-Back that she'd tucked into the top flap of her rucksack.

"This trail is called the Back Breaker, and for good reason," Hank started. "It changes elevation frequently, at drastic grades. I will not, however, tell you how long it is. The way is clearly marked, so don't worry about land navigation." He stared down the trailhead, his eyes as intense as ever.

"This is your inaugural march, a rite of passage, and your last training requirement." Laura nodded, jaw set with determination. "At two locations, there will be water available, since we don't want you dropping out there, oh and no time limit. But hurry."

He finished speaking, the faintest glimmer was visible in his eye as he hopped back into the truck and drove away. Laura was alone. She let out a long exhale, looking at her gear. *No time limit, but hurry*, she thought, shaking her head at the obvious contradiction. Laura was already sore, stiff, exhausted, sleep deprived, and her feet were killing her. On the plus side, she'd been long since acclimatized to the elevation, no thanks to the rough training she'd received. She took a moment, stretched a little, trying to loosen up. Then, hoisting her ruck onto her back, she marched down the trailhead, rifle kept at the low-ready.

Hours passed, the sun was high in the sky, and Laura crested yet another steep hill. She hurt, bad, but sucked it up and slowly made her way along the trail. As she was about ready to descend again, she noticed a jug of water, and gladly refilled her drained canteens. She made sure she'd had enough to drink before continuing on her way. The next set of miles that passed went so without incident; Laura was content to distract herself with the beauty that surrounded her. She happened upon the last water station, once again draining down what she had before topping it off, taking a few minutes to rest and ease her heavy burden. Birds sang around her, somewhere nearby concealed by the large trees that encapsulated the beautiful forest. She hoisted her ruck again, determined to finish, and set off. She had long since lost count of her pace, as well as forgetting what the total mileage she'd converted it into was, as her mind began to slip into a state of deprivation. She was feeling very hungry, and a little faint, not to mention the constant ache throughout her body. She lingered on the thought of her discomfort a little too long as she descended a slope and, twisting her ankle, she slipped. Struggling to regain her balance as momentum carried her down the steep decline, she ended up tumbling down. When she finally came to a stop she groaned in pain, struggling to push onto her hands and knees. She let her ruck slip off and rested against it, muttering to herself in agony. She protectively held her ankle for a moment before training kicked back in. Now focused, she reached into her ruck for some extra medical supplies, finding athletic tape. She removed her boot, then sock, and then proceeded to wrap her ankle with the tape. She replaced the sock and boot and then slowly attempted to stand. She made it up, but it still hurt very badly. Laura looked around, irritated and unable to vent to anyone, before taking a few long calming breaths. She needed to finish. She wasn't going to let this get in her way. She eventually got the ruck back up, as well as her rifle, and continued on her walk, albeit slower.

She limped on, unsure of just how much further the trail went, but she resolved not to quit. She noticed that the sun had begun to dip behind the mountains, and with it, the temperature dropped as well. The cold spurred her on, increasing her hobble as she struggled up another hill. It seemed as if the trail and hills were endless, causing her to imagine that she'd only ever crest at the top of a mountain. Her heart sank as she spent more time endlessly climbing up, higher and higher. Now her imagination trailed to an image of Hank, the great Valkyrie, watching her struggle, laughing like a madman at her. She channeled the intense pain her body felt to diffuse the image, allowing her to refocus.

"Just a few more steps," she began to tell herself, every few seconds or so.

She zoned out, continuing to mumble the phrase over and over again, limping along the trail until she stopped. She'd crested the giant hill. About a hundred meters away, she could see someone standing by a large fire. It was the end of the trail. She moved, filled with a renewed vigor, slowly at first until she realized that she'd broken into a slow run. She lowered her head and charged on faster, desperate to reach the fire. She looked up, panting, able to see the illuminated face of Valkyrie. He raised his palm, essentially ground guiding her until she was about twenty paces away before closing his fist to indicate a halt. Laura slowed and halted in compliance, gasping for air, unable to contain the confusion on her face. Hank lifted a finger to his lips in a quiet "*Shush*," motioning for Laura to drop her gear. She obeyed, thankful to be rid of the burden, but was still perplexed at what he was doing. Hank glanced to his left, then his right, and let out a sharp whistle. Suddenly, a burst of movement from the ground revealed that Laura was surrounded by Ghosts clad in ghillie suits. She was startled at first, but the shock melted away with relief as they began to cheer and shout. Laura put her hands on her hips, leaned over with exhaustion as she continued to breathe heavily. She straightened back up, allowing an exhausted smile before she was hoisted into the air by her new comrades. They continued their cheers as they carried her over to a lawn chair set by the fire, lowering her into it gently. Laura was appreciative as someone propped up her feet using a nearby cooler. Seemingly out of nowhere, Doc appeared and began to tend to her. He quickly removed her boots and treated the blistered, bloody feet, before re-wrapping the ankle and putting ice on it. Laura wondered if they'd been watching her progress the whole time. The ghillie clad Ghosts began to remove their suits, back down to their duty uniforms.

In the lull moment, Jamie, Rev, Spectre, Park, and Jackie appeared to join the celebration. Laura beamed exhaustedly at her friends and mother. She glanced over to Hank, who'd been watching her. He smiled and nodded at her, expressing approval in his own way.

"I think it's time for the Grog!" shouted a new voice, eliciting cheers of approval. Laura recognized the voice and turned to look as Titus stepped out of the darkness. Her heart skipped a beat.

"What do you think *that* is?" Jackie whispered to her.

Laura shrugged in response. Out came a table, a large metal bowl, cups, and an assortment of bottles. Behind the table, an older man appeared. He was average height, built like a man half his age, clean cut with greying hair.

"Ghostmaster, I formally request permission to brew the Grog!" Titus addressed the man. Laura squinted at the name tape and rank on his uniform, revealing to her that this was Colonel Nelson, commander of the Ghost Teams.

"Permission granted!" Nelson replied. Hank was the first to step forward, snatching a bottle off the table, he began to pour its' contents into the bowl.

"Ghostmaster! I add Stealth to the Grog!" he announced. In like manner, Doc went forward.

"Ghostmaster! I add Swiftness and Violence of Action to the Grog!" He was followed by one of Laura's instructors, Sergeant York.

"Ghostmaster! I add Subtlety and Poise into the Grog!" and another, "I add Tenacity and an Iron Will!"

"I add Loyalty and Honor!" and so it went. Then Titus stepped forward.

"Ghostmaster! I add salt to the Grog as a reminder of those who have fallen!" A moment of silence was observed. Titus spoke up once more. "Ghostmaster! All of the ingredients have been added to the Grog!"

"Captain Hansen, is the Grog fit for human consumption?" Nelson replied. Titus took a cup in hand, filled it and then downed it in its entirety. He then held it upside down over his head before turning back to face Colonel Nelson.

"Ghostmaster! The Grog is fit for human consumption!"

"By all means, let us serve our newest Ghost the Grog, and welcome her into our community!" Nelson commanded.

"Yes, sir!" Titus responded.

He took another cup, filled it as well as his own, both to the brim and walked it over to Laura. As he moved, the others present also served themselves some Grog. Titus handed the cup to Laura, their eyes meeting. As tired as she was, she could see he'd been run ragged as well. His eyes, however seemed to convey joy. His face brightened as they held each other's gaze. He raised his cup, as did the others.

"To you, our new Ghost, do we swear as your brothers and sisters to always be loyal, true, steadfast by your side as a shadow follows the form," he said loudly, before quietly adding, "Will you join us?"

"Yes," she replied, her voice tired.

The Ghosts let out a single loud war cry before drinking down their Grog. Laura's eyes darted to Hank and he motioned discreetly for her to drink, grinning. Laura lifted the cup, getting a strong whiff of the strong alcoholic aroma and followed Titus' example by draining it and holding it upside down above her head. The Ghosts cheered and applauded, some laughing as Laura coughed at the strength of the Grog.

"Welcome to the family!" Nelson called out amidst the noise. Food was brought out, as the ceremony quickly became a party, many of the Ghosts helping themselves to more Grog.

Jackie leaned over, asking "Was it any good?" Laura looked over at her and shook her head.

"It felt like something was trying to strangle me all the way down!" she laughed.

"Yikes. I think I'll skip out then," Jackie replied. Titus returned with a hot dog, smiling at Laura as he handed it to her.

"Here, some protein at least, I'll get Doc to grab you something healthier." Laura accepted it, bashfully thanking him. Colonel Nelson appeared, offering congratulations to Laura for a job well done.

"It is no small thing to successfully complete this selection process," he said.

"I guess I'm just a little too stubborn to quit, sir," Laura replied. Nelson shook her and Jackie's hands, and then addressed Titus.

"I hate to rain on the celebration Captain, but you and I have more work to get done."

Laura watched Titus' face. His countenance didn't betray any emotion as he acknowledged his superiors' order, but Laura could see the flicker of disappointment in his eyes. He offered her a sad smile and disappeared with the Colonel. She wanted to catch up with him, as it was beginning to feel as if fate itself was trying to keep them away from each other. Just to figure some things out with him was all she wanted. She slumped a little in the lawn chair, declining more Grog as it was continually offered to her.

"What's wrong, sweetie? Too much celebration?" Jackie asked her. Laura gave her a mopey look.

"No . . . it's nothing. I just really want a few minutes to talk to . . ." Laura trailed off. She hadn't ever shared with her mother how she was beginning to feel about Titus.

"Titus?" Jackie smiled at her knowingly. Laura nodded, too tired to put up much of a fight.

"That poor boy, Colonel Nelson has him working all the time. He is usually cooped up back at the Haunted House night and day, as well as going out on Ghost Walks," Jackie said, watching the bonfire crackle.

"How do you know that?" Laura asked, genuinely caught off guard. Jackie smiled at her.

"Well, we've had lunch together a number of times while you've been gone. He'd keep me updated on what you were doing, and eventually, he'd talk about what he's been up to." Laura stared at her mother, noticing a twinkle in her eye. "I think he really likes you, Laura."

Laura couldn't help but let her jaw drop slowly. She already knew, or at least strongly suspected, that he had feelings for her. That was no surprise. What really caught her was that he'd been spending time with her mother, so much so that even she came to such a conclusion.

"Hmm," Jackie started studying Laura's face, her tone playful. "And now here you are, in the middle of your celebration, sad that he had to leave . . . hmm . . ."

"Oh mom, knock it off," Laura played the annoyed daughter. But then, she couldn't help but smirk under her mother's scrutiny.

"Oh! I knew it!" Jackie exclaimed in excitement. "Oh, he's such a good man, dear, you'd be adorable together!"

Jackie's voice was just loud enough to catch the attention of Jamie, who then rushed over to join the conversation. Doc and Hank watched as the girls did their trademark high pitched excited voices as they discussed relationships, Jackie and Jamie hopping in place a little. The two men looked at each other and rolled their eyes. Hank downed another cup of Grog, patted his friend's shoulder, and walked away.

Laura slept the entirety of the next day, waking only to use the restroom and eat a few bites of food before returning to bed. Her ankle was not doing well, so the next morning, Jackie made her get out of bed to go see the doctor. Laura received a special boot to keep her foot in, designed not only to keep light pressure on the injury, but it also incorporated a built in circulating liquid system that kept proper warm/cold cycles going. After seeing the doctor, Laura made her way to the Haunted House. She felt entitled now, as a full-fledged Ghost, to two things. One was a big cup of hot coffee. The second was a nice long conversation with Titus, as she'd been placed on his team. She moved slowly, despising the injury that held her back from keeping a brisk pace. Although she wasn't a tall person, she normally moved with a sense of urgency whenever she could, and not being able to annoyed her. She eventually arrived at Haunted House, which was formally designated the Tactical Operations Center, but she'd never heard anyone call it by the latter before. She nodded at the two guards manning the entrance as she tapped her ID card on a nearby panel. A green indicator light flashed, allowing the large glass sliding doors to open for her, and she hobbled in. Herein lay the thinktank for all the clandestine operations involving the Ghost Teams, as well as representatives from the Underground Railroad, and more liaisons like Jamie, from Texas and other allied nations. Laura quickly spotted the large kitchenette adjoining the main corridor within Haunted House, making a beeline for it in search of coffee.

"Hey Laura, hold up a second!" She heard Spectre call out. She turned and saw him and Park approaching.

"Hey Ben, Hollywood, what's up?" she smiled. Park had something hidden behind his back, which he did not reveal.

"Hey, so, we know how much you like coffee, and now seeing that you're a Ghost and all, we figured it was time for you to get an awesome callsign. Here" Park presented a large mug from behind his back. Laura took it and looked it over. It was decorated with their unit emblem, a shadowy skull-faced ghost holding a scythe, and in black lettering over it was her new callsign.

"Ronin?" she read aloud.

"It means a samurai without a master, a warrior who is independent," Spectre explained.

"Thank you, guys, this is really cool. I like the name, too." Laura smiled appreciatively. Park grinned as she studied the mug.

"Yeah, I still think Sleeping Beauty is more applicable, but the others wouldn't let me put that on the mug." They laughed together.

"You know, Hollywood, the last day or so it was very applicable!" Laura chuckled.

"Well, we've got to run. I've got an urban assault course to run today, and Park has . . . well, whatever he calls work," Spectre joked.

"Whoah there, hot shot, it's called Cyber Ops. Look it up," Park scoffed, feigning an insult.

"Right, I'll see you guys later," Laura shook her head, smiling.

She was happy to see that her friends still had the same playful dynamic going on, despite not all being together in the field currently. She finally made her way to the kitchenette and was rewarded with a mugful of coffee. She sighed happily as she sipped the hot liquid, savoring it.

"Lieutenant Collins!" Laura spun on her good foot at the sound of her name. She saw Colonel Nelson walking down the corridor.

"Sir!" Laura responded, giving her commander her attention.

"I believe you'll want to sit in on this briefing," he said motioning her to join him. "I was going to call you, but lucky me, here you are," he added, with a light chuckle.

"Lead the way, sir," she replied, curiosity filling her.

"You'll have to forgive me, I'll need to use you as an example part of the way through," he said as they walked down the corridor. Laura raised an eyebrow, questioningly. "Don't worry; it'll make more sense in context. It'll probably answer a lot of your questions," he added.

"If that's the case, I'm fine with it, sir," she offered. He nodded, ushering her into a large conference room.

"Have a seat, lieutenant. Oh, here," Nelson moved to help her take another chair to set her foot up with, placing her towards the back of the room. Despite his being her commanding officer, Laura felt at ease with his fatherly demeanor, and appreciated it. She'd heard enough about his reputation by now to learn that he genuinely cared for every one of his soldiers.

"Thank you, sir," she smiled, taking another sip of coffee.

He walked over to the computer, quietly busying himself with final preparations for his presentation. A few moments passed in silence, Laura content to calmly finish her coffee, until the door opened allowing several people to file into the conference room. Laura shot a questioning glance toward her commanding officer, to which he gestured that she should remain seated. The newcomers took seats closer to the front where Nelson stood, exchanging greetings and handshakes. Laura didn't recognize any of them but could tell that they were high ranking officers and some elected representatives.

"Ladies, gentlemen," Nelson began to speak, drawing the low murmur in the room to silence. "As newly appointed tactical staff and senate committee members, please allow me to first and foremost welcome you."

He moved toward the computer and pressed a key. A projector screen flashed to life, displaying a tactical map of the continental US. The map itself was overlaid with data representing various zones of control, US versus PSRA.

"I will be going over with you a short summary of what we're dealing with: our enemies' capabilities, key strategic locations, and more importantly, I'll be giving you a glimpse into the way they think."

The next slide came into view. Laura leaned in, genuinely interested in the bigger picture. Colonel Nelson proceeded to share with his audience troop and armor numbers, observed new technologies, tactics and strategies employed by the PSRA forces to date. Furthermore, he elaborated on the enemy's more frequent and aggressive incursions into the greater Rocky Mountain zone, seemingly in search of the US' rumored "Home." So far, they'd not shown any indication that they were close to hitting their mark, but the prospect was alarming. The US was simply running out of time, and sooner or later, would need to reveal itself preferably on its own terms.

"From what we can tell, they are becoming more aware of just how wrong they were about this region. Up until recently, they'd believed that this was home to nothing more than loose bands of rebel factions, but now, with how much more frequently we've had to conduct Ghost Walks, it would appear they've grown suspicious." After spending more time on the subject, Nelson finally moved on to another matter.

"Now, those of you who are being transferred into the tactical staff, I believe I owe you a glimpse into our enemy's mind." He began to click through a myriad of pictures of various labor camps and execution centers, allowing the gravity of what was being seen to sink in.

"There is an elite class of Party members within the PSRA. They are comprised largely of family members, close political allies, and friends of those who founded the initial Socialist Party. They have engrained within the lower classes of people an innate sense of duty to put the Party before all else. In a brief summary of their guiding principles, the individual must: uphold the socialist path, uphold the leadership of the Party, and uphold Marxist, Leninist, and Mao thought. These principles take precedence over human rights, and many of the lower class, non-Party citizens lack even legal recognition of human rights. Lieutenant Collins?" Nelson gestured toward Laura. She sat up, uncomfortably.

"Yes, sir?"

"Would you mind expounding on your first-hand observations as a former Peace Officer?" Nelson asked. Laura cleared her throat, not totally unprepared, yet still uncomfortable under the scrutiny of those being briefed.

"Well, sir, during my time I was witness to such things, yes. Non-Party citizens often lacked such things as simple as due process, or even worker's rights. Everything is as mandated by the Party. There is no free speech, no lawful gatherings of any kind, no religious activities; it is diametrically opposed to what we have here." She took a deep breath, looking to Nelson.

"It is this elite class that our Ghost Teams, working in tandem with the Underground Railroad, seek to undermine," Nelson picked back up. "History has shown us that this regime will throw countless lives away to achieve their goals. They've been largely successful in systematically brainwashing the masses with state-controlled media, causing these poor souls to believe fanatically in the Party. Lieutenant, would you care to comment?" Laura sat up again, hands folded before her.

"This Party is indeed fanatical. The only reason I sit here before you today is that I was able to escape their machinations. They operate on some twisted idea that if an individual commits a crime, their family must pay for it on a multi-generational scale. My father, as a young man, committed a speech crime and was sent to a labor camp for five years and . . . more recently . . ." Laura paused, feeling a little shaken.

"More recently . . . executed to forward some Party agenda," she scanned the room, seeing the obvious shock registering on her audience's faces. "My mother and I were targeted next . . . but, to make a long story short, we escaped." Nelson finally spoke up again.

"Now, this system was put in place under an attempt to "sanitize" the gene pool of their citizens . . . almost qualifying as a twisted eugenics experiment to breed out disloyalty," Nelson paused, allowing for the audience to regain their composure in the light of such information.

"This is the measure of our enemy's resolve. They will stop at nothing. They will sacrifice everything and everyone but their own fellow elite. I will open the floor to questions at this time," Nelson finished.

Laura felt no small sense of relief to be free from the briefing. She stuck around afterward, graciously answering questions from the various attendees who wanted to learn more about her life before leaving the PSRA. Colonel Nelson was appreciative to her for allowing him to put her on the spot like he had and going beyond what he'd expected. She didn't mind so much, as any information she could volunteer would be helpful, if not actionable at some level. She really felt the appreciation when Nelson went and brought her a fresh cup of coffee. After parting ways with Nelson, Laura went to give herself a tour of the Haunted House in order to familiarize herself with it. As she wandered around and watched the various goings-on, she became lost in thought. She wanted to scour the library soon, as well as various intelligence pieces that had been accrued, to garner a deeper understanding of how things came to be. Her history books only gave her a synopsis of events, but what she wanted was an in-depth look. Her ankle was a hindrance to her, causing her to continue to move slowly as she clumsily hobbled around in her boot. She finished her mug of coffee, looking down to be sure that it was empty, almost out of disbelief. She eventually made her way to Ghost Team One's area and found Titus' office. The door was shut, so she knocked and waited. No response came, so she knocked again and tried the handle. It was locked. A young junior enlisted man was walking nearby, noticing Laura trying the door.

"Ma'am, I saw Captain Hansen in the armory about fifteen minutes ago," he said.

"Oh, thank you, Specialist," Laura replied.

The young man went about his business. Laura made her way toward the armory, hoping to catch Titus before he left on whatever assignment he'd been given. When she arrived at the armory, it ended up being much slower than she'd have liked. She was informed by the armory sergeant that Titus and a small squad of Ghosts had just left for the flight deck. Laura double-timed it as quickly as her boot would allow, finally catching the squad as they were loading onto a helicopter.

"Titus!" Laura called out. Titus turned, stopped what he was doing and closed the distance for Laura's ankle's sake.

"Hey, Laura, how are you? I heard you got roped into a meeting," he said, genuinely interested.

"I'm fine, the brief went long, I . . . just wanted to have a chance to talk for a minute. I haven't gotten to see you at all," she said, her heart starting to beat a little faster. Titus looked sad as he replied.

"I'm really sorry, Haunted House has had me hopping all over; there's something big coming down the pipe soon, I just know it. I really wanted a chance to talk to you, too," he studied her face. She held his gaze, unsure now of what to say.

"Laura," he said softly, his eyes brightening a little. "I haven't forgotten, nor do I regret anything from that day we ran off and played hooky, if that's part of your worry." Laura felt a little smile break across her face.

"Well, then . . . once you get back from this Ghost Walk, you owe me a proper picnic," she said, heart pounding harder.

"Of course," he replied, smiling in return. Laura glanced behind him, noticing that his squad was on the chopper but watching them.

"Um, Titus, are they waiting on you?" she asked, noticing that he was very much distracted by her presence.

"Hmm? Oh, yes, they can wait another minute," he said. They both began to blush a little as their eyes were locked.

"How long will you be out?" she asked, breaking the nervous pause.

"A week. We're running a sweep to the west, as there's been an uptick of PSRA raiders in the area. But you probably were just briefed on that," he chuckled.

"Titus, please be careful. You may be Ghosts, but you're not bullet proof," Laura said, a little worried. Her gut was beginning to tie up with anxiety.

"Don't worry; we'll be back before you know it. With any luck, that ankle will be all healed up so you can get a rematch in on that race," he assured her. Laura nodded with a smirk.

"Yeah, you better watch out though, I'm sure I'll smoke you next time," she said.

"Sir! Hate to interrupt, but we've got a schedule to keep!" one of the Ghosts on the chopper called out.

"Get her spinning up!" Titus replied.

As the helicopter began to come to life, Laura walked with Titus over to it, not yet wanting to leave his company. Titus started to climb aboard and froze. He turned and watched her begin to walk away to a safe distance from the chopper. He raised his index finger to the door gunner to indicate "one moment" and dismounted the chopper. Once he was down again, he called out.

"Laura! I forgot to give you something earlier!"

She turned back toward him, but he was already there. He stooped down a little, gently pulling her chin upward as he planted a kiss to her lips. The squad in the chopper came alive with cheers as they made their approval known loudly. Laura was shocked, as waves of new feeling surged through her. Once Titus began to pull away, she grabbed his face and kissed him again in excitement, eliciting more cheers. Both were grinning from ear to ear as they finally said goodbye and Titus boarded the chopper. Laura watched it slowly lift off the ground, the squad still being rambunctious, slapping Titus on the back and waving at Laura as well. She held his gaze as long as she could, as he did to her, until the chopper disappeared down the long tunnel. Laura just stood, staring after it, savoring the exhilaration of the moment for as long as possible. She felt happier than she'd ever felt before, allowing herself to embrace each wave of emotion. She was sure that he'd come back for her, and they would share an adventure together exploring the depths of their relationship. Finally, she turned and walked back to her home.

Chapter 15

SIX DAYS HAD PASSED, Laura's anticipation mounted. She had spent the time as if in a daydream. Jackie had all but called it when Laura had returned from the flight deck, and as giddy as she could possibly be, Laura told her every detail. And, of course, it didn't take long for Jamie to guess either. Laura had a glow about her wherever she went. Now that she was free of the boot, Laura made it a habit to stop by Haunted House to await the scheduled check-in calls that the Ghost Squad, callsign Night Walker, made at 0600. Occasionally, the OIC would allow Laura to receive the calls, logging the status and location of Night Walker. And so, Laura stood by in mission control, waiting to hear either Titus' voice, or that of the RTO. This would be the last status check before they would call again tomorrow for a pickup. Laura glanced at the mission clock and then at her watch. Both read 0602, the seconds continuing to tick. Colonel Nelson nodded at the comms sergeant.

"Night Walker, Haunted House, status report, over." Nothing but static filled the air.

"Night Walker, Haunted House, do you copy?" Laura glanced at Nelson, who remained stoic. The comms sergeant continued his attempts to hail them, unsuccessfully. Nelson took the hand mic.

"Ghost One, Ghost Master, do you copy?" Still nothing. Laura started to grow nervous, anxiety sneaking its way into her mind. It was now 0609 and still nothing.

"Sergeant Miller," Nelson began as he handed the mic over. "Try to raise them every five minutes until the next checkpoint. Inform me if they respond before then, otherwise, I'll be back at the next checkpoint time."

"Yes, sir."

Nelson then glanced at Laura. She could see the wheels turning in his mind as he stared with his arms crossed. "With me," was all he said to her as he walked away. Laura fell into step with him.

"For the record, I'm not worried yet and you shouldn't be either," he said as they walked. Laura was caught off-guard, unaware that she'd even shown anything back in mission control. "They have four hours until the next window, and it is very possible that they've just got a bad signal, or they're currently engaged in activity that necessitates radio silence. If that's the case, they will call back once they're clear." Laura nodded in understanding.

"Sir, with all this enemy troop movement, I just have to know . . . what does your gut tell you?" she asked candidly. Nelson stopped, turned to her and held her gaze steadily. He was silent for a moment.

"Scramble your team, suit up, and stand by the flight deck, lieutenant," he finally said. Laura snapped to, replying with a hearty "Yes, sir!"

"I will let you know the instant they either miss or make contact. Mount up!" Laura moved with a purpose to the armory, sending an urgent rally signal to her team mates as she went.

Within minutes, Rev, Spectre, Doc, Valkyrie, Park, and Jamie had assembled in the armory. Laura calmly explained the situation as they loaded up weapons and tactical gear. Ghost Team Two led by Lieutenant Perez, had also been scrambled. They had originally been the planned exfiltration team. The Ghosts hustled to the flight deck; loading onto three fast moving choppers they called "Screamers," awaiting word from Colonel Nelson. Laura sat next to Park, who had a real-time display of Night Walker element's projected position based on triangulation from the mission data. Park's fingers typed frantically over the virtual keyboard as he continued to input time and speed into his algorithm. He next overlaid their own mission data onto the old one, to give them a better sense of where to begin should they receive the go-ahead. Laura's team occupied Talon One, Perez's had Talon Two, and Talon Three was a designated med-evac bird with accompanying medics. The Screamers were fast attack-troop transports, each outfitted with an impressive array of mass casualty inflicting weapon systems. There were two twin rotary guns outfitted on the nose of the Screamer, rocket pods protruding from arms off the chassis of the bird, and door gunner positions on either side, wielding .50 caliber machine guns, updated versions of the old M2 platform. No one spoke for a long time; their mood was serious and somber. Laura looked at her watch for what she figured to have been the millionth time, before she glanced up to meet Jamie's gaze.

"You okay, Laura?" she asked, concerned for her friend. Laura's gaze fell.

"I guess. Maybe I'm just crazy, you know? They could have just not been able to make contact. It doesn't necessarily mean something bad happened." Laura spoke the words but could not bring herself to believe them.

"That very well could be the case, and say they do call in at this next window. We'd have all gotten dressed up for nothing," Jamie said. "Or, we do go, and find them with an inoperable radio, or something."

Laura nodded in agreement, and then looked over at Hank. He was wearing his trademark thousand-yard stare, boring a hole in the deck with his eyes. Laura felt that she could read him better now, after spending so much time under his tutelage. They way he sat, where he was looking, the extra intensity in his eyes and face told her that in his mind, he was preparing for a fight. Then, as if he'd read her mind, his eyes shot up to meet hers, and then back down. Laura understood, glancing at her watch again. They had fifteen minutes until the next checkpoint; the pilots had just about finished their pre-flight checks. Laura keyed her mic, checking to see if it was live, then hailed the Ammo Holding Area.

"Boom Shop, send it," came the reply.

"Boom Shop, Ronin. Request your fastest runners with an extra load of mags and grenades for Talon Element," Laura said.

"Roger, Ronin. Extra party load for Talon Element en-route. Over."

"Ronin out." Doc and Spectre looked at Laura, eyes widened slightly. Rev shook his head and began to say a prayer.

"Lord, we ask you to watch over us as we go to find our missing friends, but most importantly, keep them safe . . ."

A group of young soldiers from Boom Shop ran up and loaded the extra rounds onto the Screamers. Once secured, they darted off back to their posts. Laura looked over at the interactive holo-screen from Park's tough case computer. He had the mission clock in-sync with mission control, ticking down now minus two minutes from checkpoint. Next, Park uploaded the countdown to the pilot's HUDs as they brought the Screamers to a launching point. Laura felt anxiety build as she watched the seconds tick down to zero. She had a live feed from Haunted House patched through to her helmet comm system. There was silence.

"Night Walker, Haunted House, over," Laura gave Jamie a worried look.

"Ghost One, Haunted House, do you copy?" Rev reached over and squeezed Laura on the shoulder, giving her a reassuring look.

"Night Walker Element, Haunted House. Please respond. I say again please respond." Still more silence. Laura's heart dropped for a moment, and then quickly filled with a steely resolve.

"Ronin, Ghost Master, status?"

"Ghost Master, Ronin. Talon Element is RedCon One, request SP time now."

"Talon Element, Ghost Master. You are clear to launch. Godspeed, Talon Element. Ghost Master out."

Laura pumped her fist forward, yelling "Go! Go! Go!" The Screamers lurched off the ground, the pilots putting the sense of urgency into their birds as they shot down the tunnel and out into the open sky. They quickly dove down and to the west, flying in a wide formation with Talon Three higher and following behind for security. They levelled off away from the mountains, putting as much speed into their movement as possible. Talon One's pilot chimed in the comm.

"Talon Element, Talon One. ETA on objective is four-seven mikes, how copy, over?"

"Talon Two, copy."

"Talon Three, good copy."

Laura took a deep breath, watching the trees as the Screamers whooshed overhead. After a few moments, her attention was drawn to the door gunner nearest her. The gunner seemed to be tracking something with his weapon, periodically squinting through the sights on his "Ma Deuce." He kept his hand ready to disengage the safety, and as if instinct told him to, he switched the weapon off safe. Laura elbowed Park, pointing at the door gunner.

"Can you patch into his HUD?" she asked. Park brought it up with a few keystrokes and he and Laura stared at the screen, trying to figure out what he was staring at. Laura moved over to the gunner.

"What is it, sergeant? What do you see?" she was glad the helmet mic filtered out much of the background noise. He didn't move, but replied,

"Not sure, ma'am . . . I just keep seeing an odd shimmer that doesn't seem like it should belong," he began; pointing out toward whatever it was that was bothering him. "When I try to focus on it, I can't see it anymore. It almost seems like it's moving with us. It's really weird!"

"Roger, keep an eye on it if you can," Laura responded, looking quizzically at Park. Park shrugged, returning to his screen, trying to filter the HUD through various tools. Unsatisfied with no results, he opened his bag and produced a small black device which he plugged into his computer.

"Jamie, are you monitoring any unusual frequencies on the net?" Laura asked. Jamie shook her head at first, and then cocked an eyebrow.

"There is something faint," she said, shrugging at Park. He interfaced with a new program, pulling up a complete readout of active frequencies in the immediate area.

"Checking for anomalies, Hollywood?" Laura asked him. He nodded.

"This is a sensor probe I built a while back. I'd brought it to help nail down Night Walker's location, but now let's see . . ." he trailed off.

He filtered out the frequencies that he knew belonged to them, leaving only one anomalous signal. He tapped his screen, bringing up more information about the signals' properties. Only one characteristic stuck out to him.

"It's moving! Shoot it!" he shouted frantically.

"If you've got a target, take it gunner!" Laura ordered. A burst of .50 rounds flew, smashing into something around fifty meters away that erupted into flame. The fireball fell into the forest.

"It's a drone!" Park announced. "Some kind of cutting edge, high-tech model of the Predator-Ling X variant, I'll bet!"

"That was some crazy good stealth tech, that's for sure!" the gunner said.

"Are there any more?" Laura asked Park.

"Let me boost the probe range . . . and . . . negative, we're alone." Laura took a deep breath, looking over at Hank. He still wore the same intense look as if he'd expected the trouble.

"All Talon Elements, Ronin. We're being tracked, I say again, we're being tracked," Laura announced on the net. "Haunted House, Ronin."

"Send it."

"Stand by to receive telemetry from Hollywood, break. Ghost Master, please advise on receipt and analysis, over."

"Good copy, Ronin, receiving telemetry. Stand by." Laura stared at Park as they waited. His face expressed a seriousness she'd never seen before.

"Ronin, Ghost Master."

"Go for Ronin."

"Ronin, it doesn't look good. They know you're coming. Recommend abort." Laura tapped her helmet.

"Say again, Ghost Master, Recommend?"

"It's your call Ronin . . . do you want to spring the trap?" Laura looked at all the faces of her comrades in the chopper. They all nodded at her, resolute to save their friends, no matter what. "Ghost Master, Ronin. We're going to Charlie-Mike. We're getting our boys back!"

"Roger that Ronin. Happy hunting. Ghost Master out." Laura heard cheers, war-cries, and some colorfully worded insults for their enemy ring out through the open comm.

"Ronin, Cobra," Perez called.

"Send it," Laura replied.

"Ronin, we're with you. Let's kick some-" Perez was cut off in his statement, as Talon Two veered hard stick right to avoid surface to air rocket fire.

"Here we go, ladies!" shouted the pilot of Talon One. The door gunners cut down the forest near the point of origin for the ground fire.

"Yeah! Get some!" one yelled. The .50's reduced the area quickly.

"How about a little in-flight music!" laughed the co-pilot of Talon One. He flicked a switch and an intense, loud kind of music with a screaming vocalist started blasting through the comm system. Laura later was informed that the genre was called "metal."

"Yeah!" laughed Rev. "Now we're talkin'!"

Automatic weapons fire ripped out from hilltops and clearings of the massive forest, and the Screamers replied in kind. The twin guns started whirring until all anyone could hear was the telltale sound of hot and massive tracer rounds exploding their way downrange, tearing apart the forest, and utterly destroying everything they touched.

"Yeah baby! I've got a special delivery for ya right here!" the copilot yelled in between firing bursts.

The Screamers weaved and juked, dumping fire and death to whatever dared expose itself. Off in the distance, they could see a small forward operating base the PSRA had been setting up. The Talon flight dove toward it, letting fly a salvo of rockets and incinerating everything the enemy had been building. Next, they swooped high, scanning the area for enemy troop movement. At this point they'd missed their checkpoint coordinates, so Park began to scan frequencies again.

"Picking up a signal . . . Got it! Friendly emergency transponder, bearing 276, approximately three clicks . . . mobile," Park announced.

"Talon Element, Talon Three. I see a convoy in that area heading west."

"Good copy, Talon Three. Talon Element move to intercept," Laura ordered. Affirmative responses chimed in and the Screamers veered onto their new heading.

"Ronin, Talon One. I see one meat wagon and four support vehicles."

"Roger. Neutralize support, disable wagon," Laura replied, glancing at the HUD feed.

The vehicles must have spotted them, or were at least warned by their comrades, as they increased speed. They made their way toward a small, bombed out town, apparently to fortify their position. Talon Two strafed the convoy, shredding the trail vehicles. As Talon One made a pass, the pilot aborted the maneuver as the lead vehicles opened fire, pelting the chopper's armor.

"Talon Two, take them!" Talon One shouted. Talon Two charged, but too late. The convoy shot into the town, taking cover around some of the taller buildings on the main street.

"Set us down over there!" Laura ordered, indicating an LZ on the pilot's HUD that was clear of enemy fire. Talon One and Two dipped over the area quickly, allowing the Ghosts to slide down on ropes. The choppers moved off to provide overwatch as the Ghosts moved into cover.

"Cobra! Take your team down that arterial street! We'll take the right! See you on the other side!" Laura gestured, making the squads jump into action. Perez acknowledged, moving his team quickly.

"Hollywood: monitor our locations and coordinate strafing runs as we cover ground!" she directed Park who remained aboard Talon One.

"Good copy," came the reply.

Laura signaled to her squad and they advanced. Emboldened by the overwatch provided by the Talon flight, the Ghosts advanced in a rapid run-and-gun fashion; quickly picking off any stragglers that survived the strafing runs as they made their way to the convoy. Almost simultaneously, the two squads converged on the vehicles occupying the main street. The Screamers had the enemy pinned as the guns ripped the street apart. Laura caught Perez's attention, signaling for grenades to flush out the entrenched enemy. Grenades were thrown around the support vehicles, blasting any PSRA troops that occupied the area into pieces. They moved in, checking bodies and kicking away weapons from the fallen enemy troops. The support trucks were completely destroyed, riddled with battle damage from the chopper's guns and grenades. Situated in the middle of the convoy was the meat wagon. Rev ripped open the back doors, covered by his squad mates. Inside, shackled to the benches, was Night Walker Element.

"We've got them!" Rev yelled, hopping in.

He was followed by one of Perez's men who began to break the shackles with a portable bolt cutter. Laura scanned the faces of the survivors, searching for Titus. He wasn't there.

"Talon Three, Ronin. Friendlies for exfil!" she yelled. She recognized the RTO, Corporal Ruiz, as he jumped off the meat wagon and stopped him. "Corporal Ruiz! Where's Captain Hansen?" she asked.

"I'm sorry ma'am, they separated us," he began, his face worried. "He made me keep the transponder so you could find us."

"Do you have any idea where they took him?" Laura pressed. Ruiz shook his head sadly.

"Ma'am, they recognized him . . . some suits came for him." Laura was about to ask more questions, but Talon One cut through the radio.

"Ronin, Talon One. We've got enemy inbound, we need to leave now!"

"Roger, we're ready for pickup!" Laura replied.

Talon Three lifted off as the last survivors loaded, followed then by Talons One and Two setting down for pickup. Laura waited for her squad to board before she made her way onto Talon One. Right as the birds began to lift off, an explosion rocked Talon One. Laura held on for dear life as the pilot tried to recover from a spin, her body being pulled out of the chopper. Another rocket explosion close by made the pilot jerk the yoke again. Laura was thrown off the chopper and into the nearby forest. She crashed through branches and finally came to a rest within a large bush. Her vision blurred as she lay still within the bush and faded. She could hear radio traffic still, although it came through very broken. Haunted House was ordering an immediate bug-out as PSRA close air support was inbound. She tried to talk, but only made a croak as she started gasping for air. The wind had been knocked out of her. She gasped again, and again, until finally, her lungs filled with air. She rolled over to her side and vomited. She could hear the Screamers engage their thrusters, making the distinct sound that gave them their name. The sound faded off in the distance, accompanied by the occasional spurts of gunfire. This area was sure to be swarming with enemy troops, she reckoned. Slowly, she moved onto all fours and then finally to a kneeling position. She took a few deep breaths and tried the radio. No good. She tried again, silence was her response. She took hold of a thin tree nearby and rose to her feet. She did her best to assess her injuries before searching her immediate area for any gear that may have been thrown with her. Her rifle was thankfully still attached to her load bearing vest, the carabiner clip having not failed. She lost a couple of magazines, however, so she'd need to avoid contact and move silently as best as she could. There was still one fragmentation grenade attached to her vest, one canteen, and her knife was strapped to her hip. She looked around frantically; searching for anything else that'd make her new task easier. Nothing, and now, she was out of time. Time to disappear. She set off through the forest, trying to make her away through the wooded areas to the other side of the town. She headed west, resolute. She would not leave Titus behind. She looked up at the mid-afternoon sky, grey with cloud cover.

"Jesus," she whispered, pushing away the awkward feeling that tried to discourage her from talking to Rev's God. "I need your help . . . please . . . help me save Titus." She was silent, waiting for some kind of reply. She didn't hear anything, but her heart felt that familiar peace. "Thanks," she whispered, marching out into the wilderness.

Night had fallen, but Laura wasn't going to stop. She didn't even feel tired or sore, probably thanks to the countless miles of ruck marching she'd done over the mountains. The conditioning was paying off big time. She needed to figure out a mode of transportation, and soon. Her adversaries that currently held Titus were most likely driving in a convoy, which given the time between their departure and now, they could have well covered at least two hundred miles. Laura prayed they hadn't, hoping that they'd elected to stop at a FOB or regional command center somewhere along their route. She heard a noise and froze. There it was again. She slowly crouched, drawing her blade. Out of the darkness came . . . a rabbit. Laura sighed in relief, allowing herself a stifled chuckle as she watched the hare bounce away. She replaced her knife into its sheath and continued on her way.

As she went, she became aware of a distant metallic clanging. She thought herself as going crazy until she heard it again. This next time, it was accompanied by loud cursing, as someone took grievance with whatever was producing the noise. She followed the sounds, eventually reaching the edge of the tree line that ran alongside a highway. She'd thought that she'd kept well clear of any roads, but she had to admit that her night time land navigational skills were wanting. She must have drifted off course at some point, however so slightly. She crept down into the drainage ditch alongside the pavement at the shoulder, moving even closer to the source of the noise. About twenty meters down the road she spotted a PSRA cargo truck. The lights of the truck were shut off, but she could see two soldiers, one with a flashlight illuminating the struggles of his comrade with changing a tire. Laura watched them work, weighing her options. She decided that this could be her opportunity to catch a ride further west and crept closer in the darkness. The soldier holding the flashlight disappeared for a moment, before returning with a road flare. He lit it and dropped it on the road near their truck. Laura listened in as the two combined their efforts to get the change done, griping about how the convoy had left them behind.

"Listen, it's only an hour to the FOB. Let's just get this done, get on our way, and get to sleep!" one said, trying to diffuse his partner's frustration.

Finally, they wrestled the new tire onto the rim and fastened it down. Laura watched their movements carefully, watching for any sign that they'd become aware of her presence. She trained her weapon on them as they began to stow their recovery gear. They didn't appear to care to practice any sort of good noise and light discipline, even being so lackadaisical that neither carried a weapon for security. They finished up and climbed into the cab. The truck rumbled to life and slowly started to roll forward. Laura moved, darting back into the tree line to avoid the flare before sprinting after them. The truck clambered along, its motor sluggish as it accelerated. Laura veered back into the road, close behind the vehicle and leapt, catching the tailgate. She pulled herself up and in, flipping the canvas closed behind her. She felt around in the darkness, touching boxes and crates. She retrieved her red light and illuminated the cargo. There was food and water! Laura tore open a box of the field rations, eating her fill of preservative-heavy food. Next, she refilled her canteen and drank until she felt hydrated. She finished, topping it off, and stowing it back into her canteen pouch. She moved in a little bit closer to the cab and poked a hole on the side of the canvas, so she could see out. The wind whipped against the heavy canvas cover of the cargo truck as it rumbled its way down the highway. Laura could still feel the peace inside her . . . as if she knew she was going the right way, despite having no intel whatsoever. Just west.

Laura attempted to make herself at least a little comfortable as the truck often bounced on its heavy-duty leaf springs. She tapped her watch face and it glowed a soft red. They had to be getting close if the two soldier's estimation was to be believed. Sure enough, a few minutes later, the truck slowed before making a turn off the road. It proceeded slowly toward a manned entry control point and stopped, the brakes hissing loudly. Laura heard the gate guards yelling at the truck crew, making some pointed statements and insults about not knowing how to change a tire. The driver's response was vulgar, and the guards waved them through, having had enough fun at their expense. The truck lumbered on through, eventually coming to a halt within a vehicle staging area. The two exited the cab, arguing about whether they'd unload the cargo or not. One suggested they sleep and make some other junior enlisted do it for them in the morning. They agreed on their lazy plan and stomped off into the darkness. Laura looked through her peephole, seeing nothing. She moved to the opposite side, poking another peephole, also nothing. She heard nothing close by either, the only sounds emanating from the distant entry control point. She slowly moved to the back, lifting the canvas, and peeked out. Satisfied with the level of darkness, she quietly climbed out, working her way through the vehicle pool. She stopped, an idea quickly popping into mind. She picked out a good number of faster moving tactical vehicles and began to cut hydraulic lines, fuel hoses, whatever she could find to sabotage. It was time consuming, but she felt that if she needed to make a run for it, this sabotage would go a long way toward helping her escape. She moved next to some hastily built crew shacks to investigate them. She heard a lot of snoring as she crept around them, feeling that this was not where she wanted to be. She froze, before quietly slipping into a deep shadow as a roving patrol walked about, quietly muttering complaints about the cold. Laura heard one of the two patrolmen yawn, obviously tired. She waited for them to pass, before moving on.

She crept on, counting at least fifty paces before bumping into something metallic. It was a helicopter! *Perfect*, she thought. She'd used some of her down time more recently to learn the basics of flying a helicopter, including some flight simulator time. As she moved around its hull, she determined that it was a gunship. Hopefully it wasn't much different in basic layout. She stopped a minute, mentally mapping the route she'd taken through the FOB, judging distances and landmarks. Continuing in the direction she'd been originally travelling, her gut leading her off into the darkness. She could make out the silhouette of a tall tent further out and eventually an official looking car. The car probably belonged to agents from the Office of Progression, she decided. There were two figures in the darkness, guarding the front of the tent. Laura snuck her way up to the back side of the tent and peeked around, recognizing the telltale OP agent tactical armor. Laura moved back out of their periphery and took a knee. She needed to gain access to this tent, obviously, but was unsure of how she'd do it. As she racked her brain for options, she heard voices inside the tent.

"Wake him up," one voice said. There was an audible crack, followed by sharp inhalations. *Smelling salts?* She wondered. What she heard next made her blood freeze.

"Tell us, Captain . . . What is the location of your "Home"?" Laura's heart pounded. She heard a cough, followed by a raspy response.

"Hansen, Titus . . . Captain, US Army-" he was interrupted by a strike. "I'm sorry . . . that's not what you asked . . ." Titus coughed and laughed.

"Home . . . my home . . . is located in the Pacific Northwest-" He was cut off again, this time by the sound of some kind of electrical device. Laura heard him grunt in pain as he was electrocuted.

"Let's try this again," the interrogator said. "We know you're striking from somewhere in the mountains! Where is your base?" another shock followed.

"Wait . . . wait . . . I'll tell you," Titus said through gritted teeth.

"Well?" the irritated OP interrogator demanded.

"Well, what's your mother's address?" Titus laughed as the sound of fists pummeled him, followed by another electrocution out of spite.

Laura couldn't bear to hear any more, but she still didn't have a good plan. She had to bide her time, wait for an opportunity to strike. It was quiet in the tent for a few beats, Laura strained to listen for anything.

"Passed out again," she heard a new voice say. "We should let the experts at Death Valley Rehab finish the job," the first voice said.

"You're probably right . . . we're not equipped to break 'em out here," said the second. Laura heard sounds of movement, the front tent flap opened followed by a car door.

"Listen up. One of you will watch the prisoner at all times. I don't care if you rotate in and out to stay warm. We'll be back at 0500 for him," the second voice ordered the guards. The car's motor fired up and it pulled away, tires crunching on the terrain. Laura waited, listening as one of the guards took his post inside the tent, the other remaining outside.

"Hey man, you want to do thirty on and off?" the outside guard asked.

"Yeah, sure," said the one inside.

Laura peeked again around the corner, seeing the outside guard fidget. He was restless, probably having already stood for hours. He kicked the dirt, as well as occasionally stretching his back in boredom. Laura felt the ground near her, finding a decent sized rock. She picked it up and threw it beyond the guard, off to his left. The rock struck some branches and rustled as it finished its flight. The guard casually took a few steps to his left, only passively curious at the noise, and stared off into the darkness, not really expecting to find anything. Laura, knife in hand, crept up behind quickly. In a silent, deadly move, she struck, slicing his vocal cords along with his throat. Her free hand pulled his head back, her knee she drove into his knees, causing him to drop slowly, silently gurgling. Next, she dragged him around the tent and crouched, ready to pounce.

Patiently, she listened for the other guard to emerge as her takedown hadn't been totally silent. Nothing. Laura crept to the door of the tent, taking a calculated risk to peek inside. It was poorly lit, a portable lantern shedding the only light from a small table in the corner. Laura saw Titus' body slumped as it dangled from the support pole located in the middle of the tent, but she deliberately didn't focus on him, as she was searching for the other guard. The second guard was seated in a chair, his body bent over a desk as he slept. *Lucky me*, Laura sighed. She positioned herself behind him, ready to strike. Her knife tracked its way across his throat in a flash, and as he awoke to drowning in blood, she stabbed under a few ribs in rapid succession. The guard slumped to the ground, clutching at the throat wound in a futile attempt to save himself. Laura's heart pounded as she turned her attention to Titus. His hands were zip-tied above his head on the tent pole support; his feet were also fastened to the pole. His shirt had been removed exposing the fresh burns on his flesh from whatever electric prod they'd been torturing him with, as well as old scars including the large one that she now noticed ran all the way down his torso. *Had he been dissected?* Laura wondered as she went to him, cutting his bonds and freed him. She struggled to support his weight as he slumped to the ground, conducting blood sweeps and checking for obvious wounds. Not seeing anything too serious, she rolled him into the recovery position and prepared to wake him up. She moved to the desk, rummaging through the interrogator's supplies, finally finding a capsule of smelling salts. Laura returned to Titus and cracked the capsule under his nose. He jerked awake, and Laura held him still, taking his face in her hand. He blinked at her hard, unable to believe his eyes.

"Hello, handsome," Laura smiled at him, eyes welling up a little.

"Am I dreaming?" Titus asked, touching her face.

"See for yourself!" Laura chuckled, helping him sit up. Titus saw the body on the ground nearby, blood pooling all around.

"Oh! Nicely done!" he grunted, allowing Laura to help him to his feet. "What's our exit plan? Is the team standing by?" he asked. Laura shook her head, biting her lip.

"It's just me out here . . . long story," she said, noticing the confusion filling his face. "There's a gunship staged about fifty of my paces out the tent, to the right. I want to borrow it," she finished.

"That'll work," he said, moving to grab the interrogator's bag, looking for any kind of medical supplies. He took the dead man's rifle, motioning to the tent flap.

"I'm ready if you are," he said.

Laura led the way, exiting the tent and moving quickly toward the gunship. The sun was slowly beginning to creep out over the horizon, illuminating the sky ever so slightly. They moved in a crouched run, Laura helping Titus clamber onto the chopper.

"The second we fire this thing up, the whole camp will be on us," Titus said, moving into the co-pilot seat.

"Wait for my signal, and then start the power up sequence. I'll be back in a few minutes," Laura said, taking off into a sprint before Titus could ask about what her signal would be.

Her first destination was the vehicle pool. She remembered seeing a fuel tanker staged nearby, and went to it, and then opened the valves to begin spilling fuel. Next, she ran toward the ECP; hurrying before the sunlight exposed her. Seeing silhouettes of nearby ECP guards, she stopped to catch her breath. They had a gun truck parked and running, illuminating the makeshift gate with its headlights. Laura pulled out her grenade. The soldiers were all standing in close proximity to each other, a fatal mistake. Laura thumbed the clip, twisted and pulled the pin, and threw the grenade at the soldiers. Her aim was true, and as she hit the deck it exploded, killing the gate crew. Someone near the gun truck jumped into the turret and started firing wildly into the forest beyond the gate. Laura sprinted back toward the helicopter as shouting and shooting filled the dawn. More soldiers swarmed the gate, shooting and throwing grenades into the forest at their unknown foe. Laura made it back as Titus spun up the engines.

"That was some signal!" he shouted as Laura got in. She frantically assisted him with switching systems on and they both put on headsets.

"Have you ever flown a helicopter before?" Titus asked. Laura replied hesitantly.

"Well, sort of. I'm good on the simulator . . ." Titus shot her a worried look and continued the startup sequence.

"Oh great . . . I'm still on the simulator too." The sun was up high enough now that Laura could see the motor pool and vehicle crews attempting to get their trucks going.

"Uh oh! We've got friends!" Titus said, pointing.

Laura looked as two confused pilots ran toward them, waving their arms. Laura gritted her teeth nervously, pulling the yoke. The gunship lifted clumsily, gaining altitude as it jerked. Titus laughed at the pilots and Laura brought the chopper around, facing the camp.

"Let's give them a real send-off!" she said.

The guns on the chopper began to whir, followed by a maelstrom of hot tracer rounds. They strafed the cluster of soldiers that'd been reinforcing the gate. Next, they launched rockets, blasting whole swathes of the FOB, which then ignited the river of fuel that'd been leaking. The fuel was like an aftershock, engulfing a whole portion of the camp including the motor pool, the fire tracking its way back to the fuel tanker. The sky lit up with a massive fireball. Small arms fire pinged against the armor of the gunship, prompting Laura to climb higher and pull away.

"Time to go!" she said, pointing the nose eastbound. They flew as quickly as the gunship would allow, heading toward friendly territory near the mountains. A few minutes later, alarms started blaring.

"Missile lock!" Titus yelled, searching for the countermeasure controls.

Laura looked ahead, seeing the missile launch and streak across the sky in their direction. She grimaced, anticipating the imminent impact. She jerked the yoke hard stick right as Titus found the switch that deployed flares. The missile took the bait, arcing barely off course before detonating behind them. The chopper shook violently, with Laura yanking the stick hard to the left. They let fly a salvo of rockets of their own. The hilltop where the SAM launched erupted into flame, destroying the launch site. They climbed higher, resuming their course. There was silence as they scanned the horizon and ground as they flew, searching for any threats. The next attack came violently, from above. Two Predator Mark V drones stripped the hull of the gunship with armor piercing rounds. Laura struggled with the controls, fighting to maintain altitude and speed.

"Oh no . . ." Laura said.

Titus looked at her and she pointed, indicating the fuel gauge. The tank had been ruptured. They were dumping fuel. Titus unstrapped himself from the co-pilot's seat and took the door gunner position. One of the drones was making another attack run. Titus fired, tracers flashing just behind the hull of the drone. He saw it break off and climb out of range. Laura dipped the chopper in an attempt to dodge sideways as more rounds punched through. Titus fired, anticipating the second drone's movements, and scored a hit. Laura cheered as she saw the drone streak by to her left and burst into flame, striking the ground. She looked up and saw the other drone charging down at them, beginning to fire. She juked hard up and left, then down. Rounds missed, but a few smashed into the nose of the gunship. Titus tried to hit it but missed the drone wide by a few feet. Laura nervously glanced at the fuel gauge. They only had a few minutes of flight time left, provided they weren't shot down, and still a long way from friendly turf. The drone climbed high again, about to make another dive toward them. Laura looked back at Titus.

"I hope you're strapped in!" she called to him.

He gave her a funny look, then realizing she was about to try something risky, double checked his harness and gave her a thumbs up. Laura scanned the sky, finally catching the drone as it started to dive.

"Hang on!" she shouted.

She pitched the chopper sideways violently, giving Titus a clear shot. He fired, and even as his rounds struck true, the drone got a few rounds off as it burst into flame. The rounds hit their tail rotor, causing the gunship to spin out of control. Laura tried the radio, hoping against all odds that friendly ears were listening.

"Mayday! Mayday! Mayday! This is Ronin! Going down! Coordinates Unknown!" Much to her surprise, she got a reply.

"Ronin, Haunted House! We see you on radar, scrambling rescue!"

"Roger, Haunted House. I can't tell you how good it is to hear your voice!" Laura tried to guide the wild gunship toward an open clearing she'd spotted in the forest. "Brace for impact!" she yelled.

The chopper crashed through some tree tops as it dropped from the sky. The hull smashed into the ground, sliding a great distance before eventually coming to rest on its side. Laura blinked, her vision fading in and out. She blinked again, unable to focus on anything. She tried to smell, seeing smoke, but her nose was wet, dripping. She touched it with her fingers, observing the fresh blood that now covered them. Her ears were ringing as well.

"Titus!" she yelled, hoarsely.

No answer. She yelled louder. Nothing. She struggled to undo her harness, fumbling with the quick release. She finally got it and crumpled out of her seat onto the co-pilot's seat. She hit her head, and despite the helmet, it made her dizzy. She crawled back into the gunner area, desperate to find Titus. She found him and gasped as she made her way into the compartment fully. He was lying in a heap, a chunk of twisted metal protruding from his stomach made her panic. She rushed to his side, checking first for a pulse on his neck, breathing a thank you as she detected one present. She talked to him, then patted his shoulder, and then finally rubbed her knuckles against his sternum, telling her that he was completely unresponsive. She found the supplies he'd raided from the interrogator's bag, dumped a quick-clot powder on the wound, and then packed gauze around it. She checked his pulse again, as well as breathing, satisfied that he was as stable as he could be in this situation. Laura checked her weapon that remained attached to her vest, looking in the chamber as well as the magazine. She sat by Titus for a moment, thinking about what she should do next. Her head bobbed as sleep tried to claim her, her eyes heavy. She blinked hard, fighting the urge to sleep until a noise caused her to snap awake again. Twigs were crunching in the forest. She clambered up the side of the smashed wreck that used to be a formidable gunship and looked out. She could make out silhouettes through the trees approaching. Laura hesitated. If she stayed put, they could toss a few frag or thermite grenades into the hull. She couldn't leave Titus there. She dropped back inside, checking the cockpit. The glass was completely gone, smashed in the impact. She steeled herself for the upcoming task. She grabbed Titus under the armpits, dragged him into the cockpit, and finally through the window. Next, she repositioned him along the hull, where he'd have some cover for the time being.

Laura could hear the footsteps from within the forest, slowly moving closer. She took a prone firing position near the smashed nose of the chopper, scanning for a target. Her sights covered a figure in the distance, slowly coming closer and closer. She positively identified a PSRA soldier. Rescue hadn't come yet. Her thumb toggled the selector switch on her weapon from safe to semi. Her index finger slowly increased pressure on the trigger until her shot burst forth. She didn't blink as the weapon kicked, maintaining her sight picture, watching as a chunk of the enemy soldier's head was torn off. Her enemy was taken by surprise, dropping prone as they returned fire, calling out distance and direction as best they could. Laura had a decent patch of tall grass around her, concealing her position at the chopper's nose. She scanned the trees for another target, her eyes tracking right to left until they settled on movement behind a thin tree. She put her sights at the edge of the tree and fired once. Her bullet struck a shoulder, knocking the soldier back. She adjusted her aim as he stumbled and fired again, striking his head. Two down, but by now they had a good idea of where to return fire. Bullets pinged on the metal nose next to her, causing her to roll back behind the hull. She moved toward the tail, staying low as the contours of the wreck dipped lower. Something caught her peripheral vision. She looked, noticing a hole in the wreck's armor where a round from the drone had punched through, and noticed movement beyond. She rested the muzzle of her rifle in the hole, aimed, and fired. A cry of pain rose in the distance and persisted, much to the chagrin of the enemy. Laura continued to move, peering around the end of the tail section. She spotted five enemy troops finish a tactical move to the wreck itself, shoulders pressed against the hull, facing toward the nose. They were stacked and ready to move around the nose of the downed bird, believing her to still be in that area. Laura toggled her selector switch from semi to automatic, and, bracing herself for accuracy, she squeezed and held the trigger. Her fire cut down all but one of the enemy soldiers, who completed the move around the nose and returned fire. Laura ducked back to cover, noticing her weapon's bolt had locked back, indicating it was ready for another magazine. The enemy soldier fired blindly around both sides of the wreck, Laura hoped he hadn't accidently hit Titus. She jammed a new magazine in the well, released the bolt to chamber a round, and moved.

Letting the rifle dangle from her vest, she scrambled up the side of the wreck once she heard the sound of her enemy beginning to reload as well. In an adrenaline-fueled fury, Laura charged across the hull, leaping out over the nose. By the time the soldier looked up, she was airborne, knife glinting in the light before it plunged into the man's chest. The force of her momentum knocked him to the ground, and, as he fell, he attempted to swing his weapon up to fire, but too late. Laura kicked the weapon as it fired wild shots in the man's panic. She was on him, yanking the knife out and then repeatedly stabbed him all over the torso. She began screaming in a blind rage, continuing to puncture the lifeless body over and over again. Laura was covered in blood and stood, scanning the forest for more threats, panting heavily. She saw movement, a lone figure crawling away in the distance. Retrieving her knife, she stumbled into the woods in pursuit. She quickly caught up to the wounded soldier and pinned his leg to the ground with her knife. The man screamed in pain. Laura twisted the figure over, fist poised to strike as she ripped the man's helmet off. Her body filled with shock and horror. She knew his face well and he knew hers.

"Laura?" Ben Fischer managed to rasp, voice weak with pain.

"Ben!" Laura's eyes filled with tears as she held his face. "Wha-how? What are you doing here?" she sobbed. Ben made a gurgling noise; his eyes misted, and coughed up blood. Laura's hand went to his chest, where she'd shot him. He'd lost a lot of blood.

"The feds came . . . threatened my family . . . my loyalty," he whispered sadly.

"Because of me," Laura's chin quivered. Ben managed a nod.

"They volunteered me for frontier military duty . . . five-year tour . . . as a plea bargain . . . said they'd give my family extra rations . . ." his breath became increasingly raspy and difficult.

"I'm so sorry! Ben, I'm so sorry!" Laura bowed her head, shaking with guilt.

"Laura . . . had I known you . . . were here," his tears flowed freely now.

"Oh God! Ben I'm so sorry!" Laura wept.

She took his face in her palms, blood smearing his cheeks. Even as he was dying, his eyes regarded her with the brotherly love that she'd often seen in their time at the precinct together. He held her gaze, reaching out to take one of her hands.

"Please . . . Laura," he coughed. "Not your fault . . . I forgive you . . . please, Laura . . . forgive yourself," now his voice gurgled audibly. "Please tell my wife . . ." he didn't finish, his last breath bubbling with blood as Laura watched his life slip away from his eyes.

Laura wept so bitterly, so uncontrollably, her body convulsing with sobs. She writhed on the ground next to her former partner, her brother, suffering wave upon wave of intense sorrow, the emotion driving her mind to madness. She eventually regained some semblance of control over herself, crawling back to his lifeless body, and closed his eyes. She retrieved her knife and then crossed Ben's arms, allowing him to lie in a peaceful state. She continued to openly cry, although her face hurt, and her tear ducts felt raw and dry. She turned, ready to return to the wreck, and time seemed to slow. She felt a hot sensation pierce and radiate throughout her back and she fell forward. She screamed in agony as the crack of the rifle shot echoed through the silent forest. Laura crawled forward a few feet as bullets began to tear the forest apart around her. She rolled onto her back, swinging her weapon up, firing blindly at her assailants. She emptied the clip, scrambling to her feet, and sprinted toward the wreck. Bullets whistled past her ears, kicking up debris as she ran. Somehow, she made it, diving around the nose for cover. She jammed a new magazine into her weapon, readying herself for the fight. Rounds continued to strike and ping against the armor of the wreck noisily. It sounded as if they'd brought crew served weapons as well, so unrelenting was the assault. Fragmentation grenades exploded close by, rocking the hull of the chopper as enemy troops tested their throwing arms.

Laura panted, her body attempted to kick back into fight mode, but it was too exhausted. She looked up into the sky. It looked so peaceful, a beautiful tranquility within the endless void of blue; so unaware and uncaring of what transpired beneath. Laura's vision blurred a little, her head dipping sluggishly as it followed her intentions to inspect herself. Her torso was soaked with blood, although she was unsure of whose blood it really was. She peeled her vest open, pulling up her shirt slightly. There was a fresh-looking crimson hole, which she absent-mindedly packed with a handful of dirt. She didn't even feel it anymore, and she didn't care. Laura took a deep ragged breath and looked at Titus. She could see his chest struggling to rise and fall, his skin was pale, and the impaling metal chunk had started oozing blood again. He needed medical attention immediately if he was going to survive. Laura didn't want to die, but if she was going to, she was glad she'd be at his side when it happened.

Struggling to her feet and face now locked into a thousand-yard stare, Laura walked around the nose of the wreck. She raised her rifle and fired wherever she saw muzzle flashes within the forest. Bullets whizzed around her, somehow missing, but close nonetheless. She kept firing until her weapon was empty and she threw it at her enemy. She drew her knife, brandishing it, and let out a cry of challenge. A bullet grazed her thigh, dropping her to her knees. She looked up, wiping her mouth with the back of her bloody hand, and rose to her feet. Suddenly, the forest erupted into flame. Laura was thrown back by the blast, tumbling back near the wreck. She rolled onto her back and stared into the sky again. She could hear the loud rumble of jets tearing through the sky, feeling and hearing the thunder and heat of more heavy ordinance being dropped. The next thing she heard was the unmistakable sound of Screamers approaching. More explosions, loud automatic gunfire filled her ears. The wind swirled as it was beat by the rotors of the Screamers, one landing nearby. She was suddenly on a body board, lifted, and carried to the chopper. She blinked, only partially aware of what was going on; dazed. Now numb. She looked at her left arm, taking note of an IV drip. She looked right and there lay Titus, next to her, still unconscious. The medics seemed to phase in and out of being as they tended his serious condition, Laura fought against the darkness that attempted to take her. She reached out with her right hand and took hold of his left, never letting go even as she faded out.

Chapter 16

LAURA'S EYES OPENED, SQUINTING under an overhead light. She blinked, trying to let her eyes focus out of the haze that slowly slipped away the longer she was awake. She looked over, noticing Jackie at her side, asleep in a recliner with an open book on her lap. It appeared as if someone had at some point put a blanket on her. Laura flexed her right hand, grasping nothing but air. She panicked a little, until a warm, strong hand took hold of it.

"Looking for this?" Laura's head, still swimming, shot over to her right. Titus was next to her, also in a hospital bed, his long arm reached out to her. His face was very tired, but the joy in his eyes and smile filled her with the same. Laura smiled back, eyes tearing up a little.

"We made it . . . thank you Laura for coming for me," Titus said softly. Laura's cheeks felt warm as they tinted, her smile turning bashful.

"I guess that makes us even, huh?" she answered. He chuckled a little, wincing in pain at the movement.

"Yeah, I guess so," he said. "Colonel Nelson told me how well you handled the mission to find us, despite things taking an extreme turn for the worse. I'm proud of you, Laura. You've become one heckuva Ghost." Laura's gaze fell, drawing a concerned look from Titus. "What is it? What's wrong?" his tone was gentle. Laura looked at him again, eyes welling up.

"I . . . don't want to talk about it yet," she finally said, filling with anguish at the memory of Ben Fischer. Titus squeezed her hand.

"That's okay, Laura. I'm here for you whenever you're ready," he said, concerned for her.

"Titus, do you ever wish you could just . . ." she started.

"Walk away from all this madness and death? Absolutely." He finished, giving her the answer.

"I believe that we're fighting a good cause, but where does it end? When? I've faced down death, and now, all I want is to live a quiet, peaceful life . . . if that's even possible," she sighed.

"I understand. I feel the same way, really. Especially now that I've found someone that I want to spend a peaceable life with," Titus said, his own eyes welling up slightly. Laura smiled at him lovingly.

"I'd very much like that," she said. Her eyes drifted down at his large scar. He noticed her looking.

"That one . . . was the worst time in my life. I don't know if I'll ever be ready to talk about it," he trailed off, shaking off the horrific memory that plagued him. He noticed her apprehension and tried to put her at ease.

"Don't worry, Laura, I'm actually quite tough," he joked, taking an overly masculine tone and smiling at her. Laura raised her eyebrows.

"Really?" she teased, tone filled with sarcasm.

"Let's see . . . I've been shot four times, stabbed twice, now impaled once, umm, blown up three times, now crashed once, and yet I'm still breathing," he counted on his fingers as he recounted his scars.

"Sounds like you're more like a bullet magnet," Laura poked. He laughed, wincing again.

"No, no, don't make me laugh! Oh it hurts!" They had a brief moment of silence. "How are you feeling?" Titus finally asked. Laura wasn't quite sure. It seemed as though she should be in a lot of pain, but she wasn't. She glanced over at the IV drip, deciding it must be something potent. She looked back at Titus and sighed.

"That good, huh?"

"Yeah, well, I don't know. I feel like I've been out for a long time," she smiled, laughing a little.

"Yeah, last time you got shot, it was a couple days!" Titus recalled. Laura nodded, the memory feeling distant. "What did Park call you, again?"

"Sleeping Beauty! And he tried his best to make it stick!" Laura reminded him.

"Well, I do have to agree on one part," Titus said.

"What's that?" Laura asked, expecting another tease.

"You really are beautiful," Titus smiled bashfully. Laura blushed.

"Oh, you're just being nice," she said, deflecting. "There's no way I'm looking good right now. They must have put the really good stuff in your IV!" Titus glanced over at his IV, chuckling.

"Hmm possibly . . . Or maybe it's making me more honest," he started to blush, smiling at her. "I think you are truly beautiful . . . bumps, bruises, and all." Laura was blushing hard now, unsure of what to say. Titus looked past her for a second, something catching his attention.

"Now, Jackie, just how long have you been eavesdropping?" he asked, laughing. Laura looked at her mother, her charade broken.

"Oh, I woke up when you two started talking," Jackie looked up, answering. "But I didn't want to interrupt you two being so adorable!" She beamed a smile at them. Laura flung a pillow at her mother, laughing.

"You're sneaky!" she said. Titus laughed harder, causing him more pain.

"Ow, stop making me laugh!" he pleaded. A few seconds later, a nurse entered the room.

"Now what is all this ruckus?" she asked, smiling wryly. "You two need to be resting!"

"Nurse Welch, we have been doing nothing but resting, and I believe a mild ruckus is long overdue! I'm not even—" Titus joked, then sucked in a huge yawn, "tired." Nurse Welch crossed her arms, cocking a knowing eyebrow at him.

"No! How could you, body? Curse your sudden but inevitable betrayal!" Titus said dramatically. Laura laughed at him, also sharing a large yawn.

"Now, you two, lay back and get comfortable. You need rest, and I outrank both of you right now," Nurse Welch admonished. "Mom, I'm counting on you to make sure they behave themselves."

"Oh, don't you worry, I'll keep them on their very best behavior," Jackie laughed.

"If you need anything, use this panel here," Nurse Welch showed Laura and Titus the call panel built into their beds.

She left, dimming the lights and reclining their beds back. Laura's eyes grew heavy, despite her resistance to sleep. Jackie noticed, giving the pillow back to Laura and adjusting her blankets to cover her more comfortably.

"Thanks, mom," Laura yawned. Jackie bent down and kissed Laura on the forehead. Laura's eyes drooped as she took long blinks, staring at Titus. His eyes were drooping as well; he smiled at her as he passed out. Before she knew it, Laura fell asleep as well.

Both Laura and Titus underwent extensive physical therapy after spending much time recovering at the hospital. They had to take things slow, not being allowed to exert themselves, which was bothersome to the two very active individuals. They acquiesced to their therapists, however, the logic being that they didn't want to inadvertently extend their recovery time. Laura noticed that Titus seemed to be healing much faster than she, which seemed odd to her given his injuries were far worse, but she didn't want to ask him. He continued to keep pace with her in their physical therapy, probably more because he wanted to be with her regardless. Laura decided that she'd ask him at a later time, as she was looking forward to having the rest of their lives to learn everything about him. Much to Colonel Nelson's behest, President Alexander personally ordered that the two be given as much time as they needed to recover both physically and mentally. Laura and Titus spent their time together as much as they possibly could; enjoying each other's company. They frequented the flight simulator to brush up on their piloting skills, as well as often stopping by Rev's favorite jambalaya diner. On multiple occasions, they inadvertently had double-dates with Doc and Jamie, as the latter couple had discovered the hidden lake as well. But, for all the fun Laura was having, there was a deep ache within her soul, gnawing away at her. She often found herself unable to sleep, and if she did fall asleep, her mind's eye was full of violence, blood, rage. Ben Fischer's dead stare. It was beginning to drain away her sanity. Often, she'd wake up drenched in sweat, or attack the air above her, thinking someone was about to kill her. Jackie would beg her to talk about it, insisting that she should see a professional counselor, but Laura would just angrily snap back that she was fine. Titus could tell that all was not well with her, as her mood continued to darken, something obviously eating at her. They sat together, silently enjoying the warm sunshine over the lake when he decided he'd try to get her to open up.

"Laura, you look like you haven't slept in days . . . what's going on?" She didn't respond. "Laura?" her head finally snapped over to look at him.

"What?" she asked, sounding startled.

"Did you hear me?" he studied her face, concerned. Laura stared blankly at him; her eyes tired, mouth open slightly.

"Uh . . . sorry, what did you say?" she muttered like a zombie.

"Have you slept at all? I don't think you're really okay," he said softly. Laura groaned, rolling her eyes.

"Why does *everybody* keep asking me that? Yes! I'm *fine!*" she stared back out at the water, absent again.

Titus tried to put an arm around her shoulder. As he did, Laura let out an angry yell and rolled herself around, drawing a blade. Titus reacted quickly, trapping her knife hand, he pinned her to the ground using his size to his advantage. He wrenched the knife away and threw it, then spun her around to look at her face. She looked bewildered, then her eyes finally recognized him, and her face softened.

"Laura! It's me!" he said, hurt, eyes misting. She gasped, tears rolling down her cheeks as she realized what she'd done. Titus pulled her close, hugging her tight as she began to sob.

"I'm so sorry . . . I'm sorry . . ."

"Shhh it's okay, I've got you . . . you're okay," Titus soothed. Neither said a word for a long time as Laura continued to cry, more softly. "Please," he whispered. "Talk to me." Laura sniffled, trying to settle down. She took a few deep breaths.

"I killed so many people that day . . . I just never . . . in the moment, they didn't even register as people. I didn't even hesitate, I just killed, and I kept killing, like some kind of monster," she shuddered, sniffling more. Her throat caught as she struggled to get more words out.

"The last one . . . I'd wounded; he tried crawling away," she choked up again, fresh tears rolling. Titus held her face, looking into her eyes as she continued. "Ben . . . I killed Ben!"

"Slow down, Laura, who's Ben?" Titus gently pressed as Laura began to cry hard again.

"Ben Fischer! My partner when . . . when I was a cop! He was like my big brother and I killed him!" Titus pulled her close again, allowing her to have a moment.

"He was bleeding out . . . he was only out there because of me . . . because he helped me . . ." Laura wept. Titus held her tight, she could hear him whispering something, but couldn't understand over the sound she was making. She felt her guilt and sorrow start to dissipate, slowly being replaced with an impossible peace.

"What else did he say to you Laura?" Titus asked. *How could he know?* Her mind shot back to the forest, Ben dying in her arms. "He said something very important to you," Titus said softly. Laura remembered; the peace itself even urged her neurons to recall.

"He . . . forgave me," Laura sniffled, feeling an intense wave of peace surge through her heart.

"What else?" Titus pressed.

"He told me . . . to . . . forgive myself," Laura answered, another wave filling her.

"Let the truth set you free," Titus whispered.

Laura sighed deeply, releasing the guilt and shame fully. She understood that it in no way made Ben's death any less tragic, but now she didn't have to carry such a heavy burden. She teared up again; shedding tears of joy this time as she let the waves of peace and love wash her heavy heart. The two stayed together as they were for a long time, enjoying the peace that certainly passed their understanding.

"Laura, there is still so much for you to do before this is over. For both of us. I promise I'll be by your side through it all. More importantly, Jesus is here for you in ways that I cannot even come close to. It's time for you to decide if you'll take the help, the friendship he's offering you. He doesn't promise an easy life, quite the contrary. It is the most rewarding life, and he promises to get us through all of our hardest moments. Even now, he is removing the guilt and trading it for peace in you. Believe in him, in your heart, confess it verbally, and he will save you from every wrong thing you've ever done or will do."

Titus looked her in her eyes. She could see the sincerity and care that filled his eyes and she trusted him. Her heart pounded, she felt nervous as something deep within her soul, at the core of her being, awakened and yearned for this truth with such intensity. She decided.

"I believe, Jesus, save me!" she declared. She gasped as her heart felt light, unburdened, flooded now with peace and joy. Suddenly, she heard someone say,

"I love you, Laura." She looked at Titus, but the words didn't cross his lips. He seemed frozen in time as she stared at him.

"I will never stop loving you." Laura's eyes darted around, scanning the area for the source of the voice. It was so peaceful yet carried an unimaginable weight of strength.

"Jesus? Is it you?" Laura whispered in awe.

"I am," came the reply.

At the sound of his voice, the mountains seemed to shake, and a sound like a strong wind swirled around her. She felt shaken to her very spirit as years of regret, shame, anger, and all the baggage of her heart disappeared. Laura closed her eyes and allowed herself to be transformed on the inside. And, as suddenly as it came, life resumed its normal course. Titus was still looking at her.

"I'm proud of you, Laura," he said, smiling.

"Did you . . . hear anything?" Laura asked.

Titus cocked an eyebrow. "No, why?"

Laura smiled, feeling warmth that lingered within her heart. "He talked to me, Titus. I heard him!"

"That's amazing! I'm so happy for you!" Titus hugged her tight. Laura pulled back for a second.

"Hey, Titus?"

"Yeah?" Laura grabbed his face and kissed him. Afterward, she looked deep into his eyes. "I love you," she whispered. He smiled broadly.

"I love you too."

Chapter 17

LAURA SLEPT BETTER THAN she had in weeks. Everyone could tell something changed in her as her overall demeanor lifted, her conduct filled with a sense of vigor and purpose. Laura told Jackie everything that happened at the lake, bringing her mom to tears of joy. Jackie, too, had made her choice to follow Jesus a few weeks before, and had been praying that Laura would as well. As Laura continued her recovery, she began to participate in a support group that met at her church for veterans suffering from post-traumatic stress and other issues. She felt that it was important to help her fellow soldiers and share her experiences with them. After some convincing, she got Titus to attend with her. He opened up a lot, and as Laura listened to him speak of things he'd seen, done, and suffered, she thanked God for helping get him through it all. She spent a lot of time studying the life of King David, read the Psalms he'd written, finding that she could relate to the man recorded in Scripture. He'd never stopped trusting and praising God, despite all the times his life was in peril, and was led through it. Once physical therapy, as well as the mandatory mental health counseling drew to a close, Laura and Titus went back to work at Haunted House, much to Colonel Nelson's relief. Nelson had been very concerned about their well-being, as he'd been made aware of their status throughout the process and welcomed them back warmly. They joined him in one of the conference rooms for a briefing on recent activities. Laura, as was her custom, essentially drained the nearby coffee pot with her giant mug, much to Titus' amusement. Nelson, after a few minutes of casual conversation, began the briefing.

"As you both saw firsthand, PSRA forces have been closing in on our turf. We have responded by stepping up our Ghost Walks, albeit in a diversionary way. Although the ultimate goal in the short-term is to throw off their recon elements trying to pin down our base, the Ghosts have been making many of their patrols, convoys, and even some FOBs disappear," Nelson took a drink of water, clearing his throat.

"Is the secondary goal to demoralize them? Turn this area into a "Haunted Forest"?" Titus asked. Nelson smirked and nodded.

"From what we've seen so far, it's been working. Now, on the other hand, we've been keeping the air clear from prying eyes thanks to Mr. Park's drone-spotting tech. It's bought us some breathing room, but I don't know for how much longer." Laura looked over at Titus, sharing a look of approval of Park's cyber work. Nelson paused a moment before continuing in a serious tone.

"The President, after much debate and deliberation has decided . . . it's time to go on the offensive. Our target is the North West Sector," he paused again to allow the gravity of the situation to set in. "It's going to be a massive undertaking, the decision wasn't made lightly, but it will serve many strategic purposes."

"There are a lot of sea ports we'd gain access to," Laura put in, analyzing the situation.

"Free, open trade with our allies would be greatly beneficial. Not to mention the people we'd be liberating have been clamoring for a change," Titus added. Nelson nodded.

"We'd be cutting off their primary aircraft manufacturing facilities as well," Nelson continued. "The initial muscle movements have begun. As of one week ago, we began moving armor and troops through the Cascade tunnel in small groups, so as not to generate any anomalous seismic activity. Simultaneously, the bulk of our forces in Idaho are staging to blitz into Eastern Washington. They will secure the rear for our forward troops and will attack first."

"I sense a ruse, sir," Laura smirked. Nelson nodded in approval, pulling up a tactical map of the operation on the large monitor screen.

"You're correct. We want to lure the enemy garrison forces out into the open in the east, having to pull many from over the mountain pass to engage our blitzing forces. Once they do, we'll have our tunnel troops split, some to simultaneously push west of the pass to cut off their supply lines and some to engage their rear in the east." Laura nodded, understanding the strategy as a whole.

"So, when do we take the Ghosts in?" Titus asked.

"Oh, trust me, Captain, you'll like that part," Nelson crossed his arms. "There are some people you need to meet first . . . follow me."

Nelson led Laura and Titus to the corner of the conference room, and a false wall opened for them, revealing an elevator. They entered; Nelson pressed a button, and then peered into a retinal scanner. The elevator

chirped an affirmatory tone and the door closed, sending the elevator shooting upward. It climbed quickly, and then came to a halt. Nelson led the two
out, Laura and Titus falling in step close behind him. They walked through
a wide hallway that had a single door at the end, which was fortified and
guarded by four large men in black suits.

"Secret Service?" Titus asked. Laura shrugged. She felt their hard stares
as her group approached. One turned, opening the heavy door for them.

"Thanks, son," Nelson said as they went through.

"Sir," was the only reply.

As they passed the threshold, Laura glanced behind her to see that
the door on this side was another false wall. *Secretive*, she thought. Nelson
led them into another, larger conference room that was filled with men
and women in suits and uniforms all seated at a long wooden table. Laura
scanned the uniforms, noticing a large number of high-ranking officers
and senior enlisted, deciding finally to suppress the urge to crack a joke to
Titus about the quantity of brass. It would be inappropriate at a time like
this. Nelson gestured for them to be seated, as there were some vacant seats
toward the end of the table, and Laura settled in next to Titus. He smiled
at her, obviously unsure of the nature of their presence in the room. Laura
smiled back, becoming slightly distracted by the loud murmur of blending conversations. Nelson, who had taken a seat on the other side of Titus,
quickly noticed an old colleague and struck up conversation. Laura's eyes
were continuing to scan the crowd, eventually being drawn to the other
end of the room where more Secret Service agents stood by a door. The
door suddenly burst open, an entourage of people filed in quickly. Someone
yelled "Attention!" bringing the whole room to their feet.

In walked President Alexander, who waved his hand dismissively and
said, "As you were." He took a seat at the head of the table, joined on his
right by an old, gruff looking man with grey hair and a dark pencil thin
mustache. Laura couldn't help but stare, incredibly curious as to the man's
identity, as he reached into his jacket and withdrew a huge cigar. He lit it
and began to puff away in satisfaction. The President sat quietly, shuffling
through a manila folder that was on the table before him. Laura felt as if she
was being watched, her eyes quickly darting back to the curious man next to
the President. He was staring at her, his gaze narrow and contemplative. She
felt awkward and wanted to look away, but then her warrior spirit kicked in,
meeting his piercing glare with an intensity that even surprised herself. The
man took a long drag of his cigar, smirked in approval, and even cackled a
little. He turned to the President, whispering something to him. Alexander
looked up inquisitively at Laura, his eyes recognizing her, before leaning
over to the man and what he replied, Laura couldn't hear. On the President's

left sat a chubby little man, balding, with rosy cheeks and a worried face. He wore a fine looking suit, he himself addressing some paperwork that'd been set before him. President Alexander sat up straight in his chair and cleared his throat, dropping the already whispering murmur to silence.

"Joint Chiefs of Staff, representatives, senators, and cabinet members . . . thank you for attending. We stand at the precipice of rebirth as a nation, in no small part thanks to the dedication of our brave men and woman at arms, as well as our steadfast friends and allies who continue to bless us with their support. If I may embarrass you a moment, my friend, Ambassador Cartwright of the Texan Republic,"

Alexander gestured to a large man seated a few places down on his right, drawing a polite applause from the room.

"Ambassador Sharon of Israel," more applause, "And last, but certainly not least, from the United Kingdom: Ambassador Tavington," the chubby man smiled and waved, "and Minster of War Davenport." The gruff man nodded, taking another long, casual drag of his cigar. The applause faded, and Alexander continued.

"I am pleased to announce today that we are poised and ready to liberate the North West Sector, beginning in what was formerly known as Washington State. It will serve as a launching point from which we can re-claim the west coast, as well as regain control of almost half of our former territory. Ambassador Tavington, I believe you have some news from the UK?" Alexander gestured to Tavington, who dabbed his scalp with a hand-kerchief, and stood.

"Good day to you. I am pleased to announce his majesty's government has agreed to provide the United States with twelve ships of war, including an aircraft carrier, pending the capture of Washington's ports." The room erupted with applause. Tavington raised a palm. "Now, mind you, these ships are older and have seen action in the last world war, but they are in jolly good shape and will no doubt serve you well as you will have new ports and trade routes to protect." Davenport interrupted abruptly.

"My colleague fails to mention, however, the Royal Navy as well as the Aussies, will maintain a presence in the Pacific. We will not be leaving you . . . high and dry, as you say," Tavington shot Davenport a glare before continuing.

"England is not ready to formally declare war against the PSRA; how-ever, our ships will defend themselves and yours should the occasion arise. We also have agreed to the continuous sale of arms, ships, and goods to aid your cause."

Tavington sat down, and the room erupted in more applause and cheers. Laura glanced at Titus; his excitement at the announcement was visible. He looked back at her and smiled big. Laura returned his smile and turned her attention back on the President.

"As we speak, our enemy continues to oppress, to steal, and to destroy lives. What we are about to do will save some of them. It is in my heart to save all of them, but that'll be the next hurdle down the road. We will fight, we will win, and may our gracious Lord bless our venture. Thank you all."

The room erupted into a standing ovation as the President stood, turned, and exited the room, followed by his entourage. Over the next few moments, the gathering of people dispersed, slowly filing out of the conference room. Laura stood, turning to Titus and Nelson.

"That was pretty amazing," she said. Titus nodded in agreement.

"Where to now, sir? Where do we fit in all of this?" he asked. Nelson smirked a little.

"Didn't I say you had people to meet?"

He led them out a different door, following a long hallway to its end, pausing to knock on a set of double doors. A Secret Service agent opened the door and ushered them inside. Laura looked around the room. There were paintings hung on the walls, as well as a few marble busts of former US Presidents. Laura noted that the room's shape was that of an oval. There were a few pieces of furniture; couches, chairs, and an old desk that looked well maintained. Laura looked at Titus, whose face betrayed the fact he knew something she didn't. Before she could ask him anything, another door burst open and in walked the President, his security detail, and Davenport, who was still working on his cigar. Laura snapped to attention, as did Nelson and Titus.

"At ease, please. You're my guests here," the President said warmly. Davenport strode quickly to Nelson.

"Roger, old chap! How are you?" he said, grabbing a firm handshake and clapping Nelson on the shoulder.

"Great, Wallace, just great," Nelson replied, grinning at his old friend.

"Jolly good to see you again! Ah!" Davenport turned to address Titus. "This must be the famous Captain Titus Hansen, leader of what we more civilized chaps call 'Hansen's Heroes'!" Davenport shook his hand vigorously.

"Well, I haven't heard that one before, sir," Titus chuckled.

"Yes, yes, of course not! You Yanks are obsessed with more dramatic names . . . Ghosts, isn't it?"

"Yes, sir. I head up Ghost Team One," Titus responded.

"Ghosts, yes . . . And now," Davenport offered Laura his hand. "The beautiful face of death herself," he smiled, studying her face. Laura shook his hand, unsure of what to say.

"You know," Davenport said. "When I saw you in the meeting earlier, I just knew you Yanks were going to win this war. Eh, Jim? Didn't I say as much?"

President Alexander chuckled, "Yes, I believe you did."

Davenport continued. "I looked into those brilliant eyes that our young captain here is so fond of and I said to myself, 'Old boy, in those eyes are the measure of their resolve. That is the face of death. Her enemies will see her and fear her. They will run, but only die tired.' That!" he pointed at her face, which had naturally reverted to her thousand-yard stare. "Is the face that will win a war," Davenport took a puff of his cigar and finally said, "It is an honor to meet you, Lieutenant Laura Collins."

Nelson piped up. "Wallace, my friend, you accuse us of being dramatic? Look at yourself!" he prodded jokingly.

"I cannot help it, Roger. I'm from the land of Shakespeare!" Davenport laughed, before patting Titus on the shoulder. "Don't fret old boy, I make it my business to know everything about people that matter," he smiled, "And, I follow the sage advice of a certain former US Defense Secretary, which is . . ." he nodded to President Alexander.

"Be courteous to everyone you meet, but also have a plan to kill them," Alexander chuckled, shaking his head. "But, Wallace, I'd think twice about that with these two. I even find myself unable to order them into separate teams, so effective are they at what they do."

Davenport laughed. "Quite right, old boy! Quite right!"

"Captain, Lieutenant, there is more purpose to this meeting than it would appear, pleasant, though as it is to have you with us. Please, have a seat," Alexander said, motioning to the couches and chairs. Laura took a seat on the nearest couch, followed by Titus and Nelson. Davenport sat in a chair, and to his left sat the President.

"Anyone care for a drink?" Alexander offered.

Laura spoke up, "Yes, may I have black coffee?"

Alexander laughed loudly. "Of course, I had a feeling you'd ask. Word has reached even my ear that you utilize your Ghost talents on unsuspecting pots of coffee, causing them to disappear from time to time! Don't worry; I had two pots brewed in anticipation!" Alexander joked. Everyone laughed, Laura joining in despite it being at her expense. Titus only requested water, Nelson also having coffee.

"Wallace?" Alexander asked his friend. Davenport puffed his cigar, pausing.

"I don't suppose you have any old scotch lying around, would you?" he finally asked. Alexander smiled and nodded. "Oh, bless your Yankee heart, Jim," Davenport sighed. A moment passed as they received their beverages.

"Now, Titus, Laura . . . we have a special mission that requires your expertise," Alexander began, turning to Davenport.

"A number of months ago, British Intelligence embedded a spy, agent John Wickham, within the city of Seattle, his cover is that of an IT technician within the PSRA cyber command. His mission was to gather any and all intelligence that could be used against the PSRA at the hands of your government, or the United Nations. We've lost contact with him, as of this morning. His last transmission, which was interrupted, warned of imminent danger. We have no idea what, but we suspect it is of supreme importance."

Alexander picked back up. "We need your team to drop into Seattle, locate the agent and uncover what he's learned about this threat. You will be given his passwords, as well as his personnel file and locations of his safehouses."

"If he was discovered," Davenport added gravely. "It could mean war between the UK and PSRA . . . a war that we're not yet ready for."

"Has there been any indication that he's fallen back to one of his safehouses?" Laura asked. Davenport shook his head.

"Unfortunately, no. There are transponders that trigger when he uses them. He simply could not be able to reach them, or perhaps they've been disabled. We simply do not know."

"Did he have an exfil plan?" Titus asked.

"Yes, of course," Davenport said. "We will provide you those details as well," he took one last drag from his cigar. "Wish I was going with you, blast old age. There's nothing like a good old-fashioned HALO jump to get the blood going." Laura looked at Titus. He smirked.

Laura felt jittery as the plane bounced in the night sky's turbulence. They'd lifted off what seemed like hours ago, their plane breaking off formation with Air Force One as it headed for the Boise command center. Much to the protest of his aides, President Alexander wanted to personally wish luck to the US forces that were beginning to stage their invasion. Davenport had accompanied him, as did Nelson, who was going to oversee the Ghost Teams reporting in there as well. The rest of the Air Force was prepping to lift off as the countdown for Operation Sapper ticked away. Although Laura hadn't been trained on the HALO jump, she was in good hands. Valkyrie was a certified jump master, and gave her a crash course, no pun intended. She felt nervous, as she'd never jumped out of a plane before. This was only her second time on a plane, to begin with, and this type of jump was high risk. She adjusted her air mask, not yet engaged, and scanned the hold of the large aircraft. They were jammed in tight, five other Ghost Teams having joined them to jump earlier along the flight path. They would infiltrate key strategic areas just east of the greater Seattle area and neutralize defenses once the invasion was well underway. They would supplement the larger pincer movement against the enemy's counterattack with a surgical one of their own. Ghost Team One would jump over Lake Washington, infiltrating the city from the lakeshore. The city itself had expanded so largely that it was impossible to safely land on the rooftops, let alone open real estate. Laura had read up on the city, learning that it was a tech center before and during the rise of the PSRA, a status which it maintained afterward. It currently was home to the PSRA cyber command, as well as tech industries and aircraft production. Taking this region would cut off one of the PSRAs legs, essentially, when it came to control of the west coast. The population, they were briefed, was increasingly becoming resistant to PSRA repression, the product of multiple generations oppressed by the ideologies that originally had been welcome and tested in the North West in the time before. There were many who now tired of what their forebears had forced on them. It was a feeling that Laura now understood well.

The plane bounced again, and Laura checked her harness, just in case. She looked at her team, appreciating their friendship. Titus had fallen asleep, as had Valkyrie, their heads dangling forward. Laura had no clue how they could sleep in such an uncomfortable way. Doc and Jamie were talking together, Park was going over some mission data obsessively, as was his custom, and Rev was praying silently. Spectre sat in silence, fidgeting with his knife. Laura glanced at Rev, deciding that prayer was a good idea.

"Hey, Jesus," she began quietly. "As you know, we're off on another crazy dangerous mission. Please keep us all safe, and, if at all possible, help us not have to take any lives. I'd rather not, but if I have to, help me to do my part in keeping my friends safe. Help us find the agent quickly . . . and, thanks for being there."

She opened her eyes, gazing at the other Ghost teams as some slept, some laughed together, others trying to pump themselves up. She saw Perez, who was sitting by an intercom control box, fidgeting with it. Laura squinted, straining to see what he was doing. He inserted a bare wire into an input port, then pulled out a small device and smirked. All of a sudden, the hold was filled with loud, blasting music. The people who were asleep woke up, but no one seemed irritated. Laura listened to the lyrics, unable to help but laugh as some her fellow Ghosts started singing along at the top of their lungs. There was more laughter and cheering as people joined in, including Rev, Park, Doc, and Jamie. The song continued, until Perez removed his device due to the hold lights changing; indicating the aircraft was within close proximity of the first jump location. The main lights went out, replaced by red ones, accompanied by a buzzing alarm. The other Ghost Teams stood, facing the ramp as they snapped masks into place, performed final checks on themselves and each other, and stepped toward the ramp. The alarm changed, and the ramp eased its' way open. The sound of the atmosphere rushing by was deafening. The lights by the ramp flashed red, then green. Out jumped lines of Ghosts, disappearing into the blackness of night. *Oh, this is crazy!* Laura thought.

Within a few minutes, Team One was the only team left to jump. They stood by, the light having returned to a red flash. They performed their final checks, ready now to jump once the light changed again. Laura stood by, watching the light flashing. It pulsed red several times before settling to a solid green. She pumped herself up, stepping forward. Against all her self-preservation instincts, she jumped off the plane. She fell, feeling both horrified and excited in equal measure. Her adrenaline rushed as she plunged through the darkness at terminal velocity, following Valkyrie's instructions on how she should position her body. There was an unending mist of clouds, allowing absolutely no visual indication of how far yet she had to fall. Her breath was rapid, so she focused on regulating it while she watched her altimeter. She sensed a presence nearby, and glanced, noticing the figure of someone, probably Titus, waving at her in the darkness casually. She waved back nervously and received a "rock on" in response. She watched the altimeter again, the reading dropping quickly. It was getting close to chute deployment time. Suddenly, she broke through the clouds. Laura saw the lights of the city shimmering in the darkness, reflecting in the waters of Lake Washington. She steadied herself, hand on the rip cord. She tugged. Nothing happened. Her hand shot to the spare rip cord, tugged, and was jolted as the chute deployed. Within a few seconds, she plunged into the cold water. While under the surface still, she unclipped the chute pack, breaking free of it to surface. She kicked her feet, heading for the shoreline close by. She could hear her friends also making their way through the dark water, taking care however, not to make too much noise as they swam. They all came ashore; quickly raiding the two supply duffels they'd dropped along with them. Now armed and disguised, they began their search.

The streets of Seattle were beginning to show signs of life as designated shift change began, from third to first. People walked out from the highly stacked residential pod towers, each one off to their assigned place of employment. Laura and the team spread out, blending into the crowd. Park took point, his computer linkup feeding him a live navigation route into his glasses. Laura scanned the growing crowds, observing the faces of the people passing by. There seemed to be a similar look, she determined, everyone sharing a common weariness. The atmosphere itself felt heavy, under some type of invisible, yet palpable pressure. Her heart felt for them, all carrying on about their daily grind, while simultaneously being exploited.

If only they knew how deep that exploitation went, Laura thought. She then took notice of the presence of Peace Corps Officers. There weren't as many roving about as she was used to seeing, but she could sense their tension as they monitored all the foot traffic. Her eyes lifted, to the grey, gloomy sky. The early morning light was still mostly diffused by the heavy cloud cover, although some rays of sunlight were beginning to pierce through.

"Citizen! Halt!" Laura froze, realizing that a PCO was directly to her right. She turned, slowly, giving the officer her attention. He stepped toward her and pulled out a display tablet.

"Have you seen this man?" the officer thrust the tablet in her face. It was a photo and description of the agent Wickham, although they listed his cover alias. Laura's game face held, relief washing over her as her own identity was not being questioned.

"No, sir, I haven't. If I do, I'll be sure to contact law enforcement immediately," she played her part of the repressed and diligently compliant citizen.

Satisfied, the officer waved her away abruptly with a rude "Move along," before accosting the next citizen to happen by. Laura looked over her right shoulder, noticing Spectre nod at her. She kept moving on, the team stopping for nothing as they closed the distance to the last safe house. Time was against them, for not only had they lost much of it in fruitless searches of the other safe houses, but the invasion of the eastern part of the state had clearly begun. The team had noticed a rapid mobilization shortly after they'd dropped in, as PSRA forces charged out of the city to join their comrades over the mountain pass. The first maneuver was well underway. Park led them into an old alleyway, wedged tightly between two older, more dilapidated looking residential pod buildings. The alley eventually came to a dead end.

"Is there a problem with the nav?" Titus asked, impatiently.

"No, it's dialed in, sir," Park replied, studying the alleyway.

He moved to the end of the alley, and then turned his head to the left. His hand reached out and touched the wall. A small panel activated, and, revealing the section of the wall to be false, a door appeared. Park punched in the access code into the panel on the door, and it opened, granting them access. Ensuring no one was watching, they entered.

Chapter 18

A SMALL STAIRWELL WAS all that lay beyond the door, which they ascended slowly. Laura held up a fist and drew her pistol as she gave an "eyes-on" gesture toward something before them in the stairwell. Everyone drew weapons, taking note of the small spatter of blood that coated the ascent. It was fresh. Laura took point, following the trail, scanning for threats as the trail led to a door. The doorknob itself was also smeared with blood. Valkyrie stepped up, using his gloved hand to slowly open the door as Laura covered him. She scanned the hallway beyond, seeing it was empty. "Clear," she whispered.

The team slowly and quietly moved down the hallway, the trail of blood leading to another door halfway down, also smeared and left cracked open. Titus looked at Spectre and gave him a punching hand motion, in-dicating him to breach. Spectre nodded, stacking up on the door. He put his left hand on the door, covering the open section with the muzzle of his weapon, and pushed the door open quickly. He rushed into the safehouse, Valkyrie, Laura, and Titus on his heels. They cleared room after room but found no one. The place was a mess, someone, most likely Wickham, clearly had come in at some point and tossed the place looking for supplies. Laura walked around the safehouse, feeling that something was not right. Despite the concealed entry, this didn't truly feel like a safehouse. Where was the panic room that British Intelligence had told them about? The others began discussing options, while Park looked at the intel again. Laura decided to search again. She glanced at the layout of the safehouse on Park's computer screen, and then moved about the apartment, trying to picture it in her mind. It did not reconcile with what she saw with her eyes.

"The panic room is in the middle!" she said suddenly. All eyes went to her, silencing their conversation. "Look! The layout itself places four rooms in a square. But it's too small, here, physically." She led them around the rooms, giving her rough estimate of the measurements.

"The layout British Intelligence shared was incomplete, obviously Wickham must have spent some time modifying this place and hadn't told anyone . . . he suspected his transmissions were being intercepted, hence the manhunt for him," Laura went on. Titus moved back to the main room, conducting his own mental measurements.

"You're right, it does seem shorter!" he said.

Laura came back out and stared at the wall. There was a large bookcase situated halfway down the wall's length, the bookcase itself was bolted to the wall. The décor piece was dark, but something caught Laura's gaze. There was the smallest blood smear near the top, and had the lighting not been just right, she'd have missed it. She reached up, touching the same place, and a small green light flashed. She stepped back as the bookcase slid backward before moving sideways and disappearing into the wall track. She stepped inside, the extra room lighting up as she entered. She heard a click and turned to see Agent Wickham struggling to hold a pistol up at her.

"For England, Alec," Laura said the password.

"For England, James," Wickham confirmed. He thumbed the pistol's hammer forward as he lowered the weapon, groaning as he clutched his torso.

Laura rushed to his side, calling, "Doc, get in here!" Doc appeared, tearing Wickham's shirt open to assess the wound. Doc looked up at Wickham, then at Laura, and shook his head.

"Yes, yes, I already know I'm done for, old boy. Bloody OP agents shot me, but at least they won't have the satisfaction of watching me die," Wickham coughed. Titus and Jamie entered the panic room.

"How is he, Doc?" Titus asked.

"He's lost too much blood. He has maybe a few minutes left," Doc answered.

"I'd better make the most of it, then," Wickham said, struggling. Jamie pulled out a recording device as Titus gave Wickham his undivided attention.

"At 0800 local time today, PSRA forces will begin an immediate assault upon Texas. It will be a two-pronged attack; a large force will strike from the west, the rest will be dispersed along the DMZ. They aim to blitz the Texan Army and strangle out support efforts," Wickham sputtered up blood.

"Beg your pardon. Knowing that any attack on Texas would likely draw US forces from the mountains, especially now that you're on the way anyway, the enemy is going to destroy your Home . . ."

"But they still don't have a good location," Titus began, but Wickham waved him off, coughing.

"They don't care about that anymore. They know you're somewhere in there . . . they plan to nuke it."

Titus snapped his fingers; Jamie immediately began to attempt to contact Haunted House, or any friendly signal in close proximity.

"I . . . I tried to call it up myself, you see . . . but the bloody fools caught on to me and jammed all signals within the city," Wickham began slipping away. "I hope you have a way to warn them. Dear God, I hope you can reach them . . ." he exhaled slowly, breathing his last.

Titus turned to Jamie. "Tell me you've raised somebody, anybody!" he said, his face ashen. Jamie's eyes were welling up.

"It's like he said! We're being jammed!" Jamie shuddered, continuing to try regardless.

"No!" Titus threw a nearby chair into the wall. "Park! Get us through that jammer, now!" he yelled.

Laura walked out into the main room, in a daze. She looked at her watch, it read 0755. Less than five minutes until the Rocky Mountains were set ablaze with atomic fire. Park interfaced with Jamie's comm equipment, desperately attempting to break through. He was sweating profusely, teeth grit as he tried all the tricks he knew. Laura grabbed Rev's hands and they began to pray. Spectre was saying something in Hebrew, offering prayers of his own. Laura let go of Rev's hands, glancing again at her watch, eyes misting. It was 0800; the seconds continued to tick on.

Ghost Team One stood in silence together in the main room. Laura's heart was sick with worry over Jackie. Her mom was supposed to accompany some of the Cyber Division techs to Boise, but Laura didn't know what time her flight had been scheduled to leave. Not knowing almost made it worse. There was a loud tumult outside, and Laura, despite her strong feelings, was curious. She moved to the window and looked out over the street. There were screens all over, beginning a broadcast from the Truth Department. She couldn't hear the broadcast clearly, but she could see the footage well enough to catch the gist. There were live feeds of the "Defeat of Texas," showcasing PSRA forces advancing through Texan territory. Laura looked down as the crowds gathered to watch. The next images shown made the crowds gasp and Laura looked up to see a wide shot of the Rocky Mountain Range being illuminated by blast after blast, the universally recognized harbinger of death: mushroom clouds rising high in the sky. Laura read the caption of the broadcast, it said, "Final Defeat of Rebel Factions." As each blast continued to blanket the mountains, Laura dropped to her knees in anguish. Titus swept in behind her, catching her before she fell further. The others slowly gathered around the window, viewing the broadcast. There was a mixed reaction from the crowds below. Cries of patriotism and cheers arose in praise of the Party's decisive action, accompanied with outraged criticism of the brutal inhumanity. Laura listened to the sounds, suddenly becoming filled with strength of resolve. She stood, looked at Titus for a moment, and, without a word, ran out of the safehouse. "*Laura!*" "*Come back!*" she heard her friends calling out to her, but she ignored them. She had to get outside, had to get into the crowd. She sprinted once she hit the bottom of the stairwell, leaving her team behind with her speed. She got into the thick of the crowd as the bulletin concluded.

"Everyone! Listen to me!" she yelled as hard and loud as she could, though winded. "Stop! Listen to me!" she screamed. Heads began to turn, citizens becoming concerned with the possibility of speech laws being violated; some attempted to quiet her down.

"Please! They are lying to you!" More heads turned. More shushing was attempted, but a louder cry arose, "Let her speak!" The crowds silenced, giving Laura their attention.

"People of Seattle! The Party is lying to you! The Rebels, the United States Army, is on its way here now as we speak!" There was some mocking laughter, but it was stifled quickly.

"My name is Laura Collins, I am an enemy of the Party only because my father was falsely accused and executed by the Office of Progression! They tried to kill me too, but the Rebels saved me, showed me a new way of life, one that I want to share with all of you!" There were audible gasps from the crowd.

"They're not terrorists! They are kind, caring toward all people, and never trample on the rights of the citizen!" At this point, two PCOs shoved their way through the crowd to Laura.

"This is illegal speech, unlawful gathering, and sedition against the Party!" One of them called to her as they approached. Laura continued, completely uncaring.

"I was one of you, once! New York West Precinct, badge number 3263827. Feel free to verify. Despite that, they still targeted me for my father's alleged crime!" One of the officers stepped forward to arrest her, but his colleague grabbed his arm.

"Wait," he said, pulling out his tablet. A second later, he showed a picture of her with her identity and termination order. "She's telling the truth!" he announced, clearly disturbed. "Why risk yourself like this now?" he asked.

Laura smiled. "Because I want everyone to know that they can be free from the oppression of the Party! Free to speak, like this, free to think what you want, with no government involvement in your personal lives. Free to have families with no quotas! No forced abortions! No generational punishment! There is so much more to this life than what you've been told by them!" Her eyes welled up.

"Right now, your chances of freedom are endangered. This attack they've carried out is a last-ditch attempt to bully the masses into submission! I promise you that US forces are on their way here, right now. Didn't you all notice the troops rolling out? You have a choice, right here, right now. This is where we draw the line. Stand for freedom, for faith, for your families, or stand idly by and allow your descendants to suffer as you have under the oppression of the Party! Make your choice!" Laura declared. There was a great murmur in the crowd.

"What should we do?" one of the officers asked, genuinely concerned, which was a sentiment that was echoed by many in the crowd.

"Get your families to safety, convince your friends to assist US forces or stay sheltered when they arrive, and for those who are willing . . . fight!" Laura answered. There was a mixture of cheers, rally cries, and even some boos, as the crowd scurried off in a frenzy to spread the word. The two officers remained.

"How can we help?" they asked. Laura smiled, and looking beyond them, she saw Titus watching her, arms crossed but smiling.

"I need you to gather as many like-minded colleagues as possible. We're going to need to get people out of harm's way, as I wouldn't put it past the Party to use civilians as human shields. Get some officers on disrupting communications for the defense forces." The two nodded and took off running to accomplish their tasks.

Titus walked up to Laura. "Now, I'd generally discourage revealing invasion plans, but . . . seeing as you've just made it that much easier for our forces when they arrive, I think I can let it slide," he said as he approached. Laura gave him a big hug and he kissed her forehead.

"Boss!" Valkyrie ran up to them. "Listen!" They strained their ears. Off in the far distance, explosions rumbled. Next, the unmistakable sound of air raid sirens blared throughout the city.

"Did our boys cover that distance so quickly?" Laura asked.

"I guess so," Titus muttered, shocked.

"The enemy just kicked a hornet's nest. Our people are fighting for vengeance now," Valkyrie added.

"Not to mention, there's some angry Ghosts making their statement as well," Titus said.

"At this point, I think Wraiths would be more accurate a name," Laura stated. Titus and Valkyrie nodded in agreement. They then returned to the safehouse formulate a new plan.

Within a few minutes of reconvening, it was decided that the team would best be put to use by attacking the fortifications being set up on the old, northernmost trans-lake bridge. Although not heavily armed, they possessed both the element of surprise and a rear flanking direction of attack. As they were in the northern section of the city, it was not a long hike to the bridge. Before setting off, Laura had re-connected with one of the PCOs from the gathering and gained his personal comm information in order to maintain communication once the jammers went down. They moved out, southbound through the city as mass evacuations were underway. Word had spread like wildfire. The distant sounds of battle grew closer and louder as PSRA forces were being routed. The air raid sirens continued to blare as a new sound caused Laura to look to the sky. She squinted, seeing small shapes screaming through the sky.

"Look! From the west!" The team stopped a moment, taking in the view.

"It's gotta be the Brits! They had naval assets headed this way," Doc put in.

"They declared war then?" Park asked, to which Doc shrugged.

There was a loud rumble to the south as targets met a fire-filled end. A few seconds passed, and the British jets blasted through the sky over their heads, dropping more ordnance on military targets nearby.

"Comms are back!" Jamie announced triumphantly.

"They hit the source of the signal jammer!" Titus keyed his radio. "Any station on this net, Ghost One. Please respond, over," he said. A brief silence followed.

"Ghost One, Steel Dragon, reading you Lima Charlie. What is your position, over?"

Titus smiled in relief as he responded. "Steel Dragon, our position is ten Tango Echo Tango five three six one one, break . . . four three three one one; currently en route to assault north trans-lake bridge, over."

"Good copy, Ghost One. Be advised, friendly airstrike inbound on that target, break. Proceed following strike, assault and hold objective until relieved, over."

"Roger, Steel Dragon. We'll roll out the welcome mat, over."

"Roger Ghost One, good luck. Steel Dragon, out." Titus waved everyone over alongside the concrete jersey barrier in the middle of the road. "Get down! Get down!" he shouted.

Civilians hit the deck as a massive explosion rumbled close by, shaking the ground. The team got on their feet and moved toward their objective. Laura saw smoldering ruins of anti-tank emplacements and machine gun nests, as well as charred corpses thrown about the area. She could see down the bridge, easterly, as there was ongoing fighting along its length.

"Alright, Ghosts, dig in until our friends can come take over," Titus ordered.

Everyone took up positions covering back into the city, scavenging whatever automatic weapons survived the airstrike. Laura sent a message to her PCO contacts, advising them to steer their people and civilians clear of the bridge. They quickly acknowledged, also informing her that civilian uprisings had overrun some other military checkpoints and positions. Laura passed along the information to Park, so he could advise higher headquarters of the updated tactical data and friendly local forces within the city. Laura looked down the bridge, seeing friendly vehicles and troops making their way toward them.

"Contact!" Rev announced, letting loose a salvo of rounds at a PSRA truck that emerged from the city.

The truck swerved, crashed, and the occupants jumped out to return fire. They were quickly cut down by the Ghosts. Within a few moments, the friendly vehicles approached. Troop transports allowed soldiers to dismount and man the defensive positions, as well as some moving to sweep through nearby buildings. An officer dismounted one of the smaller tactical vehicles and approached Titus.

"Sir, General Steele requests your team back at command ASAP."

Titus nodded, and he and the team hopped into a truck bound back across the bridge. It felt odd to Laura to be moving away from the front lines, especially as curious soldiers stared after them as they drove by. The truck rumbled up the end of the bridge, pulling off the road on a makeshift off ramp that had been blasted through the freeway wall during the battle. They drove up into a residential area, dodging between some trees as they continued.

"Clyde Hill," Titus said to Laura.

They dismounted after approaching the remains of the bombed-out PSRA regional command center, finishing the journey on foot. They moved through the courtyard, a bustling hub of activity as logistics personnel hurried about to coordinate support for the fast-moving attack force. Their destination was the main building of the complex. Laura looked around as they walked, noticing a triage area that'd been set up. Medics and doctors had their hands full as they tended the wounded as quickly and efficiently as possible. She also noticed a group of captured PSRA troops being marched toward a holding area. They finally passed the threshold into the command center, and Laura found it just as busy on the inside. They were led into a large room where a group of commanders and other personnel were gathered together around a live tactical map of the operational theater. Laura looked at all the different symbols slowly moving block by block through the city. Friendlies were denoted by blue, enemy red. Almost systematically, the red symbols and zones of control were being extinguished.

"Ah, captain! Over here," an old stocky man wearing glasses waved him over. "All of you please," he added. The team gathered around the general. "So, I'm guessing the nuclear strike is what our British spy had to share?" Steele asked. Titus nodded, his gaze falling. Jamie played the recording of Agent Wickham's final words. The general was silent for a moment, processing.

"So many lives . . ." he muttered sadly. "What terrible luck . . . although it does explain why we've been able to handily route the enemy here. Despite our baiting show of force, they weren't at all prepared for us, having diverted so many resources to the attack on Texas."

"How are things going on that end, sir?" Titus asked, Laura noticed Jamie biting her lip nervously. Steele shook his head.

"We've got nothing, no eyes or ears on that situation. I hope to God they're holding out."

"Could the nuclear strike affect their communications as a result of the electromagnetic pulse?" Laura asked. Steele nodded an affirmative.

"Sir!" a junior officer nearby called out. "The British are coming!" he pointed to the tactical display, indicating a new group of signals entering Puget Sound.

"Excellent. They certainly wasted no time," Steele said.

"The UK has officially declared war?" Titus asked. "We figured they were making the initial bombing runs."

"You're correct, captain. Once the nukes fell, the PSRA attacked Royal Navy targets in the Atlantic and ran the Panama Canal. The British people took to the streets in outrage once news broke, and in one of the shortest emergency meetings of Parliament, the UK formally declared war and retaliated against enemy assets across the globe. Israel too, declared war, and have begun an impressive cyber-attack. The UN is in emergency session as well," Steele explained.

Laura glanced back at the tactical map, the last flecks of resistance centralized around the port of Seattle. It was quickly snuffed out by a naval bombardment followed by US ground forces moving in the secure the area. Cheers erupted as confirmations came in that the city of Seattle, its' greater east side and surrounding areas were now under US control. General Steele talked the Ghosts through the reports as they came in, shaping an updated big picture of the invasion. The enemy was now in full retreat east of the Cascades, destroying bridges along the Columbia River as they crossed southbound, in an attempt to consolidate the next areas of engagement. The only surviving bridges left were the ones crossing the river into Portland, far to the south. The PSRA still maintained a sizeable garrison there. Enemy forces that did not cross to the south were moving to reinforce the route down the interstate corridor, gathering in Olympia and other cities further south. The PSRA didn't have much of a Pacific fleet, especially now that they'd lost a large number of ships in their run of the Panama Canal. Many of these ships would most likely be recalled to protect ports in California, assuming they weren't sunk along the way by British and Australian submarines. Laura felt an appreciation for their allies, especially in light of how swiftly they responded. Her mind, however, and the minds of her friends, was fixed on Home.

"Sir," she interjected, addressing the elephant in the room. "Has there been any word?" Steele shook his head, his eyes expressing deep sorrow.

"I'm sorry, lieutenant . . . there has been nothing so far."

"The EMP . . ." Laura sighed.

"What about the tunnels?" Titus was grasping at the wind at this point, unwilling to give up hope.

"So far, the only ones that we've been able to check have collapsed and are heavily irradiated. It seems that the enemy tested some kind of new nuclear bunker buster," Steele's voice was grave. They were all silent for a few moments, no one able to put to words what they were feeling. "Captain, I'd appreciate it if you'd stick around for a while. Maybe look over some of the plans we're cooking up?" Steele finally said.

"Yes, sir, that'd be fine. Is there a place my people can rack out for a while?" Titus responded.

"Yes, of course," the general replied.

He arranged for one of his aides to escort Laura and the rest of the team to an area where they could rest, eat, and re-supply. They encountered several of the other Ghost teams that'd dropped ahead of them and exchanged accounts of the action. Not after long, however, the desire to catch a few winks of sleep overrode conversation collectively. Laura sat against a wall and let her head slump forward. It didn't take her long to pass out.

Chapter 19

COMMOTION CLOSE BY CAUSED Laura to stir. Her neck ached from the way she'd allowed her head to dangle while sleeping. She rolled her head and rubbed her neck, trying to loosen it up a little. Glancing at her watch, she noted that she'd caught about two hours of sleep, for which she was grateful. The rest of the team still slept, Rev snored loudly. Laura decided against trying to go back to sleep and went for a walk. It was eerily quiet, she noticed, she was unable to hear any more gunfire or explosions. There were far fewer people bustling around the command center as well. Laura found a stairwell that denoted roof access and ascended. She exited out onto the roof, taking in the evening sun as it shimmered over the waters of Lake Washington, watching the gentle roll of glimmering waves. It was a beautiful sight contrasted among the scars of battle-damaged city scape. As she stood, the faintest sounds of battle reached her ears, and she turned to look south, seeing the horizon illuminated both by waning sunlight and flashing explosives. She heard more rumbles and turned around; facing north as she determined that there was fighting in that direction as well. Perhaps the main battle group had split in half? It stood to reason, as there was much ground to cover in both directions.

"It was called the 'Emerald City' a long time ago," Titus' voice echoed from her right. She looked at him as he approached.

"Hey, you," she said, smiling at him. He joined her, taking in the view of the lake. Laura glanced up at him, studying his face. He looked tired, but calm amidst the circumstances, his eyes regarding the view as one would an old friend.

"Your mom is okay, Laura. She got out in time, along with many others," he finally said.

"Oh, thank God," Laura sighed audibly.

"She's in Boise, supporting cyber-ops from a safe location. Her team will be out here in a few days to start data mining the enemy cyber command facility," he added. "Still no word about Home, though . . . just silence." Laura leaned her head on him and he put an arm around her.

"You're from here," she said softly.

"Yes," he answered. "Well, about a twenty something mile drive north of here anyway . . . that was a long time ago now."

"What happened?" She felt him draw a deep breath, recalling the memories.

"My family left after some pretty bad food ration cuts. It seemed as if it would never end," he sighed. "They chased us; over the mountains . . . I . . . was the only one to make it." He trailed off.

"You okay?" Laura asked, putting her arms around him in a gentle hug. He nodded, but Laura didn't totally believe him. "Maybe once this is all over, we can go find your house? Maybe fix it up?" she said, touching his face so he'd look her in her eyes.

He smiled a little. "Yeah . . . I'd like that."

"Maybe, if things quiet down a little, they'll let us take some leave and sleep for a week," she laughed softly. He chuckled a little as well, his gaze still locked on hers.

"Hey . . . um, no never mind," he stopped himself.

"What is it?" Laura asked.

"Nothing, don't worry about it," he sounded a little awkward, eyes diverted. Laura cocked a suspicious eyebrow, but let it go.

"Okay, if you say so." She thought she heard a sigh of relief. There was an awkward silence that followed, until Laura broke it by deciding to shift their focus back on the war.

"So, will there be another mission for us soon?" she asked.

"Potentially, yes. Right now, we're on stand-by pending big army asking for help. Currently, they're pushing into Fort Lewis, so we may have to go play in the woods should things start taking too long."

"Gotcha. Have you slept at all, Titus?"

"No, not yet. I'm okay, though. They had some coffee available a bit ago, but it tasted like tar."

"Oh, gross!" Laura laughed. "You'd better follow that up with field rations to plug you up!" They shared a laugh together. "You know, despite all the horrible things that have happened, I feel good about our chances," Laura started, once their laughter subsided. "If they've committed the bulk of their forces to fighting Texas, we should be able to sweep up behind and catch them ultimately in a crossfire."

"Yes, that sounds like the optimistic appraisal of the situation," Titus said. "I just hope that we finish this with as few lives lost as possible." They were silent again, watching the sunlight fade away in the west.

Days passed in a blur, as Laura and Ghost Team One flew by chopper from one assault to the next, all over the western interstate corridor. They aided to secure strategic territory from the oil refineries and aerospace manufacturing facilities in the north, to the port of Aberdeen and eventually Vancouver, to the west and south respectively. Despite the high-pace operational tempo, Laura did not skip a beat. She was focused and driven, operating at peak efficiency, as they completed their missions decisively. Better still, there was a minimal loss of life on both sides. PSRA forces that were cut off from support would often lay down arms and surrender, as their will and motivation to fight had been effectively broken by the speed and effectiveness of US forces. Word spread quickly through the enemy ranks, thankfully, that the US troops did not torture or murder their prisoners, in stark contrast to what the Party propaganda machine had previously led them to believe. As PSRA troops were taken to detention areas, it wasn't uncommon for there to be US troops who were extended family members of the captured soldiers. These impromptu family reunions served to boost morale overall, winning more support from the liberated civilian population. Laura witnessed, often as they liberated a town or city, men and women, young and old, volunteering in droves to aid the cause however they could. Washington State, as a whole, was now back in US hands.

US forces now staged in preparation for a move across the Columbia River, conducting air strikes and artillery barrages to soften the enemy defenses. Colonel Nelson's Ghost teams based in Idaho were kept busy, supplementing the artillery strikes with lightning raids, in an attempt to disrupt supply movements and destroy enemy reconnaissance elements. Word had finally reached them that the Texan eastern lines had been pushed back a few miles, the fighting intense and very much entrenched. On their western front, Texan forces held their ground, although they fought defensively. PSRA troops from the west had split, diverting resources back to aid in the defense of the west coast. Fallout calculations had come in as well. Strong winds spread the nuclear fallout into Utah, parts of Arizona, and Wyoming. Refugees fled en-masse, flooding westward and north. Laura was able to reconnect with Jackie, as her team arrived from Boise, and the data mining operations were begun. Laura hugged her mom tight, allowing tears to flow. Jackie had a pleasant surprise for Laura, having had the forethought to bring a duffel of Laura's clothes and other things. They shared all the events that had transpired since last they spoke, but Jackie eventually had to join her team and bade her daughter goodbye.

With plenty of time before she had to meet up with her own team, Laura seized the opportunity to get clean for the first time in days. Feeling refreshed, she went to grab some hot chow. A forward support company had settled in the courtyard of the regional HQ, supplementing the triage center and logistical support area. Laura grabbed a disposable tray as she filed through the chow line, receiving a baked potato, corn, a small helping of chicken, and a slice of bread. It was army cooking, but she preferred it over pre-packaged field rations any day. Laura carried her food toward the designated recreation area, which essentially was nothing more than a large room filled with a few old, worn couches, and a television screen. Laura sat down, the couch creaking loudly as she settled into it. She ate in silence, which was promptly interrupted by raucous laughter. In walked Rev, Doc, Jamie, and Park. They flopped onto the remaining couches, one activating the TV screen. Laura absent-mindedly continued eating, oblivious to the fact that someone was talking to her. There was silence, and she turned and looked, noticing her friends were now staring at her with amused looks.

"What?" she asked. They all laughed.

"You were totally gone for a minute there!" Rev told her.

"I asked you a question, silly," Jamie said.

"Chhh! Earth to Laura! Come in, Laura," Park said, imitating a voice over a radio. Laura rolled her eyes at him.

"I'm sorry, what's up Jamie?" she asked, giving her friend her undivided attention.

"Oh, nothing important," Jamie laughed. "I just wanted to know if the chow was any good." Laura took another bite of chicken and shrugged.

"It's okay. The chicken tastes a little strange," she said between bites.

"Oh, they say that in the Army, the chow is mighty fine! A chicken jumped off the table and choked a friend of mine!" Rev sang, laughing.

"Don't forget the coffee! It looks like muddy water and tastes like turpentine!" Doc added, continuing the melody.

They laughed together for a moment, eventually becoming distracted by the TV. Park had set up a receiver that allowed them to pick up the BBC news channel. It currently was reporting on the conflict between the UK and PSRA. Images of ships firing their weapon systems flashed on-screen as the reporter narrated events. A map of the PSRA east coast appeared, populated by small icons denoting a naval blockade being set up by the Royal Navy.

"Gotta hand it to them . . . they do it big," Doc said.

"I wonder how it'll pan out on that front, seeing as the Brits don't possess the manpower the PSRA can muster," Jamie put in.

"I'd think the Brits would wait until we and other allied nations can get out there before landing troops," Rev surmised.

"Any word from the UN?" Laura asked.

"Nothing yet, still deliberating," Doc said, his voice dripping with disdain. "They're behaving very strangely for having witnessed multiple nuclear strikes which killed some member nation's ambassadors."

"Maybe they're hesitant to jump into a fourth world war?" Jamie asked.

"Or maybe someone powerful is holding a gun to their heads," Laura spoke up. All eyes were on her.

"What do you mean?" Doc asked.

"Think about it . . . at the collapse of the old US, the PSRA maintained control of some of the US bases all over the globe, right? Including those with tactical nuclear warheads? They could, in theory, be threatening the UN by demonstrating their willingness to utilize the nuclear option, discouraging any more foreign involvement in their conflicts. It doesn't hurt that China is playing big brother, both ideologically and logistically, to the PSRA as well," she explained.

"Whoa, where did you come up with that?" Doc asked, visibly blown away.

"I've been studying history and geopolitical relationships in my spare time," Laura stated, a smug smile forming.

Rev chuckled. "Spare time! Hah! Just means you ain't working hard enough!"

"Well if I've learned anything, it's how hard you work at snoring loudly!" Laura shot back. "You sound like a huge idling truck!" Everyone laughed. Rev smiled, taking the roasting.

"I'm not even gonna argue that," he said. Suddenly, Spectre burst into the room.

"Briefing in ten, get ready!"

"Looks like we're back on the clock," Doc said. Laura shoveled some corn into her mouth and followed her team as they rushed out of the room.

Chapter 20

"WE'VE GOT A BIG problem!" Laura heard someone; she wasn't sure of whom, yell nearby. She blinked, foggy beyond her belief. Suddenly there was a hand under arm, pulling her up. It was Titus; she saw blood on his face, and a wild look in his eyes.

"Ronin! Wake up! Let's go! Laura! Move!" he yelled.

Laura blinked again as he dragged her along, her ears ringing, sounds nearby muffled. The sounds of gunfire sharpened. She roared in frustration, shaking her head. As her vision cleared up, she witnessed Titus spray gunfire downrange. He pulled her down with him into a freshly blasted foxhole, and they both crashed down hard.

"Doc! How's she look?" Laura blinked again; Doc was staring into her eyes as he flashed a light over them.

"Concussed!" he yelled in response. Laura saw that it was just the three of them in the foxhole. She struggled to remember what had happened, where everyone was.

"That mortar really rung her bell, boss!" Doc said, joining Titus in returning fire. Titus fired, and then ducked down.

"Laura, I need you to fight!" he ordered, with urgency in his tone.

She nodded, although staring blankly at him. Her gaze went down, noticing she still had her hands firmly clasped around her carbine. Training kicked in, and she proceeded to check the chamber, then the magazine. She popped up and fired where she saw muzzle flashes in the darkness. In the brief seconds she'd taken to expose herself and fire, she'd snapped a mental image of the area she could see. It was partially wooded; some old houses and dormitories were wrecked or aflame. A large broken dome provided the roof of an old bombed-out structure nearby. Then it clicked in her mind. They'd reached their objective at Rocky Butte. Although it didn't qualify as a mountain, it possessed a commanding view of the Columbia River, the bridge crossing, and Portland's airport. More details flooded into Laura's mind. They'd penetrated into enemy territory in an attempt to knock out enemy anti-air emplacements, as part of a prelude to crossing the river. The flaming remains of a pair of mobile SAM trucks led Laura to draw the conclusion that they'd been successful thus far. Now they were pinned, with enemy support elements more ready to respond and counter-attack than friendly intel had been led to believe. Laura popped up again to return fire. Her peripheral vision caught more glimpses of the immediate area. She noticed muzzle flashes nearby, centralized within a similarly shaped fox hole, indicating the rest of the team's location. A few blasts thundered and she ducked back down as enemy grenades detonated short of their mark. This was shortly followed by an earth-shaking boom, another massive mortar shell detonating, ripping apart the ground. Laura recovered from the sonic shockwave and reloaded her weapon. She looked at Titus, and his gaze met hers.

"Laura . . . Don't try it!" he shouted, as if reading her mind, but it was too late. She scrambled out of the fox hole. "Covering fire!" Titus yelled as he and Doc sprayed a salvo of rounds toward their foes.

Laura sprinted toward the nearby wood line, praying the darkness shrouded her movement. She crouched behind the trees. No one had noticed her, she decided, as no one was shooting in her general direction. All enemy fire was concentrated at the mess of fox holes she'd just left. Laura moved, trying to zero in on where the mortar fire was coming from. She could see where the enemy had drawn their lines as bursts of light filled parts of the woods and the nearby access road. Laura skirted around the extreme limits of the enemies' lines, heading down the slope until she heard the telltale *whump* of mortar tubes launching their payload. She saw two mortar crews firing as quickly as they could, the tubes glowed a dull red from the heat. Laura laid prone, crawling closer until she reached a good distance from which she could effectively fire. She waited, watching as the mortarman dropped a shell down the tube, ducking as the whump carried it off. She aimed her weapon, tracking her sights over the opening of the tube. As the mortarman placed the next mortar, she fired. The bullet struck the shell, detonating it and vaporizing the mortar crews. Her ears rang again, and she waited to see if anyone would come to investigate. Nobody came. *Maybe they think the crew cooked off the round*, she thought. Laura stood, making her way back uphill, but this time she followed the road. As she went, she began to see the backs of the PSRA troops as they fired from their positions of cover, and she crept up behind them. She well-proved the title of Ghost, moving silently and lethally as she began to slay her enemy, knife in hand. She worked her way uphill, cutting throats, slashing arteries, even once throwing her knife into an enemy's eye. As she retrieved her knife, one soldier caught sight of her in his periphery. As he turned, sweeping his weapon at her, she dropped him with two rounds. The unexpected gunfire drew the attention of more enemy combatants, and Laura found herself pinned behind a vehicle. She looked for an avenue of escape but was unable to find any. Suddenly, as quickly as she'd been zeroed in on, all shooting stopped. Laura peeked around her cover, seeing that her assailants were down. She moved out of cover, signaling "no shoot" by waving her left hand near her face. As she'd expected, from the shadows emerged Titus, Doc, and Rev. She rushed over to join them, and allowed Doc to perform a quick blood sweep on her.

"Are you okay?" Titus asked, noticing the blood covering her.

"It's not mine, I'm not hit," she answered.

"Geez, boss! Look at her handiwork!" Rev said, flicking his flashlight on a body nearby. Titus toggled on his night vision goggle and saw the corpses letting a bloody trail downhill.

"I guess we know who it belongs to," Doc said, whistling in approval.

"Back up the hill, we need to bug out before more goons arrive," Titus ordered.

They ran up the road, and after a moment Doc called out "Omaha!" their running password. They joined the rest of the team, forming a secured perimeter as Titus received a liquid, ammo, casualty and equipment, or LACE, report from Valkyrie. Satisfied with everyone's status, Titus contacted Haunted House. They were advised to stand by as a Screamer was inbound to their location. The lightning raids on anti-air batteries had been a success, allowing US air power to dominate the skies. Laura could hear and see the destruction begin to rain down upon enemy assets from her view on Rocky Butte. She squinted in the darkness. Friendly forces were crossing the bridge and amphibious vehicles were in the river, beginning the assault on the airport. It was now only a matter of time before Portland itself would be liberated.

Laura rose from her cot, feeling as stiff and sore as ever. She'd barely slept, as her new "home" for the time being, was a large crew tent situated a few hundred meters of off the runway of Portland's airport. The constant noise from vehicles and aircraft was intolerable. She got ready for the day as best she could, given the limited access to supplies. Logistical support was doing their collective best, but given the rapidly moving front lines, it was difficult to keep up. Laura found herself wandering the grounds, aimlessly. She felt stressed, exhausted, and her mind kept flashing through the events of the night on Rocky Butte. *So much death and destruction*, she thought as she felt her hands begin to shake. Looking down, she saw that they were covered in blood. Laura panicked, wiping her hands on her uniform furiously, but when she looked again there was no blood.

"I'm going crazy!" she mumbled to herself, exasperated.

She took a knee, trying to center herself, trying to get her heart to stop pounding and her palms to stop sweating. More images tore through her mind's eye, the screams of the dead filled her ears. The faces of people she'd killed.

"Stop . . . please . . . make it stop," she started to sob. She fell to her hands and knees, tears flowing freely, her heart and mind were filled with anguish.

"Oh, Jesus . . . please help me," she whispered.

Laura felt a gentle hand placed on her shoulder. Warmth seemed to melt away the pain, and she reached out to the presence. A hand took hers, pulling her to her feet in an instant, but when she opened her eyes, no one was there.

"Be strong, I am with you," she heard within her heart.

"H-hello?" Laura whispered.

"Ma'am? Are you okay?" Laura spun around, hearing a different voice. There was a small group of soldiers, four in total, approaching her, concern on their faces.

"Oh, yes . . . I'm okay, I'm good," Laura said, wiping away the tears from her eyes. The group had closed the distance now. There were two young men, no more than eighteen, and the other two, a man and woman, both looked around Laura's age.

"Are you sure, ma'am?" the woman asked. Her name tape read Olson; her rank patch indicated by three chevrons that she was a sergeant. "We noticed you collapse there a moment ago, do you need a medic?"

"No, thank you though, Sergeant Olson. I'm fine, really," Laura answered, composing herself fully. She could see the concern in Olson's face even so.

"Say, aren't you Ronin? From the Ghost Teams?" one of the young privates, Miller, spoke up suddenly.

"Miller! Customs and courtesies!" Olson snapped.

"Sorry ma'am," Miller said, awkwardly.

"It's quite alright," Laura said. "And, yes, Ronin is my callsign." The junior enlisted men got excited.

"Told you!" one said, punching his friend in the arm.

"Please, ma'am, excuse their enthusiasm," Olson sighed, trying not to be embarrassed by her soldiers. "It's not every day that the Joes get to meet one of their heroes."

"Hero? Oh, well I don't know about that, um," Laura was taken by surprise, unsure of what to say. Olson smiled, taking a small step forward.

"Now ma'am, before you go saying that you aren't, just listen up. Back at Fort Lewis, we were pinned down out in the woods, totally cut off from our platoon. You Ghosts came out of nowhere, cutting down the enemy left and right. I got hit, and as I went down, I saw you take down not just the one that shot me, but his two buddies with just a knife and some of those cool ninja moves. You dragged me out of the mud to the casualty collection point yourself. Me and my boys here owe you our lives. Thank you." Laura met Olson's gaze, seeing her eyes had misted. Laura still felt embarrassed and shy but smiled at the sergeant.

"You're welcome. I'm sure you'd have done the same for me," she said.

"Yeah, but it wouldn't have looked as cool!" the other man, a corporal, said. They all shared a laugh.

"Say ma'am, we're about done with this foot patrol. We'll be grabbing chow next and visiting some buddies at medical, if you'd care to join us?" Olson said.

"Yeah, I'd like that," Laura said.

She joined the patrol, and as they walked, the young privates could not help but bombard Laura with questions. She couldn't help but laugh at some, taking the opportunity to humorously embellish details at others, getting a rise out of her audience. They made their way to the chow hall after formally concluding the patrol, seating themselves with the rest of their platoon as their company cycled through for chow. The other soldiers were equally excited to have Laura join them for chow, the Ghosts having become something of a legend at this point in their campaign. Laura graciously fielded their questions but couldn't help but notice one particular private, named Akeman, seated across from her. He projected an air of arrogance as he simply stared coldly at Laura while she interacted with the other "Joes" and tried to enjoy the mealtime. There was an eventual lull in the conversation and Akeman suddenly spoke up.

"How many of the "*Pissers*" have you killed?"

Laura froze for an instant, slowly setting down her fork as she raised an icy glare to the young man. Sergeant Olson stood from her seat, about to chew out the disrespectful private.

"Akeman, you little shi-" Olson began.

"How many? I've wasted ten," Akeman pressed, more loudly.

Laura suddenly snapped, grabbing the man's head with one hand, she slammed it into the table while with the other she drove her knife into the wood, mere centimeters from his nose. The color drained from his face as he whimpered in fear. Laura maintained a tight grip on his head, her fist closed around a clump of hair.

"Why? Do you want to be next, private!?" she yelled in his ear.

"N-n-no ma'am." He mumbled. She released him, glaring hard at the shocked faces that stared at her.

"Don't ever ask that question again!" She stood tall, withdrawing her knife from the table. "Everyone listen up! Don't you *dare* become complacent! Complacency kills! Yes, we've enjoyed success against our enemy, but you better remember, they are tough and worthy of our respect! At the end of the day, they are just people . . . just normal people, no different than you or I. They have families, friends, loved ones . . . Some of you may even meet distant relatives!" Laura took a deep breath, her anger subsiding, but her voice remained firm and authoritative.

"A while back I went after a friend that'd been captured, ended up taking many lives that day . . . sent them to whatever eternal destination awaited them . . . but the last one . . ." tears misted her eyes. "When I looked into the eyes of the last one, I saw the face of my closest friend, my brother, from before I fled New York." The oxygen seemed to be sucked from the chow hall. "This is a fight between neighbors, friends, brothers, and sisters! Never forget that! Don't you ever forget that." Laura sheathed her knife and exited the chow hall. As she left, she could hear Olson begin to yell.

"Akeman! You insubordinate piece of trash! You're gonna spend the next month cleaning latrines with your tongue!" Laura wandered the area of operations aimlessly, feeling somber. She couldn't believe the inhuman ignorance she'd witnessed, and it infuriated her.

"Hey! Laura!" she heard Park call out. She kept walking, pretending not to have heard him. "Laura, wait up!" he ran after her.

"What?" she stopped, hands on her hips.

"Uh . . ." Park started, shocked at her uncharacteristic hostility. She crossed her arms, impatiently waiting. "So, it looks like you called it," he started.

"Called what, Park? I'm not in the mood for games," she sighed.

"Yeah, I can see that. Well, the PSRA just publicly announced to the world that its enemies would '*suffer the same fire as the rebels*'. Israeli intelligence has confirmed that the remaining PSRA missile bases world wide are now at high alert, ICBMs are fueled and ready to fly," Park went on, with a worried look on his face. Laura's mouth dropped. "That's not even all of it," he continued to fill her in on what he'd learned.

Laura ran, searching desperately for Titus. She followed the main service route that led toward the Ghost's area of camp, covering the distance quickly. "Titus!" she called out. He stood rigid, arms crossed, staring at the river in the distance. He sighed heavily as she closed the distance.

"I sometimes have to stop . . . take some kind of account of all this mess," he began, his tone low and sad. "I just replay everything, you know? All of it, good and bad."

"What are you talking about?" Laura interjected, breathlessly.

"I need to remind myself why I'm here, now. Whether or not I can change what is," he paused.

"Titus, everything has happened for a reason, right? You're here because you *can* change things," Laura took his arm. Titus nodded, looking at her with sad eyes. "Is it true? About?" she whispered.

"Yes," he said, quietly. "Multiple sources confirmed the entirety of the PSRA western divisions heading this way, including an entire Zealot Division. The fallout from the nuclear attack blew in such a way to create a no-go zone cutting them off from the Texan western front."

"What's a Zealot Division?" Laura asked.

"The best of the best within the PSRA's ranks . . . well trained, well equipped, and very fanatically minded. They almost worship the Party, and will stop at nothing to win."

"What can we do? How long do we have?"

Titus shook his head. "We dig in, although despite the influx of recruits we'd still be outnumbered ten to one. We may have two weeks tops, if we're lucky," he sighed.

"Isn't there a battalion of British Royal Marines on the way?" Laura asked.

"Yes, but that doesn't exactly improve the odds in a meaningful way," Titus responded.

"Titus! Screw the odds! We've come so far, accomplished so much!" Laura cut in, staring him down hard. "C'mon, I dragged you out of a FOB deep in enemy territory with an entire division between us and home! What would Rev say? Have faith!" Titus blinked, the wheels in his mind beginning to turn.

"That's it!" he said. Laura cocked an eyebrow.

"What's it? Faith?"

"Yes! Well, in a way,"

"Huh?"

Titus took her hands, becoming animated. "A while ago, Rev was talking to me about Gideon. The odds were horribly stacked against him, yet God *decreased* his forces down from thousands to three hundred men and delivered an army of over ten thousand into their hand!" Laura nodded, tracking. "All we have to do is take small groups and hit them at every natural chokepoint between them and us! We don't have to defeat them in one big engagement-"

"We just have to delay them long enough for help to come!" she put in.

"Exactly! We will hit, run, hide, and repeat to get them to give chase, slow down, divert and delay. We'll knock out their supplies, disrupt their communication, and confound their best laid plans. By the time they reach our front lines they'll be battered, sleepless and nutritionally deprived, and most importantly, broken and without the will to fight!" Titus seemed excited now, capping off his train of thought by grabbing Laura and giving her a big kiss.

"You're my inspiration! C'mon, let's go pass this up the chain!" He took her hand and ran.

Laura waited anxiously for Titus outside the command center. He'd been in there for the better part of an hour after making the initial pitch of his plan to General Steele. Laura had her hands in her pockets, poking the same patch of grass with her toe repeatedly.

"Hey," she heard a gruff voice. She looked up and saw Valkyrie.

"Hey, Hank," she replied, continuing to poke the grass.

"I heard about the chow hall," Hank said, a softness etching its way through the gruff tone he usually employed.

"Oh yeah?" Laura said, cocking an eyebrow. Hank stood still, arms crossed as he stared her down. She returned the gaze, noticing the slightest smirk cross his lips. "What's so funny?" she asked.

"Bet that kid wet himself," he chuckled a little. Laura couldn't help but smile as her imagination took over. "I mean, it was a serious situation, but still," he shook his head, unable to stop chuckling. Laura studied him, as this was a rare sight for Hank.

"I would've done the same thing; given the circumstances . . . those kids will learn, usually the hard way."

"It changes you," Laura said. Hank looked at her with a sad understanding in his eyes.

"Taking a life is no small thing, and if you're not careful, you'll lose that part of you that feels . . . it drains away the soul every time." Laura nodded, knowing fully well his meaning.

"How long have you been in this fight?" she finally asked after a period of silence. Now it was Hank's turn to kick a patch of grass.

"Most of my life, come to think of it," he said, grimly. "My Pa taught me to hunt, shoot, and survive from the moment I was big enough to hold a .22 rifle. But at some point, we stopped just hunting game . . . started hunting men," his gaze turned to the horizon.

"I was only eight the first time," he trailed off, his face becoming downcast. "For all the training one can receive, nothing can ever prepare you to take a human life," he stepped closer, putting a firm hand on her shoulder. "Laura, I'm sorry you had to take your partner's life. There are no words." Laura's eyes misted up, and she smiled sadly at her mentor.

"I'm okay, Hank. When I sank to my lowest point, I found freedom, peace; all the things Rev talks about. It's real. I gave my life to Jesus on that day. Now I know that no matter how bad things get, he will pull me, us, through it all."

Hank smiled. "I wouldn't have made it this long without him watching my back," he replied knowingly. Laura smiled; glad to hear that she had this in common with her friend as well.

"So, what are your plans for after the war?" Laura asked, feeling a small measure of joy in the midst of their storm. Hank let out another small chuckle, running his fingers thoughtfully through his beard.

"Well, I suppose I'll build a farm out in the middle of nowhere. Enjoy the peace and quiet, you know? Put my hands to something productive."

"That sounds really nice," Laura said, imagining the scene.

"Well, what about you?" Hank asked.

"Me? Oh, I haven't thought about it much," Laura said. Hank crossed his arms.

"Oh yeah? Tell me another story," he laughed.

"What?" Laura asked, innocently.

"Okay, I can believe you haven't thought about *where*, but I know for a fact you've been thinking about with *whom*," Hank pressed humorously.

"Oh, great, you're going to razz me too, now, eh?" Laura chuckled.

"Nah," Hank smiled. "I think it's a good thing. Wherever you go, you just keep that man close. He's a good one. Oh, and make sure to have lots of little ones, get his hair nice and grey for me, will you?"

Laura punched Hank's shoulder, laughing. "Geez, Hank! He hasn't even asked-"

"Asked who, what?" Titus emerged out of the command center. He had a suspicious look.

"Nothin', boss. We're just messing with each other," Hank said, giving Laura a subtle wink. She smirked, and then turned to Titus.

"So, what'd the general think of the plan?"

Titus nodded, looking satisfied. "I gave him the initial pitch and then he halted everything and got the President on the line. We had a good, long conversation with him and Minister Davenport and they agreed to the plan, albeit with a few alterations."

"Wow! Okay, then! When are we getting the warning order?" Laura asked.

"Soon, first the general has to get Colonel Nelson and the rest of our Ghost Teams on their way in a hurry. In the meantime, we're going to go over the maps and start planning our target areas. Come with me," Titus said. Laura and Hank followed him back into the command center.

After studying the maps and hashing out details, Laura was filled with confidence that their plan could work. It would require reallocating some key strategic resources, but at least they had a fighting chance. All available Ghost Teams and fast-moving infantry attack squads were directed to occupy key areas around the major highway and interstate corridors. They quickly began to set traps and ambush points. Laura, having read up on history, put to use the lessons learned during the US global war on terror. They set up improvised explosive devices, hiding them wherever enemy troops had to tread. At each key ambush point, weapons caches were set up, mainly stocked with anti-tank weapons and other demolition type devices, although some were equipped with remote anti-air batteries. Road blocks were built, using whatever was handy; trees were cut down and laid in the roadways, rockslide areas were rigged to blow. Park rigged up a common detonation trigger, utilizing a tertiary communication frequency, so that any friendly could detonate traps. Adding to the overall ruse, US troops in the Portland garrison made a highly visible show of force, the goal to cause the enemy to believe they were digging in and thereby giving them a false sense of security that their transit north would be relatively safe. Friendly ships were inbound and would provide whatever long-range strike operations they were capable of, however limited. The enemy was not unprepared, however. The PSRA army made their way north from California, carefully covering their movements with a mobile anti-air screen, nullifying for the most part friendly air strikes. With them also, travelled what remained of their air power that'd been stationed in the west. US command flagged all enemy SAM trucks as high value targets, for if they took out enough of them, friendly air support would be made possible. Great care was given to make the fast attack forces appear to be normal patrols as they pushed south as rapidly and discreetly as they could. US forces worked hard, 24/7, to set up the elaborate snares along every major northbound route through the former state. Ten days passed, and the work was finished. The enemy was about to cross into Oregon.

Chapter 21

LAURA LAY PRONE UNDER some bushes, watching through binoculars for any sign of movement. The Ghosts were situated on a wooded peak overlooking the Interstate a few miles north of the Californian border. Next to her was Valkyrie, who was utilizing the scope of his sniper rifle. Below them lay the first trap of Operation Mire. A long body freight truck and two box trucks were parked chaotically on the road, as if abandoned in haste by frightened civilians. They were loaded with fertilizers and other dry flammable chemical materials, procured from local farms, as well as conventional explosives. The enemy would most likely think little of them, as news of the inbound PSRA forces had driven out whatever civilian population remained. Park sat concealed in the brush, scanning the airwaves for enemy surveillance activity, particularly for the stealth drones they'd encountered before, as well as monitoring for communications. They had stashed some drones of their own at other cache sites. These were smaller, yet carried a powerful payload of armor piercing anti tank missiles. Further downhill, Rev and Spectre were wielding semi-auto 40mm grenade launchers. Doc and Jamie were staged nearby with the getaway ride. Titus leaned behind a tree, concealed partly by brush, but mainly by his ghillie suit. They all looked like bush monsters clad in such attire. Laura caught a glint of light in the distance. She squinted, straining to make out what it was. She tapped Hank's boot with hers, and almost instantly he saw and trained his weapon toward the silhouette. Within seconds, the object turned, revealing the profile of a scout helicopter.

"Scout moving in . . . let's see how thorough his sweep is going to be," she said finally.

The chopper closed a great distance swiftly, weaving left and right over the Interstate corridor in anticipation of enemy ground fire. When none came, the chopper hovered in place for a few seconds, only about a hundred or so meters away from the Ghosts' position, buffeting them with the wind from the rotors. They could see the pilot and crew visibly scanning around them before the chopper continued its way north along the Interstate.

"Looks like they bought it," Rev said quietly.

"Contact. Enemy armor. Three tanks and six APCs following," Valkyrie broke in. The armored vehicles drove on, pushing up to the ambush site.

"Must be the advance party ahead of the main body," Spectre said.

The vehicles weaved their way around the "abandoned" trucks; turrets aimed covering their respective sectors of fire. Suddenly, the column halted, engines still idling. Back to the south, the first elements of the main body appeared; tanks, APCs, and other various tactical vehicles. A few meters ahead of the lead vehicle in the advance party, the Ghosts had laid a decoy, which had caused the tactical pause as someone in the vehicle noticed it. On the rear tank a hatch popped, and out clambered a man yelling into his helmet microphone, stomping toward the lead vehicle. He could tell that they were sitting in a bottleneck, but despite his yelling he could not get the lead vehicle to begin moving again. Laura and Valkyrie monitored the commotion, their attention now turning toward the main convoy. A tank in the lead also had a hatch popped open, with what appeared to be a high ranking officer barking orders over the NET. To add to the confusion, half of the APCs opened up and troops spilled out. It quickly became clear that someone along the line ordered them to check out the trucks. The first yelling man attempted to wave them off, frantic, as he could tell that things weren't right about their situation.

"Valkyrie," Titus said.

"Already got my sights on the convoy commander," Hank replied.

"Take him."

Laura watched as in an instant the man's head completely plastered onto the metal hatch behind it, and the now decapitated body slumped forward. Not a second after the .50 caliber rifle fired, Titus detonated the explosives. The earth shook violently as the massive blast filled the air, fire and shrapnel destroying everything within the deadly radius. Valkyrie began putting rounds into the engine blocks and wheels of faraway support trucks, furthering the delay the enemy would suffer. The 40mm launchers opened up as well, walking a trail of destruction along the burning remains of the advance party. Any troops lucky enough not to be evaporated by the main and ensuing trailing blasts fired in a wild panic, at nothing in particular.

"40's out," Spectre reported.

"Roger, let's move," Titus replied.

They clambered their way out of sight, before rushing down to the waiting getaway vehicles. They sped away down an old forest service road, thick black smoke rising over the canopy of the forest behind them. They allowed themselves some cheers, fist bumps, and even a bit of relief. Titus took a deep breath and said ominously, "Varrus . . . give me back my Legions."

A few hours passed as they made their way many miles to the north, where the next ambush site and weapons cache waited. Park had been relaying their HUD signals to Command, who had also celebrated the first successful strike of Operation Mire. In the subsequent hours as they'd travelled, they received footage from the teams operating east of them that had also encountered enemy movement up that highway corridor. Further surveillance reports were coming in stating that the enemy had been seriously delayed on both routes, costing them many hours to move wrecked vehicles out of the way and service damaged ones. Furthermore, they had to narrow their convoy movements as huge sections of paved road had been replaced by deep smoking craters. Despite the good news, the Ghosts still had to manage to buy even more time for the Royal Marines to land. Laura personally felt confident that they could accomplish the task, given the early success they'd experienced. Between the first and second ambush sites, they had planted several more small IEDs, less in hope of causing damage and more in delay and fear. Still they waited at Site 2, with night beginning to fall in the forest. Night was a Ghost's best friend, which tipped the scales of the next engagement in their favor. Here at Site 2 they planted mines on and off the roadway, while laying in wait with anti tank weapons.

"What better roadblock could there be?" Doc had joked earlier.

The silence of the night was broken as a mine loudly made its presence known out in the distance. The enemy was getting close. Boom went another. They were even closer now. The rapid pattern of explosions and the rumbling of a very loud motor struck Laura as odd, and she scanned down the road with her night vision scope. Barreling down the road was a tank, a bulldozer style ram fixed to its front end, marked with obvious signs of heavy blast damage. It hit another mine, rocking it slightly, but not badly enough to kill it or throw tread. The tank was being used for route clearance, and it swerved in search of more mines to hit.

"Spectre, Doc. This one's yours," Titus spoke into the comm.

The two men sprinted in the darkness after the tank, which rumbled past their location. Then, the tank slowed as another explosion finally crippled it. It threw tread and ground to a halt, the motor sputtering. Spectre and Doc silently climbed the vehicle, waiting for their chance. Not long after, a crewman popped out in hopes of repairing the tread and was quickly "assisted" out by the waiting Ghosts. Seemingly without sound, they laid the lifeless body out of sight and reset. Another crewman climbed out and met the same fate as the first.

Rev let out a little cackle as he shook his head. "Man, they make that look way too easy!"

Apparently, the tank commander was frustrated by being ignored by his crewman and also clambered out in hopes of setting things straight. He too was quickly dispatched. Doc removed the man's helmet and keyed the radio, sending a message for maintenance assistance. Within a few minutes, the rumblings of loud diesel motors were heard in the distance. Already Doc had entered the tank and rotated the turret rearward, while Spectre beckoned the oncoming vehicles with a red light.

"I like the idea, guys, but be very careful. One hit on that armor and you're toast, Doc," Titus chimed in.

"Roger, I figure I'll get three shells off before ditching. This thing has an auto-loader!" Doc replied, laughing.

Doc waited as a support vehicle and two APCs passed by the primary ambush point, where the other Ghosts were staged. He paused a moment, then sent a shell straight through the lead APC. It erupted as the massive round smashed through the light armor, incinerating the occupants in an instant. Spectre fired off his anti tank weapon as well into the next vehicle, while the other Ghosts began sending fire into the trailing convoy. Doc sent another shell downrange in the commotion, striking the support vehicle. Trucks and armored vehicle were now ablaze, cooking off ammunition within, causing a fresh wave of blasts. Doc fired off his third shell. Almost instantly a return shell whizzed past the turret, and Doc scrambled out.

"Time to go!" he shouted, as Spectre was already on the ground almost to the tree line. No sooner did Doc's boots strike the ground the tank was hit with another shell.

"That was too close, my friend," Spectre said as he gestured Doc to follow him into the woods.

"Break contact! Move to Rally Point Charlie!" Titus ordered. The Ghosts rushed into the forest as PSRA forces began to immerse the ambush site with heavy weapons fire. They made another clean get away.

An hour later, they regrouped in a part of the forest pre-designated as Rally Point Charlie. Every Ghost conducted a quick blood sweep of a comrade before plopping to the ground, physically exhausted. Laura retrieved a canteen they'd stashed at the rally point and drained it.

"Is everyone ok? Any hits? Injuries?" Titus asked. Heads shook, before panting mouths emptied more canteens. "Good, let's take ten. Catch your breath and restock."

Each Ghost complied in turn, grabbing ammunition from the cache so they could reload weapons and stock up on fresh magazines. Park retrieved a hard case from some nearby bushes and opened it. Inside was a mini drone which Park quickly set up. The tiny rotors whirred to life, launching the drone into flight as it disappeared into the night.

"I'm going to scout out their forces nearby, if any," he muttered tiredly. Titus stood over his shoulder glancing down at the control monitor.

"Good thinking, Hollywood. If you come across the convoy, make sure to look for mobile SAMs. Command needs to know how many they're bringing," he said.

"Roger, boss," Park replied.

"Hey boss, guys, tune into the Haunted House Freq!" Jamie suddenly announced. Hands shot to comm switches. Laura patched in, just in time to hear Ghost Team Two update command on the situation to the east.

"I repeat! PSRA forces along our sector are turning around!"

"Good copy Cobra One, Haunted House out."

There were some quiet cheers shared among the group, but Laura had a bad feeling about the situation. She flicked her comm back to their shared channel.

"They triggered a nasty landslide!" Jamie relayed more information. "The highway is completely impassable for miles!" Laura made eye contact with Valkyrie, who must've been thinking the same as her.

"Guys," she started, "they'll have to come into our sector . . . they're only about three hours east of Site 2 on the arterial highway. That's a whole extra division we weren't counting on." The cheers faded into silence.

"That'll be fine," Titus finally said, albeit with an air of uncertainty, "Our primary mission is to delay the enemy. Perez and his team bought us a lot of time in the long run."

"I understand that," Laura said, slightly irritated, "But if that's all we accomplish, they'll still reach Portland with most of their strength. They won't be demoralized, just annoyed. And, we all know that even with the Royal Marines coming in we'll still be badly outnumbered." All eyes were on her. Titus stood, staring at her contemplatively with arms crossed.

"She's right," Valkyrie said in the brief pause. "We need to break them, absolutely destroy their morale. Make them wish they'd never left home."

"What do you have in mind? We're already hitting them psychologically; wasn't that the point of the IEDs?" Titus asked. Valkyrie looked at Laura, who said cryptically,

"Let's take a Ghost Walk . . ."

Chapter 22

Laura felt exhausted already, utilizing a slow surge of adrenaline to blink away her sleepy eyes. She thought to herself: *if I don't get to sleep, then neither does the enemy.* Their Ghost Walk took them back in the vicinity of Site 2, where they'd ambushed the suicidal route clearance tank before. The site was mostly clear of the rubble of battle, yet some crews were still hard at work to move the bigger burnt hulls of the tank and APCs. More vehicles continued on passing by in smaller convoy elements, mostly comprised of logistical support vehicles and troop transports as the main body had most likely passed through some time ago. Titus came up alongside Laura, whispering.

"Why'd you bring us back here? You know I trust your judgment, but Command is going to want to know what's going on; why we're breaking from the schedule." Laura pointed at the crew working at the charred hulls.

"We're going to make them disappear," she said quietly.

Titus nodded, the ominous statement sinking into his understanding. In order to move more quietly and also to allow some rest for the team, only Laura, Titus, Spectre and Valkyrie came on the Ghost Walk. Laura led the others, creeping closer and closer, staying low in the darkness. A pair of road flares provided the only light for the crew as they worked. The crew had two guards posted to keep watch over them. Laura identified them as the first to go and drew her long blade. In the span of a few seconds she and Valkyrie crept up to their post and silently took them away. A moment later, one of the crewmen noticed them missing.

"Ey! Rawlins! Franklin! Where are ya knuckleheads? I swear if you're shamming again, I'll get the sarge to bust ya down," he trailed off his tirade as he heard rustling in the trees nearby. Titus and Spectre rustled again, causing the man's head to turn in that direction.

"Hey! Is that you guys? C'mon stop messin' around! It ain't funny!" The man tapped his partner and they both stepped into the forest. Laura waited, and surely enough, the other crewmen noticed that the others hadn't come back.

"Whoah now, what's going on out here?"

They were on edge, setting down tools and equipment and grasping for their rifles. Laura tapped Valkyrie. They moved onto the road in a blur, appearing like wraiths before the men, lunging and slashing as they came. Titus and Spectre came from the other flank simultaneously, and the whole ordeal was over in mere seconds. Bloodied bodies littered the road.

"Now, for more demoralization," Laura said.

She and the others dragged the bodies to lie shoulder to shoulder across the road in an impromptu roadblock. Next, she cut off a bloody shirt off one of the dead men and painted the side of their recovery vehicle: Turn Back. Valkyrie and Spectre quickly rigged booby traps utilizing hand grenades, setting them underneath the bodies. As they finished, almost by some morbid timing, headlights appeared in the distance. The next convoy was on its way through. Their attack had only taken a few minutes in total.

"Time to move," Laura said. They disappeared into the black forest once again.

Titus reported in to Command what they'd done. The Command staff was shocked at first, but Colonel Nelson quickly agreed with the decision and argued to the rest that such brutality was necessary to breaking the enemies' will to fight, especially as they now had to contend with a Zealot Division. After gaining approval from higher authorities, Nelson directed the Ghost Teams to adjust their tactics accordingly. With the landslide blocking the eastern highway, the Teams responsible for that sector were quickly rerouted to the main Interstate corridor. With the extra help, the Teams were able to rotate attacks on a sustainable schedule. Team Two, led by Perez, came in to relieve Titus' crew. Team One then moved further north, to another cache, where PSRA forces had not yet reached allowing them a few hours of sleep and a decent meal. Laura hadn't noticed before just how hungry she was, and when she'd thought about it, she realized it had been almost two full days since she last ate. The group was very somber, a general feeling of remorse had settled in over the issue of nightly Ghost Walks, and more importantly, what they had done during such night incursions. It was one thing to neutralize an enemy in a stealthy manner, even with a blade, but Laura felt wrong about arranging corpses, booby trapping them, and leaving cryptic messages for the enemy to find. Furthermore, she thought about what would happen when all of this was over. In that hopeful future, people who had served on both sides would have to coexist.

Laura didn't want to make life afterwards a living hell for the survivors of the current one they were struggling in. She took out her blade and studied it thoughtfully. After a deep sigh, she next extended her left forearm and looked at the lightweight armor section that covered it. She didn't want to count the notches she'd carved into it, for there were far too many, and pain filled her heart. She clenched her jaw solemnly and etched yet a few more notches while blinking away tears. She had the distinct feeling of someone watching her, and noticed Titus some distance away gazing at her intensely. He turned away, muttering something as he stomped off into the woods. Laura groaned and stood, following after him. She eventually caught up to him, moving quickly to overtake his long strides.

"Titus, what's wrong?" She asked. He stopped and turned to face her, his countenance filled with anger. He roughly snatched her forearm, displaying the notches.

"Keeping a body count? What, are they just some trophies to you? Not even human beings?" he finally fumed. Laura was taken aback at the implications.

"Whoah, hold on a second! Are you accusing me of being some kind of psycho or something?" her reply came back equally fierce, if not the least bit perplexed sounding.

"Then what is this? How do you explain it?" His grip on her arm was solid as he shook it. She eventually wrenched her arm out of his grasp.

"Let go!" she glared. He shook his head in disgust and turned away.

"No! Hey! Don't you go acting all high and mighty, like your hands are so clean!" she barked at him. He turned, glaring.

"I may not be innocent of shedding blood, God knows, way too much, but I'm not enjoying it!" At that Laura slapped his cheek; the sharp clapping sound pierced the forest. Her eyes burned with fire.

"How dare you!" her voice seemed to pack the extra punch that sobered the shocked look on his face. "Do you really think I'm that sick? That I'm somehow becoming a monster right before your eyes?" Titus was silent, his gaze still locked onto hers, yet lacking the conviction it did a moment ago. Laura couldn't help but take his silence as an affirmation, and slapped again, harder.

"This!" she displayed the notches, "is a tally I keep so I know just how many times I need to fall on my face and beg God to forgive me! Beg Him to not let me have my soul absolutely destroyed! I keep this tally so that once this war is over I can go beg forgiveness from that many widows and their children for taking their loved ones away, starting with Becky Fischer and her kids!" At this point Laura could no longer hold back her tears and she let them flow.

"And now here is a man standing before me, the man who claims to love me, who now won't look me in the eyes because he thinks I'm a blood hungry monster!" She began to sob. "I hate this! Every single second of it! Every single time I damn some soul to Hell, I share in their torment!" She dropped to her knees, her eyes raw and no longer able to produce tears. She just shook.

"I never asked for this life! I just wanted to be a good cop . . . a decent daughter that would maybe fix things with her father . . . God, I just wanted to someday meet someone and have a family and a normal life!" Titus sat by her and took her hand, silent as he listened, ashamed of his assumptions.

"Titus, I don't want to do this anymore! I just can't . . . anymore." At that he pulled her into his embrace and held her.

"Laura, I'm so, so sorry . . . I'm sorry. I never thought about how you felt in all this; I was selfish. I disagreed with your plans and tactics and never considered the toll it would take on you." He let tears of his own fall.

"You are not a monster. You are a wonderful, brilliant, caring person that's been thrust into the worst of the human experience. More than anything, Laura, I do love you . . . with all the pieces of my heart." They were silent for a few moments, listening to the breeze whisper through the trees.

"I love you too," Laura finally said, no longer physically wracked with grief. "I just wish we could disappear, start over somewhere else. Put all of this madness behind and never worry again if today will be the last."

"Yeah, I wish that too." Titus whispered. The peace they felt finally lingered for a moment, yet too briefly. Laura's ears perked up at the sound of someone shouting in the distance.

"Boss!" It was the voice of Valkyrie, sounding closer now. Laura and Titus stood, moving toward the sounds of Valkyrie running through the forest.

"Here!" Titus called. Hank burst out of the trees, a grim look on his face. "I figured you'd turned off your comms," he said. "We've got to move, now!"

"What's going on?" Laura asked as she and Titus followed Hank back through the forest, slipping their ear pieces back in.

"The enemy is blitzing through, and to make matters worse, they've begun carpet bombing the forest along the Interstate corridor. We're out of time . . . we've got nothing left that can slow them down, not that many, and not that fast." They burst through the bushes surrounding their cache site, the others already ready to move. Jamie reported to Titus:

"Haunted House is sending a Screamer to get us, ETA two minutes."

Laura adjusted the sound level of her comm as the traffic coming through was loud and frantic. She next shoved as many magazines and other gear into her assault pack as she could, and then joined everyone in a circle as they performed quick functions checks on their weapon systems. Each Ghost quickly checked and adjusted each other's armor, or straps on packs, as well as other quick pre combat checks. Already steadily growing was the rumble and concussion of approaching bombs, completely obliterating huge swaths of forest. Thick black smoke filled the horizon as acres upon acres began to burn.

"Looks like they got tired of our haunted forest," Rev said, straight faced.

"Any word from the other teams?" Spectre asked. Jamie and Park shook their heads.

"The NET has been a mess for the last twenty minutes; I can't lock down their freq," Jamie said somberly.

"They'll be alright, they're as tough as they come," Doc said unconvincingly.

"They got clear in time, you'll see," Titus said with the confidence of a commander.

Although the situation was grim, as it usually was, the team trusted his word. Laura scanned the sky, thinking that she'd spotted something, but was unsure. Then the rumbling of heavy bombs started to get significantly louder. Closer.

"Um, how close is that chopper?" She asked disconcertedly.

The ground was consistently shaking now, and Laura felt as if her ears were going to pop as a wall of fire trailed past them, missing their position by about two hundred meters. They'd all hit the deck, now scrambling to find any semblance of cover or protection. As the bombs finally passed by, everyone rose to their feet. The next sound filled them with relief, the Screamer was finally inbound. It quickly descended, performing a touch-and-go, allowing them just enough time to jump aboard and strap in. The chopper shot off in seconds, wasting no time in their flight northward. Laura patched into the chopper's comm channel.

"Aww, looks like I missed all the fireworks!" The pilot said.

"You didn't miss much! Y'know, other than permanent deafness!" Rev replied. The pilot and copilot both chuckled.

"We'll make some of our own here soon enough," came the response.

Laura looked out the gunner port on her side of the chopper. The sky was choked with black smoke, largely blotting out the sun. Out in the distance, fires raged out of control as the deep green forests now blazed a hot red-orange. Laura jumped, jerking her face away from the gunner's port as bullets pinged off the hull. Both door gunners opened up the .50s they manned, punishing whoever decided to use the chopper as target practice.

The Screamer weaved through the air as the ground fire intensified. What followed next caused Laura's heart to sink into an ocean of dread. Alarms began to clang through the comms, signifying a missile lock. The copilot cursed loudly as they bobbed abruptly to the right, just as a surface-to-air missile screeched mere feet off their left. The missile's trajectory caused it to arc hard as it attempted to re-acquire the target, but ultimately it slammed into the ground, sending a wave of heat skyward. The pilot pushed the Screamer as fast as mechanically possible, trying desperately to get as close to friendly lines as they could in the event they should crash land.

"Hang on back there! We're going to make a crazy approach!" The pilot yelled.

"That's okay; I think my stomach is still lagging a mile behind us!" Park replied, his eyes squeezed shut and his face turning a shade of green.

The chopper banked hard to the left, and Laura realized that they were coming closer to the enemy's eastern flank. After about thirty seconds, enemy vehicles were visible and on the move, headed north on their blitz. The copilot started to expend the aircraft's entire vast array of devastating weaponry at will, leaving a blazing trail of destruction in their wake. The door gunners continued to strafe and cut down anything not heavily armored.

"Let's make them pay for missing!" the pilot shouted, and the flight crew let out a war cry. More bullets assaulted the hull of the chopper, some armor piercing ordnance ripped through. The Screamer began to smoke and pitch side to side as a never ending hail of bullets continued to swat against it.

"I gotta put us down! Hold on!"

Instead of being fearful, Laura just huffed in frustration. She'd already crashed once before and that was enough for her. The chopper labored as it slowly lost altitude despite the crew's attempts to hold it up and steady. Luckily for them, they'd passed beyond the range of the ground fire that'd knocked them out of the sky, at least until the enemy's front lines came to them. The Screamer was headed with much curse-laden guidance for a peak nearby, where an arterial road crested the top, putting them just a couple miles from the Interstate. Alarms were sounding within the heavily damaged chopper, and despite its condition, the pilot was actually able to set it down right as the engines finally failed. The location they'd dropped onto possessed a commanding view of now charred and burned forest, along with smoldering ruins of buildings that had been flattened by the bombing runs. Laura pulled the release on her five point harness and hopped out of the downed bird. The road leading up to their perch was in as bad of shape as everything else in sight, pocked with huge craters and chunks of rock and concrete strewn about.

"They won't be able to get anything with wheels up this hill," Laura said after surveying the area. Hank quickly eyeballed the top of the rocky peak next to them, searching for a good nest.

"Listen up team," Titus called out. "HQ says to dig in here until help can come. We have an armor brigade en route that'll be hitting that eastern flank here very soon. Now some extra good news," Titus grinned, relief visible on his face. "The Brits are here, landed early! They brought some serious artillery with them. We're going to have a front row seat for them shelling the whole grid once it starts filling up with enemy forces." There were cheers among the team, and the hopes of survival skyrocketed.

"So, once the bad guys realize we're up here, don't you think they'll just roll over us? Can't Haunted House spare another bird?" Doc asked, slightly nervous still. Titus shook his head.

"It is a bit of a raw deal, but no, there are no more birds to spare. Not only that, but they can't risk losing another one even if they could. We still don't have eyes on their SAMs. I'd rather dig in and wait from a defensible position than start hiking toward friendlies and get overtaken on the way." Doc shrugged, agreeing after thinking through that perspective. Laura pointed at the chopper.

"We can use the .50's if they spot us," she said.

The door gunners, Sergeants Mills and Ibanez nodded enthusiastically, and set off to prepare the weapon systems. Everyone got to work immediately, stripping the chopper of equipment and setting up firing positions. Laura heard Valkyrie's voice over the comm.

"Contact, ten o'clock! 1500 meters! Four scout VIX." Laura looked up at the peak face, wondering how he'd gotten up there so fast. She took a look through her rifle's scope.

"They're heading straight for us; must've seen us go down," she commented.

"Watch your sectors of fire!" Titus ordered by way of reminder, as everyone hunkered down lower into their fighting positions.

"More VIX on a northerly heading," Valkyrie continued, "Looks like the beginning of the main body. Scouts are one click out . . . 800 meters," and so on.

Laura kept listening to Hank call distance and direction until the vehicles were approximately 200 meters away, at the base of the hilled roadway. The vehicles paused at the base, obviously assessing whether or not they could ascend the road with the huge craters present. A moment passed, Laura ever training her scope on one of the doors of the trucks, and the scouts quickly dismounted their vehicles and prepared to move uphill on foot.

"Hold fire," Titus whispered, "Steady." The scouts began to move cautiously uphill, two squads worth. "Pick a target, left to right according to your sector . . . three . . . two . . . one."

In unison, the Ghosts, with the helicopter crew, fired one shot each, effectively cutting down both squads. The remaining scouts further downhill fired back, scrambling for cover around their trucks, or clambering to bring to bear the machine guns mounted on top of the trucks. Sergeant Mills opened up on the .50 and quickly tore the trucks apart. Valkyrie quickly silenced another squad's worth singlehandedly from his elevated position, and Rev fired off two 40mm grenades to mop up the rest. A momentary silence settled, the Ghosts quickly re-readied weapons and checked themselves for damage. Valkyrie disrupted the calm once again.

"Contact, ten o'clock! 1200 meters! Two APCs, one tank!" he called as a tank shell whizzed by the chopper, just nearly missing.

"Whoah! That was too close!" yelled the pilot, Chief Taylor.

The APCs halted behind the wrecked scout vehicles, with top mounted guns peppering uphill in hopes of catching something. Troops poured out the rear decks, sprinting toward whatever piece of cover they could find. Mills harassed them with the .50, while also being sure to button the APC's sights.

"I've got a 'lil something for ya!" Jamie shouted, and produced an anti-tank rocket.

She got a positive lock on one of the APCs and fired. The rocket punched into the armor and incinerated the crew. Rev continued to let fly more 40mm grenades until he was out, then switched to his light machine gun. He added to the storm of automatic fire crashing its way downhill. The enemy blanketed the hill with fire, but as they were firing up such a steep hill, they found that they could not effectively suppress the Ghosts. Laura continued to methodically take aim and fire single shots whenever she acquired a target, slowly but surely thinning out the opposition. Nearby, Titus, Doc, Park and Spectre did likewise. Time seemed to freeze as the fighting endlessly continued. Valkyrie kept them apprised of incoming forces.

"Oh no," he said.

"What!?" Titus shouted.

"Two choppers inbound!" Valkyrie replied. Laura stole a glance as well before returning her attention downward.

"Do we have anymore rockets or anti-air anything?" she asked.

"Negative!" Jamie replied.

"Here we go," Mills said, turning the .50 to engage the choppers after Ibanez swapped his barrel. No sooner did he begin to depress the trigger, the choppers erupted into flames. Over the sound of battle, the unmistakable roar of jet engines was heard as two US fighters tore across the sky.

"Yes!" Doc yelled, "We've got air superiority!"

Laura was tempted to look, but was now too focused on the near-battalion's worth of troops flooding the area, including a company of Zealots, all intent on storming their hill. Grenades were blasting very near to Laura's position, and she shook her head while hunkering down for a moment to reload. She glanced at the .50, the barrel was glowing red hot, nearly transparent, as it spit more and more lead downrange. Suddenly, a large blast rocked the hilltop, killing Chief Taylor and his co-pilot Chief Watkins.

"Mortar!" Rev boomed.

"Wait one," Valkyrie replied. A pair of successive shots of his rifle rang out. "Mortar squad down." Titus surveyed the battleground, quickly deciding what next to do.

"Doc! Hollywood! Rev! Fall back beyond the .50!" he ordered.

The men, being in the forward fighting position, complied. Everyone else intensified their fire, attempting to suppress the onrushing, maddened enemy soldiers long enough for their comrades to move. A tank shell suddenly struck the rocky face of the peak next to them, causing a small rockslide to crash downward onto the Screamer and entrenched Ghosts. Laura luckily dodged the bigger boulders, but some of the smaller rubble pelted and smashed into her. She yelled in pain, crawling her way out of the mostly filled in crater she'd occupied. Some big rocks had tumbled their way downhill as well, scattering the enemies' advance temporarily. Rev took advantage of the confusion and picked off a number of enemy troops in rapid succession, throwing a hand grenade to add to the chaos. There were subsequent cries of pain as other members of the team had been injured in the slide.

"Rev! Give me a hand! We need to get the wounded to cover!" Titus yelled as he dragged Park away.

"Roger that!" Rev acknowledged, moving with incredible speed to assist the injured.

Laura, who'd taken refuge behind a large rock, picked up a spare rifle that'd been staged nearby and emptied the clip as some Zealots attempted to take more of the hill, charging well beyond the Ghost's now abandoned forward fighting positions. The rifle clicked, bolt locking to the rear indicating an empty magazine. Laura dropped the rifle, drawing her 9mm pistol she fired two shots into an enemy soldier that'd gotten within feet of her. The man fell, but as he went down another took his place. The new one fired, hitting Laura center-mass on her chest plate. She was knocked over backward, gasping for air, and returned fire squarely in the man's face. She felt a hand under her arm. It was Rev, dragging her back behind a boulder.

He propped her up, handed her his spare pistol magazine, and disappeared again around the rock. Laura could hear his LMG open back up, and then suddenly he was back, dragging Doc, and repeated the process until each Ghost, most of whom were pretty battered from the rockslide, was out of the field of fire. Laura scrambled to her feet as he brought the last one out of harm's way, and when he returned, he smiled at her and collapsed. Laura dove to him, realizing that he'd been shot multiple times and had lost a lot of blood. He began to cough, spitting up blood as he spoke.

"Don't worry little sister . . . I'll be fine. You make sure they make it outta here, you hear? You win this thing for me." Laura vigorously nodded, tearing up. She watched her friend's face as it filled with a peace that was beyond words.

"Oh, Jesus! I'm so happy to finally see you!" Rev exclaimed joyfully, tears in his own eyes, as his life slipped away.

Laura pushed herself onto her feet, checked her weapon, and rounding the boulder, she opened fire. In a flurry, she took out four more enemy troops before they realized what was happening. As they spun to return fire, Laura dove behind an enemy, allowing him to take the bullets meant for her. She intended to make them pay dearly for every square inch of this hill. As she hit the ground she emptied her clip into the other soldiers. She grabbed a rifle off the ground, spinning to engage the next target. Bullets zipped past her ears, some even grazing her armor. She rolled behind another boulder to evade the fire. The ground suddenly began to quake harder than she'd ever experienced before. Laura stole a look into the valley below just in time to see heavy artillery rounds begin to obliterate everything. The PSRA forces were now caught in an immensely large kill box of British fire. Laura stumbled out to re-engage her foes in the mayhem. She fired at them as they tried peeking out of cover until . . . click. She was totally out, without a spare weapon anywhere in sight. She quickly rolled back behind cover as bullets pelted close behind her, but then she heard them go click as well. A brief silence followed, at least on the hill. Then Laura peeked in time to see a grenade being lobbed, as if in slow motion, sailing through the air at her. Then, still slowly, the butt stock of a rifle swung out and batted the grenade back toward the enemy. It exploded as the enemy dove for their lives. In a daze, Laura looked up. Titus, out of nowhere it seemed, sprinted toward the enemy, tackling the first one as he tried to get on his feet. The second one stumbled, falling over backwards into a crater. Titus let rain his fists down on the man he had tackled, until, with a surge of furious strength, he lifted the man overhead. He let out a maddened cry and dropped the man's back onto his awaiting knee. Laura winced as she heard the audible crunch. The man slumped to the ground as Titus released him. Titus then turned, stumbling after the second man, who, having just witnessed the brutality of his foe decided it would be better to leap over the guard rail and escape, tumbling roughly downhill. More artillery barrages ripped across the valley, trailing its way south, enveloping PSRA vehicles who tried in vain to evade the massive blasts. More US jets roared overhead, dumping off more heavy ordnance in supplement. From the east, US armored vehicles began to appear to mop up the rest of the enemy. Titus dropped onto his knees, exhausted, and visibly battered. Laura came alongside him and took his hand.

"We did it," she said to him, looking into his eyes. His face washed with relief as he nodded, and clutched his side. Laura helped him onto his feet, and noticed he was bleeding. A bullet had found its way through. Laura grabbed the aid kit from his tactical vest and began treatment.

"Thanks," he said quietly.

A few moments passed and he started arranging pickup from HQ. Laura rounded the boulder, finding that Hank had already begun tending to everyone's injuries. Laura lent him a hand with the rest, helping Spectre especially as he regained consciousness. No one spoke, although Jamie couldn't keep herself from tears as Doc solemnly began laying a poncho liner over the body of Rev. It was at that moment that Titus came limping around the corner. He hadn't realized before, when he'd come after Laura, that Rev was down. Now, the emotion sank in. He threw himself on the ground near his closest friend, and bitterly wept. Laura sat with him, pulled his head onto her lap and cried with him.

Chapter 23

GHOST TEAM ONE WAS listed as currently "Not Mission Capable," as most of the team had sustained serious injury during their stand on the hill. Titus had surgery to remove the bullet from his side, Doc had a few broken ribs, Park was shot in the arm, and Spectre, Jamie, and Laura received various heavy bruising and head trauma from falling rocks. Hank was the only one to escape with minor scrapes and bumps. The two Sergeants manning the .50 cal had also sustained head trauma from the rockslide, but would make a quick recovery. Worse than all the physical injuries sustained was the emotional toll of losing Rev. Everyone was taking it very hard, especially Titus and Laura. Everywhere she looked, there was mass celebration of the miraculous victory US and allied forces had achieved. The PSRA Army was almost completely obliterated, with surviving pockets either fleeing south, deserting, or surrendering. Laura couldn't bring herself to join in the excitement, the cost for her and the team was too bitter a price to pay. She had trouble staying focused during the After Action Review of the battle as a whole, only snapping back into reality as she debriefed her team's contribution. She made her report while maintaining a stiff military bearing, but in her heart she wanted to be anywhere else. She craved time away to process everything, to be with her teammates as they recovered, to be there for Titus. He would be out of surgery soon, and Laura wasn't going to let anything stop her from being there when he woke up. Laura scanned the dimly lit room, studying the faces present. Most were in high spirits as they reveled in their collective achievements. Her gaze fell on Lt. Perez, as well as some of the other Ghost Team leaders present. They all were both grim and silent, eyes filled with a fresh, real pain. Every team had lost dear friends, and some teams didn't make it back at all. Team Nine led by Captain Singh had infiltrated the enemy's main body in a successful attempt to destroy many of the mobile SAMs, enabling US air assets to regain air superiority, leading ultimately to victory. It was a one way mission, a selfless sacrifice that made a profound impact on the war effort as a whole, but one that was only truly felt by the Ghost community. Laura stared at a nearby monitor that was displaying known casualties by name, the ever growing list populating faster than she could read. She felt a gentle touch on her arm and turned.

"Lieutenant . . . Laura, how are you doing?"

It was Colonel Nelson. His eyes were filled with compassion and concern, his tone soft and fatherly despite the visible grief and exhaustion that hung heavily on his countenance. Nelson had personally led a number of lightning raids, and given his ever demanding responsibilities as battalion commander, he'd probably not gotten a chance to sleep yet. Laura's eyes quickly surveyed the room and she realized that most everyone had cleared out, leaving her standing there in a trance for an unknown amount of time.

"I'm . . . I'm okay, sir," Laura replied, unconvincingly.

"Master Sergeant Bridger . . . Rev . . . he was a good man, easily one of the best I've ever known," Nelson said, voice filled with remorse.

"Sir, I'd like to do something for him, well, for everyone we've lost," Laura finally said. Nelson raised an eyebrow.

"What did you have in mind?" he asked.

"Well, I think we should have a memorial . . . our way," she said.

"Absolutely," Nelson nodded, "I'll see that you get whatever you need. Just let me know."

"Thank you, sir." Laura managed a small smile. Nelson began to walk away, and then turned.

"Oh, and Laura? I think there's someone who would like to see you. Take care now."

"I'll tell him hello for you," Laura offered as she watched Nelson leave the makeshift conference room.

Laura left, heading straight for the hospital. She was able to catch a ride from some medics who were on their way to pull shifts, and after thanking them she proceeded to Titus' room. He was still asleep, the lights in the recovery room had been dimmed, and Laura was sure to be quiet as she entered. She sat, watching him sleep peacefully for the moment, although she doubted that he'd be able to maintain that peace once he regained consciousness and heard about the other Ghost teams. Laura really didn't have the heart to tell him such bad news, but she steeled herself to the idea as it would probably come best from her. Laura reached up and rubbed her own neck, the amount of tenseness she felt was giving her a headache.

"Quit worrying so loud," Titus whispered, a smirk forming, "I'm trying to sleep." Laura smiled at him as he peeked open an eye at her. She reached out and squeezed his hand.

"How are you feeling?" He thought about it for a while.

"Umm, I'd have to say numb for now. Lots of painkillers, I guess."

"Oh, well that's nice," Laura chuckled, before adding finally, "We really need to get some alone time, you know? At a bare minimum I'd like it to *not* involve one of us being stabbed, shot, or crashed!"

Titus winced as he laughed. "Oh, it's so true! We've got to switch it up a little!" Laura's smile grew as she watched him.

"Say, we are Ghosts after all, we could just vanish for a few days," she said. Titus' face changed slightly as he studied her a moment.

"Laura, I've been thinking a lot lately." Titus sat up a little, shifting to face Laura before continuing. "After all the loss we've experienced, and the absolutely limited time we get to share; I mean, who knows if we'll even see tomorrow, really? I . . . I just don't want to wait around and miss something great because of some misguided sense of proper timing-"

"Titus, what are you talking about? Are you having an existential crisis, or are you on too many painkillers?" Laura teased.

He scoffed with a small grin. "No, it's not that, I've really given a lot of thought to *us*. I'm done just waiting around for circumstances to be favorable, you know? I'm done missing out on-" At this point, he started to attempt to get out of the bed.

"Hey, wait just a second there, speedy!" Laura said, gently pushing him back down into bed.

"But, I've got to . . . its important-" he tried to argue, sitting back up, but Laura wouldn't hear of it.

"Titus Hansen, you lay your butt back down in that bed, that's an order!" Laura laughed. He gave her a half worried look. She cocked an eyebrow as her cop senses started kicked in.

"C'mon, you don't have to get out of bed to ask me anything, unless . . ." her eyes widened, her head catching up to her heart. It began to race. Now Titus had a very amused look on his face as Laura now looked like the deer in headlights. He reached out and took her face in his palm gently.

"Okay then . . . Laura Collins, will you marry me?" In the span of a millisecond she sprang forward and kissed his face and lips excitely. He started laughing. "Am I to take that as a yes?"

"Oh my gosh! Yes! Sorry!" she laughed before kissing him again.

"Good answer!" he laughed harder, wincing from the wound. Laura helped him sit upright so she could hug him.

"Here," he reached over to the bedside tray, and retrieved a small black silicone ring, and put it on her finger. "It's not fancy or anything, but it'll do until I can get you something proper." Laura beamed, holding up her hand, taking it all in.

"Oh, it'll do fine!" she said, hugging him again. "I love you so much," she said.

"I love you too," he replied.

Laura ended up sitting with Titus the rest of the afternoon, only leaving after he succumbed to sleep once again. She then went and visited the other members of the team to see how they were doing. It didn't take long for each person she was visiting to notice her overall change in demeanor, and became inquisitive. Laura would smile and lift her left hand. Jamie most of all about lost her mind, squealing and speaking in such excited tones that Laura's ears began to hurt. The whole team was excited for her, as a bit of happy news did much to raise their beleaguered spirits. Hank even smiled when Laura shared the news with him and simply fist bumped her saying "About time," playfully.

After Titus was discharged from the hospital, he and Laura were inseparable. They took on the responsibility of planning and coordinating the upcoming memorial for the Ghost Teams, as well as volunteered extra time to meeting with newly liberated civilians at gathering places to assist with their orderly transition into their new lives. By order of the President, the Ghost Teams were allowed a long respite in order to return to peak combat efficiency and strength. With the help of British forces and the fresh supplies they'd brought, US forces pushed down into northern California, encountering scattered and meager resistance along the way. Although the fighting was far from over, the balance of power on the western theater of combat had swung heavily in favor of the US and her allies. Laura, having spent far too long reading daily activity reports and intelligence briefs, closed down the computer terminal she'd been utilizing. Rubbing her eyes, she realized that she'd been staring at the screen for far too long without blinking. She absent mindedly reached for her coffee mug and sipped, sighing in disappointment that it had gotten cold. Laura tipped the mug back anyway, finishing the cold coffee regardless. She set down the mug and picked up her Bible that she'd set close by. She was still looking for an appropriate passage to share during the memorial, which would be starting that very evening. As she read, she sensed someone enter her area.

"For a Ghost, you sure aren't that sneaky," she said without looking up.

"Well, I never thought to lay claim to such a lofty title anyway," came the reply, and Laura instantly recognized her mother's voice.

"Mom!" Laura jumped up and threw her arms around Jackie, who laughed.

"It's so very good to see you too, sweetie."

"How'd you get to come down from Seattle?" Laura asked, offering Jackie a seat.

Jackie sat, smiling and said, "I wasn't going to miss the memorial, and, thankfully, my supervisors could all sympathize. So, here I am, for as long as I want." Laura nodded, offering a knowing look. Jackie broke the brief silence.

"So, how is everyone doing? I've been kept so busy I haven't been able to keep in touch." Laura bit her lip with a deep breath.

"Well, everyone is recovering from the physical injuries, but," she trailed off.

"But losing a dear friend, a loved one, isn't something that will heal quickly," Jackie finished, her voice shaky as she only too well knew that pain. Laura's eyes filled with tears as they met her mother's. Jackie scooted her chair closer and hugged Laura tight.

"I miss him," Jackie said, tears streaking down her cheeks. They were quiet for a few minutes, before Jackie finally asked, "Now, what is that on your hand?"

Laura had a quick laughing shudder through the tears. She sniffed, holding up her left hand so her mother could see the little black silicone ring. Jackie gasped in excitement, wiping tears off her face.

"When?" was all she could ask.

"Um, three days ago," Laura grinned, wiping away her own tears as well.

"Well about time! I was about to light a fire under his butt! He asked my permission weeks ago!"

"Weeks?!" Laura laughed, "That explains some things!" Jackie pulled her daughter close for another hug and Laura groaned in fake pain.

"I'm happy for you," Jackie said. They shared more laughs and stories, enjoying one another's company until it was decided that they both needed more coffee. At that, they headed straight for the chow hall.

Epilogue

NIGHT HAD FALLEN, AND the Ghosts had assembled. They gathered together in a quiet place, far outside the city of Portland. It was an open field with some sparsely placed trees, and located in the midst of their gathering place was a large old stump of a tree that had been felled many years prior. On the top of the stump, which stood around eight feet high, was an oil lamp that Park had rigged up for the occasion. He built it with an interchangeable fuel tank, so that the small flame could always be kept burning. Standing just in front of the stump were Laura, Titus, and Nelson, all facing the assembly. Also standing nearby were the volunteers who would handle the 21 gun salute, as well as a bugler who'd play Taps. Nelson looked at the assembly, his eyes slowly tracking from left to right as he took a single, deliberate step forward. His face was grim as he stood then at attention. His voice rang out into the night.

"Ghosts! Atten-tion!" The whole assembly snapped to.

"Tonight we honor our fallen brothers and sisters who paid the ultimate price so that we can continue to fight, to serve . . . and most importantly . . . so that we can live. I will not stand before you and say do not mourn, or weep, but the opposite. I encourage everyone here to feel free to express themselves however they need to, to come to grips with what has happened to our family. I only ask that no one carries a burden of guilt or shame for having lived, when our friends did not. They would not want you to. They would want you to honor their sacrifice by living the best possible lives that you can," Nelson's voice was heavy with emotion at this point. He took a deep breath, clenching his teeth. "At ease!" he commanded.

The Ghosts went to parade rest and turned their heads toward the Colonel.

"At this time, Lieutenant Collins will read for us a Scripture befitting our comrades, and then Captain Hansen will lead us in prayer," Nelson then nodded to Laura. Laura cleared her throat as a knot formed in her stomach.

"In John's Gospel, Jesus says: '*Greater love hath no man than this, that a man lay down his life for his friends.*'" Laura's eyes misted. "Tonight we've come to say goodbye to such friends . . . and that we love them dearly . . . Titus?" she couldn't keep going.

"Let us pray," Titus began, bowing his head; the entire assembly following suit. "Lord Jesus, we come to you tonight in desperate need of you. Please, for the love that you've proven to us, fill our hearts with your peace that passes beyond understanding. Let every heavy heart be lifted, every tear wiped away. Let us feel your goodness and your presence here with us tonight. Lead us and guide us, Lord," Titus' eyes welled up and a tear streamed.

"We come to your throne of grace, asking for your help, mercy, and grace in our time of need . . . comfort us, but especially the families of our fallen," he paused, sniffling away tears. "In your name we pray, amen."

"Amen," the assembly spoke in unison.

Nelson took the floor again. "At this time, we'd like to invite the representatives of each of the fallen to come forward and speak when I read off their names . . . Sergeant Amy C. Wilkins!"

Lieutenant Perez came forward and faced Nelson, snapping a crisp salute before Nelson handed him Sgt. Wilkins' dog tags and knife. Perez, choking back tears, began to share about Sgt. Wilkins' life, detailing her accomplishments, friendships, family and how she died. There were sniffles and tears as the hardest Ghosts tried to maintain their composure, especially those who were closest to her. When Perez finished speaking, he turned to the tree stump. He jammed the blade into the old trunk and hung the dog tags on the knife. He saluted toward the tags, and then returned to his team.

"Specialist Frankie J. Ibanez!" Nelson bellowed, sorrow laced in his voice.

Up came Sgt. Juan Ibanez, the brother of Frankie. He followed the protocol, but as he spoke he couldn't keep it together. Laura's heart wrenched, she felt for this soldier who'd lost his little brother. Ibanez finished speaking, bawling openly and turned to the tree. He let out a pained, agonized cry as he jabbed the knife into the trunk and hung the dog tags. His team leader came and put an arm around his shoulder, helping him away. Colonel Nelson called the next name. And then the next . . . and the next . . . and the next . . . until there were dozens of tags hung, moving everyone if they weren't already, to tears. Laura could feel the stab of each knife driven into the stump. Finally, Nelson called out,

"Master Sergeant Jack "The Rev" Bridger!"

Laura hesitated, and looked to see as Titus moved to receive the dog tags and knife. After receiving the items he faced the crowd. Laura put her hand on his back, gently rubbing before removing it. He gave her a weak smile, and then began to speak.

"Jack, or Rev, as we all knew him by was the best picture of how to live and love in this life," Titus choked back a bit. "He always made time for people, it didn't matter how tired or busy he was, or whatever . . . he just really knew how to love people. More than that, he was an amazing husband and father. His . . . his family have already departed this world . . . I remember, when it happened . . . he had just lost everything . . . and yet, he found strength to go on, to draw from. He'd always preached at me about God, and Jesus, before . . . but when I saw him at his lowest and yet so peaceful . . . I couldn't believe my eyes. It was because of him that I gave my life to Jesus Christ, as so many of us here can relate. He truly walked the walk; truly followed Jesus. Rev was my best friend; he was my brother. He died saving us . . . and I can take comfort in knowing that he's finally, truly happy . . . finally reunited with his wife and kids, enjoying eternity in the presence of his heavenly father." Titus was now openly crying and looked upwards. "Hey buddy, tell Annie and the kids hi for me."

Titus moved to plunge the knife, but hesitated. He looked out into the crowd, taking in the faces of his team, his gaze setting upon each one in turn. As Titus' eyes locked onto Hank's, the grim man set his jaw and nodded, a single tear streaming from each eye. Titus turned and offered the knife to Laura, giving her a loving smile.

"Here . . . you were his little sister." Laura took the knife, tears flowing down her cheeks. She turned to the stump and stabbed, burying the blade almost to the hilt. Titus then hung the dog tags and he and Laura both saluted.

"Ghosts! Attention!" Nelson called the assembly back to order. Off to the side came the voice of the honor guard sergeant.

"Honor guard! Present . . . Arms! Ready, aim, fire!" Seven rifles fired in unison. "Ready, aim, fire!" The second volley rang forth, and then the third. As the final volley echoed in the night, the bugler blew Taps in honor of the fallen. Once the song was over, and the command to order arms was given,

Nelson spoke again. "Let this place forever be sacred ground, over which we will keep a constant vigil. Much like the Tomb of the Unknown Soldier in our nation's history, we will post a watch to safeguard the legacy of our fallen heroes . . . Assembly dismissed!" Nelson brought the memorial to a conclusion. Not a single person moved. Nelson surveyed the formation, perplexed. Titus stepped forward.

"Sir! All Ghost Teams request permission to keep the first watch!" Nelson smiled, a tear ran down his cheek.

"Permission granted."

"Thank you, sir!" every Ghost replied in unison.

The formation broke and reformed around the tree in a circle, every Ghost facing outward. Laura joined the perimeter, everyone adjusting to allow room for their fellows to join in. Titus came and stood by Laura and then Jackie appeared on Laura's other side. Laura looked and saw Nelson also joining the formation. She then grabbed both Titus' and Jackie's hands, and leaned her head on Titus' shoulder. The Ghosts kept watch all through the night.

www.ingramcontent.com/pod-product-compliance
Lightning Source LLC
Chambersburg PA
CBHW050405030726
47503CB00006B/2034